INVERCLYDE LIBRARIES

D0474503

KILMA

1 4 OCT 201	2 3 MAR 2015	1 9 MAR 2015
1 2 JUN 2015	2 7 OCT 2015	2 0 FEB 2016
2 9 MAR 2016	1 3 MAY 2016	
3 1 MAY 2016		
1 2 JUN 2017 SOUTH WEST		2 5 SEP 2017
1 9 SEP 2019	1 4 JUL 2022	

INVERCLYDE LIBRARIES

This book is to be returned on or before
the last date above. It may be borrowed for
a further period if not in demand.

For enquiries and renewals Tel: (01475) 712323

Inverclyde Libraries

34100 003201170

Andrew Clover has always been a Jack-of-all-trades. As a comic he was Perrier-nominated, as an actor he played the clown in *Ashes-to-Ashes*, his 'Dad Rules' column was a hit in the *Sunday Times*. But what he truly loves is books. A year ago he moved to the remotest countryside intending to write a romantic comedy – a sequel to *Learn Love in a Week*. Instead he found himself writing this.

Praise for *Learn Love in a Week*

'Loving a woman, raising a family and living a life have never seemed so funny. A brilliant and hilarious novel'
Giles Coren

'The funniest book about relationships I've read in years'
Lisa Jewell

'A saucy modern fable that offers food for thought about what is really important' *Daily Express*

'Funny, well-observed and moving' *Candis*

ANDREW CLOVER

The Things I'd Miss

arrow books

First published by Arrow Books, 2014

2 4 6 8 10 9 7 5 3 1

Copyright © Andrew Clover 2014

Andrew Clover has asserted his right under the Copyright, Designs and Patents
Act, 1988, to be identified as the author of this work.

This book is a work of fiction. Names and characters are the product of the
author's imagination and any resemblance to actual persons,
living or dead, is entirely coincidental.

This book is sold subject to the condition that it shall not, by way of trade
or otherwise, be lent, resold, hired out, or otherwise circulated without the
publisher's prior consent in any form of binding or cover other than that in which
it is published and without a similar condition including this condition being
imposed on the subsequent purchaser.

First published in Great Britain in 2014 by
Arrow Books
The Random House Group Limited
20 Vauxhall Bridge Road, London, SW1V 2SA

www.randomhousebooks.co.uk

Addresses for companies within The Random House Group Limited can
be found at: www.randomhouse.co.uk/offices.htm

The Random House Group Limited Reg. No. 954009

A CIP catalogue record for this book
is available from the British Library

ISBN 9780099580454

The Random House Group Limited supports the Forest Stewardship Council®
(FSC®), the leading international forest-certification organisation. Our books
carrying the FSC label are printed on FSC®-certified paper. FSC is the only
forest-certification scheme supported by the leading environmental organisations,
including Greenpeace. Our paper procurement policy can be found at:
www.randomhouse.co.uk/environment

MIX
Paper from
responsible sources
FSC
www.fsc.org   FSC® C016897

Typeset in Scala Regular (11.5/16.5pt) by SX Composing DTP, Rayleigh, Essex
Printed and bound by CPI Group (UK) Ltd, Croydon, CR0 4YY

The
Things I'd
Miss

CHAPTER 1

I rowed with Simon last night. He went off and slept in his special room above the garage. Alone in the marital bed, I have a fitful sleep, and a confusingly beautiful dream which involves Hugh Ashby, my first real love.

Bang. I'm woken when the front door slams shut.

Now . . . I'm not a Morning Person, even at the best of times. Stumbling from bed, I see it's dark and windy outside. As I tramp downstairs, all the bad words of the row fly back to my head like bats. I feel tense and twisted with guilt.

But then I reach the kitchen and see Simon, who seems absolutely fine.

He's a cheery, unflappable man, my husband. He looks a bit like Jean-Paul Belmondo in *À Bout de Souffle*, and a bit like a human Staff Bull Terrier. He's got a wide mouth, and a strong square jaw, and he sticks his chest out and does everything with a swaggering, bustling gusto. As I enter the too-bright kitchen, he's busy cooking a giant Man Breakfast. He turns from the stove, brandishing a spitting pan of bacon, which he crunches down on some eggshells.

'Morning, babe!' he calls happily.

I'm wondering . . . should I say sorry for last night? Should he? Where should I start? Then I notice the time, and I start there.

'Darling!' I begin. 'It's five forty-eight in the bloody morning!'

'*I know!*' he says. 'We should have gone *twenty minutes* ago!'

I whimper: '*What?!*'

'It's Saturday!' he explains. 'I *really* need to open up!'

Simon got sacked three months ago – he was an analyst in renewable energy – and he coped in brusque manly style: he got spectacularly pissed, then disappeared. He returned *four days* later, saying he'd had a 'literally amazing time with Edmundo', and he'd bought a café called Kiters' Paradise. (It's not how any woman would picture Paradise. It's in Hythe on the Kent coast. It sells coffee and flapjack to a crowd of kite-surfers.)

'There should be quite a few people out,' Simon assures me. 'It's high tide, and there's a very strong wind!'

He places a coffee in front of me.

'Anyway,' he tells me, 'I've got the boys up.'

What?! The day has just got significantly more complicated. 'The boys are up!' I say, a bit squeakily.

'Yeah!' confirms Simon. 'They're eating breakfast.'

I lean round the corner into the dining area, and there they are – my boys.

Hal (8) is eating toast, while reading *Cooking is Fun* – his favourite book. He's a gangly boy, with the large watchful eyes of a deer. Tom (5) is sitting next to him, eating Cheerios. His nose needs wiping. Seeing me, he pauses with milk dripping off the spoon and he grins. He then begins doing what he normally does on glimpsing Mum: he starts discussing dogs.

'Mum,' he begins, 'can we get another dog?'

I look at the one we have already. He's a beagle called Kipper who's got a habit of running head first into doors. I can see an argument for replacing him; it's not something I want to get into now.

'We've already got a dog,' I say. 'And a newt.'

'But we could get *another* dog,' suggests Tom. The subject of dogs is something of a hobby-horse for him. Once started on it, he doesn't leave off.

Simon pours milk in my coffee.

'Hang on,' I whisper to him. 'Why are the boys going to the beach?'

'They love the beach!' he says. 'I thought you all did!'

'We do,' I agree. 'But not when there's a high wind, and it's still dark. What are they going to do?'

'Oh . . .' He shrugs. 'You'll think of something!'

'What?' I say. 'Do you think *I'm* coming?'

'Why wouldn't you come?' says Simon.

He seems surprised. His eyebrows are thick and black like caterpillars. They are raised in innocent astonishment.

'What am I supposed to do?' I plead.

'Whatever you want,' says Simon. He beams at me. He is almost insultingly cheerful. 'Or don't go, if you don't want.'

'Actually I'll have to go!' I reply. 'Because otherwise you'll just leave them!'

'No, I won't!'

'You'll say you're keeping an eye on them,' I whisper, 'but you'll go kite-surfing off!'

'It'll be fine!' he says. 'Edmundo will keep an eye on them.'

'Exactly,' I say.

Edmundo is Simon's partner in the Kiters' Paradise project. He's a very talkative Spanish man, with a shaved head and a thick beard, who used to deal weed on an impressively large scale. He's not an ideal nanny.

'Give me five minutes,' I say. 'I'll come.'

Simon beams. He's ludicrously proud of Kiters' Paradise. He's delighted I'm coming.

'Excellent,' he says. He gives me a brief manly hug.

I'm still trying to be cross with him, but for a moment I do feel good.

Eight minutes later, I'm heading for The A-Team van.

Simon adores *The A-Team*, and, six months ago – 'so I can carry all my kite-surfing equipment' – he bought an exact scale model, which is parked outside the house. It is black, with a side door, and, for some reason, it's a left-hand drive.

As I walk over, the back door slides open.

Hal is smiling at me from the middle row of seats. With his left hand, he's cuddling Kipper, who's sitting on the seat beside him. He gives me no trouble at all.

Trouble comes from Tom.

As I lean in through the windowless sliding door, Tom shouts: '*Mumma!*' He is on top of his car seat, squatting like a mad snotty frog. '*Mumma!*' he shouts again, and he spreads his arms wide. He's playing a game that Simon taught him. '*I am de Love Monster!*' he says in the Love Monster accent (slightly Polish). '*Take me! I am yours!*' he shouts, and then he *launches* himself at my neck.

It's flattering, of course. I'm glad he's pleased to see me.

But it feels less like a hug, and more like a tackle. And it makes me smack my skull on the doorframe. I'm actually really cross, but I don't say. I detach myself from Tom, and put his seat belt on. No one this irritated should have to contend with a child's seat belt, but I manage. I go round to the front seat, where Simon is turning on the radio. It's Jeff Buckley singing 'Lilac Wine', one of the most heavenly songs of all time.

'*DJ Monster!*' shouts Tom. (At school, Simon's name was DJ Monster. I don't know why.) '*DJ Monster! I. Don't. Like. This. Music! Play the Monster Mix!*'

Simon was asked to do the music for my brother's wedding – a job to which he's been touchingly devoted. And, yes, that's sweet, but he's been working on it for two months. On the rare moments he is home from Kiters'

Paradise, he disappears to his room above the garage, where he works on the Monster Mix: he remixes classic TV tunes, to a very phat drum and bass.

As I put on my seat belt, Simon presses play.

The Monster Mix starts with *The A-Team* theme. Drums beat. A chopper sounds. Simon turns and catches the boys' eyes and they listen excitedly to the famous voice-over introduction. When it gets to: 'If you have a problem . . .' they start lip-synching along. Simon loves this line. The Monster Mix repeats it *twice more.*'

Bloody hell, I think, I really do have a problem; I don't think it can be solved by the A-Team.

The chorus kicks in . . . 'DUM Dum DUMMM . . .' Simon shows off by revving the car backwards very fast. I instinctively turn to check the boys are all right. It's fine. They're in seat belts. But Kipper isn't. As Simon zooms backwards, the dog slips from the seat, his head crashes into mine and he gives me a big French kiss. I get slobber on my mouth.

'For God's sake!' I shout. 'Can you stop?'

Simon cuts the engine. The music stops.

'What's the matter with you?' he asks.

'I have just been snogged by a dog!'

Obviously I've said the wrong word.

'But we could get a new dog,' suggests Tom.

'We cannot get a new dog,' says Hal, speaking for me. 'Because we've already got one. And a newt. And you *promised* to clean out the newt's tank!'

'I have *started*,' snarls Tom, 'to clean out his tank.'

'What?' I say. 'Have you?'

'Yes!' he growls. 'I have put him *in the bath*!'

What?! There's a bloody newt in the bath?!

'Look,' says Simon, 'are we going to the beach?'

'*No, we are not!*' I shout. 'Boys, get out of the van!'

'I should have opened up already!' pleads Simon.

'Just go on your own!' I snap. 'Be back by twelve!'

It's now 1.42. Simon's not yet home.

The whole house is in chaos. Action Men are fighting on the floor. Plastic dinosaurs are roaming each surface. The boys are now fractious from their early start. They're also hungry. We've so far eaten a whole packet of HobNobs. (I ate most of them; I need to deal with that.) I'm now trying to cook corn, fried chicken and rice, though I'm hampered by a significant factor . . .

I have no rice.

I texted Simon and asked him to bring some home. 'OK,' he replied, 'I'm just having a quick chat with Edmundo. Bit of work to discuss.'

Simon and Edmundo are in the throes of a full-on Man Crush. They spend all hours excitedly discussing Kiters' Paradise. They want to Expand. They have Grand Plans to do more food. They want to project the football on to an outside wall, so men from all around can gather to watch, like a herd of curious cows.

I *really* need to work myself.

I'm a painter. I teach art three days a week at a secondary school in Ashford, but in six months' time I'm having an exhibition at the Horsebridge Gallery in Whitstable. They've been e-mailing all week. They're doing their brochure. They want me to give them the title of my exhibition, and a few words about it. The trouble is, it's hard to give the title when you haven't got one. And it's hard even to *think* of one when you're being followed round by two small boys, and one of them is cooking, and the other has been discoursing, for several hours, about dogs.

He's just paused.

It's delicious, like having a pneumatic drill outside, which suddenly stops. I see what's happened. Sitting on the floor stroking Kipper, he's just found a felt tip, and he's now started drawing a dog. That's no surprise. That's all he ever draws. The trouble is, he's drawing on the cupboard door. I should probably stop that, but right now I'd let him burn the cupboard door, if he stayed quiet.

My phone rings.

I can't find the phone, of course.

I try all the normal places. I look on the shelf. I look in my bag. I look in the bathroom. (There's a bloody newt in the bath!) I've just found the phone in my studio, when it stops ringing. I feel a stab of rage about that.

But then I see it was my mum who called, and I feel relief.

I look round the studio. I've barely visited in three days, and the air is thick with reproach. There's a dried earwig stuck to the window. My old paintings are lolling, unloved, against the wall. They're shit. Well . . . They're technically good, I can see that, but they lack that haunting Peter Doig quality that tells the viewer these pictures mean something, that there's a *story* behind them. I'm sure my pictures used to have that. How do I find that again?

I don't think I can find it in a phone.

I eye the greasy screen guardedly. I want to check my messages. The voices in my head are shouting: '*Don't check your messages! No good comes from checking your messages!*' But I can't resist it. I open my e-mails.

It's like unblocking the pipe under the sink. I'm blasted by a toxic torrent. I've got twenty-eight e-mails. They're mostly spam. There are two from students who want to consult me about uni. There are three from the Horsebridge. They really want that title. I see instantly that most of the messages are asking me questions I can't answer; *all* of them make me tense. One of them is actually from my mum – the arch maker of shame. She's marked her message 'Urgent'. Ugh . . . I hate it when people do that. It means the messages are already stressful: I don't want to look at them.

It's as if my mum senses I'm near. She rings again. I get a mental image of her, hovering by her phone, with her short grey hair, modelled on Judi Dench's. Bracing myself, I answer.

'*Hi!*' she says, already sounding manic.

'Hi, Mum,' I say, going quiet and still. I do that with Mum. I'm like a vole hiding from an owl.

'Do you want me to pop over later?' she asks.

The short answer to that of course is: no.

Mum pops over two or three times a week, and she very rarely pops without bringing crap. Last week, it was two deckchairs and a Breville sandwich maker.

'I've got this stuff of Dad's for you to look at,' she explains.

I admit it: the word 'Dad' raises a crumb of curiosity. But Dad left in 1976: whatever he left behind – I'm sensing it wasn't his best stuff. I'm seeing a squash racket, *The Joy of Sex*, and some shoes.

'Mum,' I tell her, 'I don't want Dad's things. They'll depress me.'

'*Why?*' she answers, much offended.

'Because they've been in your attic forty years, and they were Dad's.'

'Oh,' ripostes Mum. 'Your dad could be quite fun sometimes.'

This is one of Mum's themes: that Dad could be fun. He loved his squeezebox, apparently. Used to play it at parties. Now . . . I'm sure Dad could be quite a card, playing his squeezebox at parties. The point is, he wasn't playing it at *my* parties.

'Mum,' I say, 'I don't even remember the man.'

'Well, I think that's a shame. Don't you think you should?'

I ignore the words 'should' and 'shame' – the classic

Mum words, her prime weapons in her campaign to hand out blame.

'And I don't want his stuff,' I continue, 'clogging up my house.'

'The thing is,' sighs Mum, 'it's in the car now. I'll pop over and just show it to you.'

Bloody hell. There's no holding her back.

'Great,' I say, with as much warmth as I can muster. 'I'll look forward to it!'

''Bye then!' she calls.

''Bye!'

I've been squatting to take the call.

Standing up, I have a brief white out. I think it's because I've always been tall, and, let's be honest, a bit overweight: I have a lot of white outs. I quite like them. They feel like a brief holiday from reality. But as my head clears, my unease returns. Why should I remember my dad? I think I've forgotten him for a very good reason.

'*Mum!*' the boys are shouting. '*The cooking is burning!*'

I snap out of it, and hurry back to the kitchen. I take the pan off the hob, and then turn back to the boys, who are eyeing me expectantly. There's a brief silence.

Then Tom fills it.

'But if Kipper *dies*,' he says, 'we could get another dog!'

Oh, God. We're back to this.

I look at the clock, and I realise Simon should have

been home almost *two bloody hours ago*. I could kill him. I just *know* he's stopped to have a drink. I've *told* him not to do that.

'*Mum*,' says Tom, impatiently. He's assuming I haven't heard him. He's incorrect about that. I hear everything. That's the trouble. '*Mum!*' he repeats, even louder. 'I *said* . . . if Kipper *dies*, we could get another dog, and I think he could be a *brown* dog, and he could be a **hairy** dog, and he could be <u>*so big*</u> I could *ride* on him, Mummy!'

The corn on the cob is boiling over.

'He could be *so big*,' says Tom – again – 'I could *ride* on him, Mummy. Do you think that's a good idea?'

'*No!*' I say suddenly. I manage not to shout.

'But why?' says Tom.

'*Because I don't want a bloody big dog!*' I reply, and I'm sorry, but I *am* shouting now.

Tom goes quiet.

For a moment I feel good. My rage has overawed him. But then, two seconds later, coming like rain after thunder, the guilt bursts over me, and I'm showered in shame. I feel like I'm a child again, and my mother is standing over me shouting: 'YOU are a very SPOILED little girl, and I need you to GO to your room!'

Both sons are looking at me, worried.

'Mum,' says Hal, 'are you all right?'

His big sensitive eyes are full of concern. He's wearing his new chef's hat, which I find incredibly endearing. I feel very bad I just shouted.

'The trouble is,' I say evenly – I've got myself back

under control – 'I'm struggling to think up the title for my new exhibition.'

'I could help!' says Hal.

'Thank you,' I say. By which I mean: no, you couldn't. I can't work out myself if I should be thinking up some fancy idea to attract interest from the art world, or if I should just paint things I like, which would end up looking more commercial. 'Also,' I continue, 'we need rice. Let's get in the car, and we'll go to the garage and buy some.'

'Mum,' says Hal, giving the Standard Child Objection, 'do we *have* to?'

His brother is more blunt. 'I do NOT want to go in the car,' warns Tom.

I sigh, and weigh it up in my mind. This is the trouble with living in deep countryside: the garage is two miles away. But if I hurry, I could get there and back in twelve minutes. That *should* be fine. And anyway . . . I *really* need to escape. If I could just have twelve minutes on my own, I could think up a theme for this exhibition. If I go one more day without one, I'll have to shoot myself.

'All right,' I say, 'you two stay here. I'll put the television on.'

Now . . . I know I'm proposing a plan which is technically illegal. But my children give it their most enthusiastic support.

'*Televizioneeee!*' says Hal, in a kind of cod Italian accent, waving his arms around like a chicken. '*Televizionnnneeeee!*' he says again. Then he realises that Tom has already run

[13]

off: he's in danger of losing control of the remote. So he sprints for the living room, as if he were the fastest chicken in all Italy and he's just seen a fox.

In the hallway, I pause by the big mound of shoes.

As you leave the house, there's that Magic Minute where you suddenly remember your wallet, and the letter you promised to post last week. My whole life is like that Magic Minute. Trouble is, it's always interrupted.

The dog arrives.

Kipper is mad keen on trips in the car, especially if we're travelling alone, which means he can go in the front. He likes to see himself as navigator. 'All right, you can come,' I say in my special doggy voice, and Kipper waggles his tale pleasingly. I open the front door, the sunshine spills in, and the two of us trot amiably towards my battered old Ford. It's not in good shape. One wheel's a bit flat, and a wing mirror has come off, leaving a nest of wires.

'Up!' I command, opening the door.

Kipper leaps up obediently, and he goes over to the pasenger seat. He places his paws on the dashboard, and he looks out, like a navigator of old, surveying the open sea. I stroke him fondly. The top of his head is delightfully soft.

'Good boy!' I tell him, and I set off.

There are three houses in our little hamlet. We live

in the first. Mrs Eden lives in the second – a bungalow. She's very old, and rarely seen. The third house is a new farmhouse belonging to some actual genuine farmers called the Newsomes. As we pass, Kipper eyes the front yard. He seems mystified as to why chickens are running round in it, when logically they should all be being bitten by dogs.

I glance at the clock. It's now 1.59.

I drive as fast as I can up the hill. Unfortunately, I meet a jeep coming down. I slow down, I edge round the jeep carefully, giving a wave. This is a strange country tradition . . . When passing someone, you must always flash a friendly wave, which is not easy, when you're trying not to slip down the steep slope into the field alongside, and you don't feel friendly.

Setting off again, I punch on the music machine.

Amy Winehouse is singing 'Back to Black', which I like even more than 'Lilac Wine'. Amy and I start singing along: 'We only said goodbye with words . . .'

But we're interrupted.

'*This is travel*,' announces a self-important man, who starts talking excitedly about a traffic jam outside Dover. '*Shut up*,' I yell – it feels good to take out my frustration on some inanimate objects! – and I hit the radio so hard I break a nail. I then step on the accelerator again.

As I roar off up the hill, my head is filling with questions.

How do you stop those traffic updates?

Why do I feel such rage?

[15]

How bad is it leaving young children with a TV as a babysitter? And how long will Tom stay watching? He'll sit there three weeks if he's watching CBeebies, but what happens if Hal has put on CBBC? If that's happened then Tom could have been driven away from the TV, and he could, even now, be heading to the kitchen, with a plan of building a bonfire out of knives and electrical equipment. Is that stupid? Because I've imagined it, does that mean it's more likely to happen?

With these unruly thoughts bouncing round my head like a car full of underage footballers, I hurtle up the hill towards the bend. And, yes, yes – *OK!* – I see I'm committing a number of errors, but that's the thing with errors: once you make one, more follow in quick succession. My actions are one long list of mistakes . . .

I am reaching the point where the road climbs through a copse of trees, clinging to the side of the hill. At this point, the road turns sharply to the right.

I glance at the clock, which now says 2.00.

I have reached the bend.

I don't slow down.

I turn the corner, travelling fast, and, as I do, *a van* appears, and that's travelling fast too.

I attempt to step on the brake.

I miss it.

I step on the accelerator instead.

I swivel the wheel hard to the left. I still fail to miss the van, however, and it smashes me, hard, on the right side of the bonnet.

Whereupon time seems to slow right down.

My car, however, does not.

It soars, at speed, off the side of the road, into the trees.

For a moment, I think: *Oh my God, I'm flying!* It seems ordinary. It seems fine.

And then the car hits a tree. The windscreen shatters, and Kipper dives through it. And then we hit another tree. Then another. We've now sailed through the little copse of trees. They have slowed our momentum. And the car lands on its bonnet.

I hear a most almighty smash as the front end concertinas.

The car still has momentum, though. It does a head-over-heels and it lands, with a further smack, on its roof. For the tiniest of moments I see the ground cramming over my head. I see a plastic dinosaur that had been on the dashboard. It leaps upwards as the green ceiling closes down.

CHAPTER 2

Everything disappears.

It's like a TV being switched off. I can't see anything. I can't feel anything. I hear a ringing in my ears like tinnitus. Then I have a brief floating feeling, and hear a faint echo of choral singing. Then I stay in absolute silence for several seconds.

And then, very slowly, I regain my sense of smell.

I smell lilac. It smells of early summer. It smells of hope. I also smell dusty floorboards.

Very carefully, I open my eyes, and I see a glass of water which contains a small sprig of white lilac. It is standing on floorboards of dark brown wood. I'm on a mattress on the floor.

I know where I am.

I'm in my room in Isis House, the place to which I moved in my third term at Oxford. A mirror is leaning against one wall. I see myself in it. My hair is thick, and badly cut. My skin however is unmarked as fresh snow. I'm nineteen. I am young and effortlessly beautiful. There's an old digital clock by the mirror, which I've not seen in many years. It says 5.08 a.m. Turning slowly, I notice that the door is ajar, but I can see my old poster – the self-portrait of Filippino Lippi. I also note that the curtains are open, and dawn light is creeping softly into the room.

Lying beside me, on his back, is a man.

'What's going on?' I try to say, but my voice sticks in my throat. I feel that I'm a passenger in my nineteen-year-old body, but I can't talk. This seems to make sense. I take a slow breath in, and, as the lilac-scented air reaches my lungs, I start to hear, quietly at first, the thoughts of my nineteen-year-old self . . . I am thinking of the party that Gemma and I threw here last night. When I slipped away at 2 a.m. it was still going strong, but I was alone. Why is this man in my bed?

I look at him. He is huge and quite astonishingly attractive.

It's not just that he looks handsome, though he does. He has long eyelashes, and good cheekbones, and full lips with a pronounced Cupid's bow. It's more that, even in sleep, he looks charming. He has a small smile, and his eyebrows are slightly raised. He looks like a music lover, who's hearing some Bach, played better than anyone's ever heard it before. He's leaning his head on his right hand and his bicep is thick and hairless. He's wearing a white t-shirt which has ridden up at his waist, so that I can see the bottom of his giant ribs which jut out, like the cliff top over a little bay. I look over the cliffs to his flat stomach. He's wearing black dress trousers, tied at the waist with a red tie. That has come undone. I can see the tops of some white pants, and a naked hipbone, and a little bit of muscular stomach. As my younger self takes a slow breath in, I catch a whiff of his scent – musky and manly and with a trace of wine – and I am suffused with a sense of longing.

His eyelashes are fluttering.

His head turns towards me, and a lock of brown hair falls over his face. I decide that I will brush it back. Very tentatively, I reach forward and lift the hair with the backs of my fingers.

His pale blue-grey eyes sweep open and look at me.

I know what he's going to say. I've been in this scene before.

Smiling, he says my name: 'Lucy Potts!'

I know his name of course. It's Hugh Ashby.

'Hello!' says, my nineteen-year-old self. 'I didn't know you came to the party.'

'I came at three,' he says, 'a bit more than fashionably late. I brought you flowers.'

'I just found them,' I say, 'and then I found you, in my bed!'

'I suddenly felt really tired. So I crept in here and fell asleep.' He smiles gently. 'Forward, I know, to creep into a girl's bed. Excuse me.'

My nineteen-year-old self is doing the sensible thing:

she's smiling at Hugh Ashby. My feelings are fusing with hers. I feel calm and expectant and light with love.

'That's OK,' I breathe. 'I've not seen you since your birthday. Been revising?'

'No. To tell you the truth, I've been mainly in bed.'

'Have you fallen in love with someone?'

'You'd be the first to know about that,' he says. That gives me a quick flutter in my heart. I remind myself he flirts with everyone. 'No,' he continues. 'I've just . . . been a bit tired recently. The nurse thinks I might be developing ME.'

'What's that?'

'It's that new condition,' he explains. 'The one known as the Yuppie Disease.'

'What's a Yuppie?'

'Young Upwardly Mobile Professional.'

'Shouldn't that be Yumpy?'

Hugh laughs at this. It's a happy baritone chuckle.

'What causes it?'

'No one knows,' he says. 'It could be viral. It could be provoked by some trauma. It could be depression.'

'You always seem fine to me,' I remark.

'That's because when I am with you, Lucy Potts,' he says, his eyes sparkling with affection, 'it's like having a robin sing outside my window.'

'You're such a poof,' I say.

He chuckles again.

'I'm not actually,' he says. 'And I could prove it.'

I look into his eyes, and I feel peaceful and extraordinarily happy. I can't help it. I must kiss him. But then something happens, as, somehow, I know it will. Beyond the foot of the bed the door is open, and suddenly music starts up. It's the thud thud thud thud of house music. Technotronic.

'Is the party still going on?' I ask.

'It was when I crept in here,' he says. 'Simon's brought over his new decks, and he's determined to use them. Gemma was dancing, which, alas, was encouraging him.'

Abruptly, Technotronic disappears, there's a pause, then some cows start mooing to an ambient beat. Hugh grins. 'Bloody KLF!' he says. 'Simon plays it every night. It's his Come Down album.'

'Do you like it?'

'I enjoy all his music,' says Hugh.

'Do you?' I ask.

He smiles. 'I'd prefer it if he played Liszt. But I love Simon, so he can do no wrong.'

'Do you really?' I ask.

'He wears ridiculous baseball caps,' he says, 'and he over-uses the word "basically". But you've got to admit, he's sweet.'

'I suppose so,' I acknowledge.

I can't even think about Simon right now. I'm actually lying in front of Hugh Ashby, and staring into his blue-grey eyes. It's like looking down into a rock pool. I feel a strange lurching sensation, as if I'm about to fall into him. I feel as if something amazing is about to happen.

The KLF is turned up louder.

'I'll shut the door,' I say, sitting up.

'Don't,' says Hugh. He holds my left hand.

That stops me, and I look at him. He folds both his big hands round mine. They are very warm manly hands. Looking at me, a trace of a smile on his lips, he squeezes the base of my thumb. I never knew a hand squeeze could be so lovely. I don't hurry him. I feel calm, I feel in love, and the older part of me knows this isn't going to last. I've been in this scene before. It's one of the memories I revisit most often. I explore around in it, always thinking the same thought: why oh why oh why oh why did I not just kiss him?

'What's the matter?' I say, smiling.

'I've waited so long to be in a bed with you, Lucy Potts, and now you're getting up.'

'I'm just going to the door. Though I could venture further. I could get us tea.'

'Tea?' he says. His eyes light up. He likes that idea.

'Would you like tea?'

'If you made me tea, Lucy Potts,' he says, 'I would like it.'

'Would you like anything else?'

'I'd like a glass of chilled rosé wine,' he says. 'But more than that, I'd just like to hold your hand.'

I smile at him. Hugh Ashby has a foppish, poetic way of talking, but he somehow does it so he sounds sincere and manly. It's partly because his voice is so lovely. It's deep and smooth like melted chocolate.

'One moment,' I say.

I'm about to go when on an impulse I lean down, and

brush the hair from his majestic brow. I leave my hand on his cheek. It's a hot night, and his skin is just clammy with sweat. I enjoy the feeling of his broad cheekbone under my palm. I consider him a moment. I want to kiss him, but I know I shouldn't. He is not in my bed, I realise, because he likes me. He's here because it's a party and he might have ME, and he needed to crash. I mustn't get this wrong. Every girl fancies Hugh Ashby. He's way out of my league.

Kiss him, I whisper to my younger self. *For God's sake, just kiss him.*

I am thrown into turmoil. I am startled by hearing a strange voice whispering inside my head, and I feel dizzy and confused. My vision briefly bleaches away as if I'm having a white out. But I still have my hand on Hugh's cheek, and it seems to anchor me. After a few seconds, his face swims back into focus. I see him, looking at me, all handsome and strong and understanding.

I see I've got him captive. And I sink my mouth to his Roman lips, and I kiss him.

Did I do that? Did I really kiss Hugh Ashby?

I know I did kiss him once, but it definitely wasn't now. I feel I've torn myself away from reality, and as a result I feel immediately faint again. But then I'm grounded by the warm feel of his cheek beneath my hand. I'm excited by the curve of his beautiful lips.

I sink slowly towards them again.

A tiny jolt of electricity runs through me as my nose rubs against his. I can smell a trace of wine on his breath.

I press my lips to his, and I feel their surprising softness and warmth. I withdraw. But already I feel like an addict. I must kiss him again. I press my lips sensuously to his, and then I reach forward the very tip of my tongue, at the very moment he reaches forward his, and we touch. I pause, as the ecstasy of love explodes slowly like an orange firework in my heart.

I don't believe it! I've just kissed Hugh Ashby!

We've declared our love. It's happening! It's an absolutely thrilling start. I decide I shall make tea, I'll brush my teeth, and then we'll see where this leads. Maybe we won't just kiss each other. Maybe we'll finish the night triumphantly making love. I get up quickly.

'No!' says Hugh, but I bolt away. I hurry towards the door, with its poster of Filippino Lippi. I dodge through it, and pull it closed behind me. As it shuts with a slight bang . . .

Everything changes.

The door has changed. The smell has changed. Now it smells of lawnmower and wood and dust.

I'm in a shed.

But where is it? It seems familiar. I look round. Leaning against the wall there's a dirty old mirror, and I look into it.

I am five.

My face is round, but it's pretty. My hair is in a disordered bob with a short fringe. My eyes are round too and very watchful. My whole body is endearing and childish and I can't help but notice that I'm wearing some superb clothes. I'm wearing my best blue dungarees – the ones with the embroidered flowers on the chest. I've combined them with my favourite white blouse, the one that has bunchy sleeves that are a tiny bit like Snow White's. It's a joyfully childish ensemble, and I'm delighted to note I've set it off with suitably eclectic footwear: Wellies. And not just any Wellies. Oh, no. I'm rocking my All Time Favourite Wellies: the red ones, with the ladybird spots, and the little eyes that peep out of the toes. Seeing them again gives me a rich warmth inside.

What is going on? I think. *Why is this happening?*

But my five-year-old self isn't thinking that. As I look around, I become aware of my thoughts. At first a quiet whispering, they quickly grow louder. I am very *interested* in the spider on the window. She's sleeping in the middle of her web. She's got a sort of cocoon nearby her, and that's filled with a dead fly. I would *not* want to sleep next to a dead fly. Ooh . . . The spider is moving slowly towards me. This feels scary. What's going to happen?

Suddenly, the door behind me is *slammed* open.

A smirking girl comes marching in. She is the same size as me. She is wearing red boots. They are Kickers. She's also wearing some orange stretchy shorts, and a hat that belongs to my dad.

I am thrilled to see her.

It's The Amazing Gemma Weakes, the greatest friend of my childhood. She lived just three doors up the road.

She went to the same primary school as me. Even after I left it, we stayed friends. We stayed in touch as teenagers. We even went to the same university. She's been the greatest friend of my life, and, seeing her now, my five-year-old voice just erupts out of me.

'Gemmaaaaaaaaaa!!!' I shout.

She bustles into the shed. 'I *knew* you were in here,' she says busily. I remember this. Gemma was *always* busy, even when playing – *especially* when playing. No one on the planet takes play more seriously than Gemma.

She grabs the bike pump.

'Ah, good!' Gemma informs me. 'I need this.'

'Why?'

She looks me straight in the face. 'When I get in the orchard,' she declares, 'there might be monsters.'

'Monsters?!' I ask. I need to know more.

'Yes,' says Gemma, nodding. 'Ones that are big and hairy and have got big . . . BIG . . . chicken feet.'

'Chicken feet?!' I enquire. Somehow that is not the detail I was expecting.

'Yuh!' she says. 'Have you seen chicken feet? They are big and scaly and *scratchy*! My dad says that chickens are dinosaurs! He's getting chickens at his new house!'

'Chickens are dinosaurs?!'

'YESSSSS!' says Gemma, and she nods her head up and down even quicker. This is quintessential Gemma. Whenever she talks to me, she always acts as if I'm a half-wit – albeit a much-loved one whose heart is in the right place – whereas she is in full possession of the facts.

'And,' she carries on, 'I am pretty certain that some of the monsters ARE going to be dinosaurs.' She looks at me like she knows I might not believe her. She attains full certainty. 'DEFINITELY dinosaurs!' she concludes.

'But . . .' I begin. I look at the bike pump. 'Why do you need that?'

'*To shoot them!*' explains Gemma, as if anyone would know that. And to show how it works, she pumps it three times. 'Come on!' she commands.

We both run out of the shed.

She turns to the side, to the gap in the hedge that leads into the orchard. You are not allowed in the orchard. Gemma, however, goes straight through.

I don't. I stop where I am.

My young self looks towards the hole in the hedge. I'm longing to go through it, but I'm sensing Mum could be watching. Meanwhile my older self is looking round in wonder. It's extraordinary. I'm in the garden of The Old Vicarage, Linton Hill, Kent. I was born in this house. This was my first garden. And I realise anyone will remember their childhood garden as Paradise, but, seeing it all again now, it is even better than I remembered. I can just see the roof of The Old Vicarage. It's a rickety, wizardy, half-timbered house, and from where I'm standing, the wonky line of its roof is just visible. My gaze caresses down the half-timbered walls and into the long lovely garden which flows down the hill into several terraces. You go down jaggedy stone steps between the levels. I'm at the best bit – the last one. It's a wild meadow area. It has long grass, and dandelions, and a weeping willow tree, and if you go under it, you feel like you're in a cool sun-dappled cave.

I turn and I look again for Gemma.

The hole in the hedge looks like a magic archway into a better world. I can see a long line of apple trees, which stretches down into the valley, and then up to the wood at the top of the hill. I know that wood! It has squirrels leaping from every tree. And in front of it is the white cottage of Mrs Lindhurst. She is the mum of Miss Lindhurst, a very pretty lady, who plays the guitar at Sunday School. We all went to that house at Christmas and Miss Lindhurst played the guitar, and my dad played the piano, and we were allowed to eat as much cake as we wanted. It wasn't horrid granny cake either (fruit cake). It was delicious springy sponge cake, and it had jam and soft lemon-flavoured icing which had tiny lemon shapes which were sweet and sour all at once.

Gemma pokes her head back through the hedge.

'I have not seen any dinosaurs yet,' she assures me.

I'd forgotten about the dinosaurs. But I don't want Gemma to know that. So I nod.

'Stay there!' she orders. 'I will FIND OUT what is going on, and then I will come back, and I will REPORT!' She is pleased with that last word. She says it again. 'I will REPORT. Do. Not. Move!'

At this, Gemma holds out her finger at me like it's a wand. She looks like a small but very busy witch.

'*Stay there!*' she commands again.

I nod at her. I want to tell her there's no way that I'm

going to move. My young eyes are noticing that a dandelion has just released three seeds and they're floating up like fairies off to seek their fortunes. My older self is relishing the miraculous novelty of all this. I am five again, and I'm at the bottom of The Old Vicarage garden, waiting for Gemma to return with her REPORT. I would not move from this spot, not for all the cake in Kent.

But someone arrives. It's Mum. She's standing at the edge of the highest level of the garden. She already looks cross.

'Lucy!' she calls.

'What?' pleads my young voice.

She looks young too and very strange. She has blue eye shadow, and blusher, and her hair is blonde and permed. It has been tied back by a green Clothkits headscarf. I remember that scarf. For years it lay in a box under the sink, and we used it to clean windows. She also has her hands on her hips, and she's staring down at me like an angry giant.

'I have *told* you we need to *go* and *buy shoes*,' she says. 'Haven't I? *Haven't I?*'

I nod quickly. I want to placate her, but at the same time I'm confused.

'Why do I need shoes?' I ask.

'You are starting school soon,' she reminds me, furiously.

'Can't I wear my Wellies?' I ask.

'Of course you can't wear your Wellies!' scolds Mum. '*We don't have much time.* We need to go.'

She turns and strides off towards the house. She's wearing a shiny red skirt and it's tight round her surprisingly shapely bottom. My young self is now boiling in confusion. I don't understand why I can't wear my Wellies to school. Mum seemed to imply I'll get into terrible trouble if I even attempt it, and this makes me think that school is a terrifying and alien place, where you must do everything correctly or you'll be subjected to terrible punishments. Is that true?

It's OK, I whisper to my young self.

But my young self isn't reassured at all. I was already scared because Mum seemed angry for no reason, and now another strange voice has appeared in my head, and that's made me feel terrified and dizzy and a bit sick. I feel like I do when I get a nose bleed. My legs feel weak. Terrified, I'm desperate to get to Mum. I know she's cross but I'm sure she can help. I hurry after her. But of course the steps are jaggedy and hard to climb at the best of times – even when you're not wearing Wellies, and feeling faint.

And I trip over.

Bang.

As I fall I shut my eyes.

When my eyes open everything has changed.

I am not climbing up the jaggedy stone steps of my childhood garden. I am going up the stairs to my bedroom in my current house in Kent. At the bottom of the wall there's a small mural done in felt tip. I can't be sure who did it, but the subject is dogs.

I pause. I think: what is going on?

Then I see I'm holding Simon's overnight bag, the one he used on his recent trip to Munich, and it all comes back. This is last night. This is the fateful row that started everything off. I'm condemned to live it out again. Taking a deep breath, I stamp crossly up the stairs and enter our bedroom. Dumping the bag on the floor, I see something which makes me more angry still. There is a patch of dog wee on the carpet.

I say: 'Bloody hell!'

'What?' calls Simon.

The bathroom door is ajar. I can see a leg with wet black hair. He's in the bath. Which means that either he hasn't noticed the wee, because he's pissed. Or he thinks I should clear it up, because, as far as he's concerned, I should deal with all canine emissions, as if I've done them myself. I am so angry, I want to get far, far away from here. But I can't. Someone has to keep this house going. I must clear up.

I go into the bathroom.

Simon sits up quickly. I think he's embarrassed I can see him naked. I don't look anyway. I feel uncomfortable about men in the bath. I just grab all the tissue I can. I bundle it round my hand, I return to the wee, and I begin dabbing. There's not much tissue, and it's quickly used up. So I take the wet tissue downstairs. I chuck it in the bin. I also find a twelve-pack of Andrex Super-soft Toilet Tissue, and I carry it up the stairs under my arm.

As I re-enter the marital bedroom, Simon exits the bathroom.

He's wearing The Contraceptive Dressing Gown – a ridiculous green fluffy gown he brought back from a business trip. He begins rubbing the damp patch with a towel.

'Don't do that!' I say.

'Why?'

'You don't rub it,' I tell him. 'You dab it. You *absorb it*.'

I nudge him aside. This is the nature of marriage: you're always struggling to gain control of something, and right now it's a patch of wee.

'You empty that bag you took to Munich!' I suggest.

Something about the bag makes him uncomfortable.

'Why did you go to Munich?' I ask.

'To see Tomas Markfield,' he says. He pronounces it in a German accent: Tom*a*s Markfield.

'Why?' I say.

'He makes the best kite-surfing equipment in Europe,' Simon informs me. 'And he is up for us selling it at Kiters' Paradise.'

'I'm happy for you,' I say. 'But can you empty your overnight bag? It's been on the stairs three days!'

He bends over to pick up the bag.

'You can start,' I say, 'by putting away the condoms.'

He freezes a moment. That's what gives him away.

'What's the matter with you?' he asks.

'There's a box of three condoms in the inside pocket

– one Featherlite, one ribbed, and one that tastes of pineapple.'

'So?' he says, now facing me for the first time. He's clearly decided to brazen this out. 'They've probably been there since Christmas!'

'I used that bag a month ago, when I spent the night with Gemma. The front pocket was empty. There's now a packet of three that you obviously bought because you were hoping to get lucky with some gorgeous German maiden.'

'Well, I obviously didn't get lucky,' says Simon. 'Since the packet's still wrapped.'

He takes it out and throws it in the bedside drawer, where he keeps the other ones.

'Lucy . . .' he begins.

'I don't care!' I say. 'Maybe that's what you should do: find some German girl who's very keen on pineapple. Find one with scurvy. She might want the vitamins!'

He says nothing to that.

'Is that what you want?' I say.

'No!' he says. 'I would prefer to have sex with *you*. Which is something you don't seem to want, since you look at me like I'm some dog that followed you home.'

I am taken aback by that one. Simon has just summarised my feelings towards him exactly; I don't congratulate him on his eloquence.

'Lucy,' he says, and places his hands on my shoulders. That's a mistake. He should never have got so close. I hit him in the face with the Andrex.

'Owwww!' he says, making the most of it. He's obviously relieved to find some grievance. He clutches his face like a footballer.

'What?' I protest. I'm boiling with annoyance.

'You just hit me with a bog roll!' he says, backing off.

'It's super-soft!' I say.

In fact, I see that was my mistake. I hit him with the extra-quilted tissue. If I'd only turned the weapon, I could have clonked him with the stout cardboard inside and he'd be spitting out teeth. I now chuck the entire roll at him. He raises his arm and blocks it.

'Lucy,' he says, 'I bought the condoms, at the airport, on the way home, because I was hoping we might have sex.'

'We already have condoms!' I retort.

'It's been so long since we used them,' he retaliates, 'I'd forgotten.' He seems to be turning this conversation round to my shortcomings. I feel less keen to pursue it. 'Besides,' he says, 'I was pissed!'

Now that's something I can attack. 'But why,' I say, 'are you always pissed?'

'Probably,' he says, 'because it depresses me to come home to a woman who is angry I've lost my job!'

'You've *got* a job!' I yell. 'You've bought a café, which cost you two hundred and fifty grand!'

'It's not just a café! It's four acres of seafront!'

'In Hythe!'

'A place that's filled with kite-surfers.'

'Please!' I shout. 'Don't talk to me about kite-surfing!'

'You don't like it! Fair enough. But loads of blokes do,

and it's free, and it's exciting. That site could be massive! We could make it a hotel. It could be the best place on the whole South Coast!'

'But it's currently a draughty shack,' I shout, 'where you spend *all* your time.'

'I'm trying to *build* something!'

'With Edmundo! Do you *trust* Edmundo?'

'Do you trust me?'

'I'm not sure I do . . .'

'See? This is why I drink! I'm coming home to someone who doesn't trust me . . .'

'It's not that I don't trust you!' I interject.

'And *who doesn't love me,*' he concludes.

And this time I don't protest quickly enough. I'm shocked to hear him say that.

'Hugh was the only one you ever loved!' continues Simon.

I stare at him. I simply don't know what to say.

'Hugh isn't even here, is he?' I try.

I've found my tongue at last, but I'm not able to mount much of a defence.

'But you think about him all the bloody time!'

'I think about him, yes,' I allow. 'Because he was a lovely, kind, talented man, and if he'd lived, he'd have done wonderful things with his life.'

'Look,' states Simon, 'Hugh is dead. End of.'

I turn away. I hate it when people say 'end of'. For a start it winds me up that they are missing out the word 'story', which is the best word in the whole language. And

I also hate it because they have never *told* the end of the story. Stories *don't* finish, not unless you're completely lacking in curiosity, and only an oaf would boast of that. Besides the story of Hugh is not finished. There are so many subplots left unresolved. *Why* did he die? And *what* might have saved him? And was it my fault?

'And maybe Hugh *wouldn't* have been dead,' I protest, 'if he'd only stayed at college. It was after that everything went wrong.'

'And how would we have kept him at college?' says Simon.

'I don't know!' I answer. 'We could have just . . . given him more love.'

'You'd have shagged him!'

'Oh, don't be so crude!' I complain. 'The point about Hugh wasn't that he was sexy . . .' Though, Lord knows, he was! 'He was clever, and a brilliant talker . . .'

'I get it!' says Simon. 'I get it! That's what you think, isn't it? If you could change the past, you think you would have chosen him.'

Did Simon really say that? Did I miss him saying that?

'That's what you think,' he repeats. 'Don't you? *Don't you?*'

Simon has his hands on his hips, and, as he approaches me, he juts his head forward on each new question. I was once attacked by a goose under the delusion I was trying to disturb her chicks. I'm reminded of it now.

'That's ridiculous!' I protest.

'Is it?' says Simon.

'You're the one with the bloody pineapple-flavoured condoms!' I shout. 'I'm not that keen on pineapple. Especially when it's mixed with latex, and stretched over a cock.'

I feel ugly swearing like this. But I am so angry. I hate this whole conversation. I hate this bedroom. I leave it at speed. I charge down the stairs. Reaching the bathroom on the first floor, I see the tub is still filled with submarines and Action Men wearing sub-aqua equipment. Sighing, I kneel down by the bath, and begin lifting them out. My hand is shaking, and I'm trying not to cry. The row seemed to come from nowhere like a squall at sea.

Having experienced it again, inside my body, I'm feeling shocked too.

If anything, I'm feeling even worse. I know that the row led to a catastrophic chain of events. Simon stormed off to spend the night in his room above the garage, and I was still cross the next morning, and then I got out of the van when he wanted to go to the beach, and then I ended up driving my car off the side of the hill. That must not happen again. I feel desperate to prevent it. Behind me, I can hear Simon angrily clattering down the stairs. What can I do?

You must stop him going out, I whisper to myself. *Get up and apologise.*

But my words don't have the desired effect. Kneeling by the bath, I was already feeling bewildered by the row. Now I feel terrified by hearing a voice inside my head. I'm wondering if I'm entering a psychotic state, brought on by stress, low blood sugar, and bulimic eating. I stand up, but maybe I've moved too fast. I'm having a white out. I can hear Simon passing outside the bathroom, but I feel powerless to stop him. Sounds are growing muffled. Vision is bleaching away. I hold a hand out towards the towel rail to steady myself, but I don't grip it, I just grab a towel. And so I don't rush out and apologise. I fall back down towards the floor.

When my vision clears, I find I'm on my hands and knees on concrete paving stones.

On the floor next to me is a leaflet for a pizza company, which has gone wet in the rain. An ant is walking over it. Beside that is a sketchbook. It is open. There's an aged photograph of some swimmers, stuck to the page with yellowed Sellotape. Where am I now? And what the hell is going on?

I kneel up. I'm outside a terraced city house.

With a dull thud of surprise, I see I'm outside Hugh's flat, which I last saw when I was twenty-two. I'm reassured by that. If I could change the past, then this is definitely the place to go. I am crawling around. What am I doing? I shift a plastic bucket filled with empty bottles. Beside that, there's one of those metal objects you use for pulling off boots. It's shaped like a frog. Under it I find a key. I pick it up, and take it to the door.

Before putting the key in the lock, I kneel down and call through the letterbox.

'Hugh!' I shout. 'It's me! Lucy! I'm coming in!'

I wait for a moment at the letterbox, but the house is completely silent. Has Hugh gone out? wonders my twenty-two-year-old self. Of course it would be amazing if he had gone out; it would also be unfortunate. I want to see him. I need to talk to him.

'Anyway,' I call, 'I'm coming up.'

I turn the key, and push open the door.

There's a huge pile of junk mail inside the front door. Pizza deliveries. Cab firms. Indian food. The stuff is an inch deep. It's not surprising people get depressed, I figure. The outside world just wants to make money out of you.

'Hugh,' I call again. I glance up towards the living room where he spends his time.

It looks unusually dark in there. The curtains are blocking the windows.

'Hugh,' I call again.

I go up to the living room.

I'm expecting to see him in the armchair to the right of the door. There's an ashtray on the armrest, filled with cigarette butts and Rizlas. But there's no Hugh.

I duck out.

'Hugh,' I call again.

I glance quickly into his bedroom – it's a fusty nest with an unmade double bed with twisted duvets on it, scattered with dirty clothes and books. I can't help but look at what he's been reading. As usual the list is eclectic. There's some Montaigne. There's a book called *Think Yourself Healthy* by Avi Goldberg

Reich. There's a book on Erik Satie, open at a page which shows a handwritten manuscript of his music. The instructions say '*Léger comme un oeuf*' ('light as an egg'). That makes me smile. Hugh loves Satie. Where the hell is he?

I head down the corridor towards the bathroom.

As I step inside, I can see something's wrong. There's a bottle of gin lying on the brown linoleum. There are also four boxes of Nurofen Plus. Beside them lie several blister packs, all empty of Nurofen Plus. Already fearing the worst, I edge in there sideways.

Hugh is lying, very still, in the bath.

Incongruously, he's wearing a suit and tie. His eyes are shut. His face looks very beautiful and quite serene. His eyebrows are lifted as if he's listening to piano music played more brilliantly than ever before.

The bath is red with blood.

In movies, when people get bad news, they instantly cry or scream. I don't. I just stare at him for several seconds. I feel as if my insides are being scooped out, to be replaced with cement. Then, suddenly retching, I swivel towards the avocado-coloured sink that's been splattered with toothpaste. I am weak. I can't stand up. My legs buckle. I fall back against the bath. I shut my eyes.

And then suddenly it's not the bath I'm sitting on.

I'm on the hot back seat of a car, and my mum is right in front of me.

Her face is enormous and red.

'I WANT NEVER GETS!' she shouts. 'You are a very SPOILED and GREEDY little girl!'

I really want to get away from her. But I am trapped in this car. I can't move my legs. There's a weight on my chest. There's an unbearable pressure in my head, and I shut my eyes in pain.

CHAPTER 3

And now I wake up, and I see it.

I am trapped in a car.

I am upside down, and the full weight of my body is pressing down on my head, which has been forced back. The steering wheel is pushing very forcefully against my chest, and my legs are numb. I know instinctively that I have terrible injuries which I cannot yet feel. For the moment I am more bothered by the pressure on my head. I'm leaning hard on it, it is swollen with blood, and it feels as if it could burst. I can smell petrol, and there's a taste in my mouth like iron filings. I begin to realise what I've been trying to avoid all along . . .

I've been in a terrible car crash.

Because I am upside down, it looks as if the sky is green and has fallen on my head. Just above my eyeline, I can see a patch of grass which has been sprinkled with jagged cubes of glass. A large bee appears. It hovers, terrifyingly near, as if inspecting the glass. I have a mortal fear it may start walking over my face.

I am just thinking this when a huge black crow appears, upside down, and bounds towards me over the grass. It seems to be bouncing off the ceiling. It stops just feet away from me. Turns its head as if sizing me up. I look at its scaly feet, its strong beak. I am terrified it's about to leap towards me and pluck out the Turkish Delight of my eyes.

It springs closer.

Panicked, I dodge away from the crow. I crawl feverishly from the car – over the grass scattered with glass. I crawl twelve feet, before I ask the obvious question: *How the hell did I do that?*

I kneel up in the grass, and look back.

Bizarrely, the car wheels are still turning, as if the crash has only just happened. The bonnet is concertinaed, and the roof has been squashed down. Through the shattered window, I can see my pale face. It is wedged against the floor. A little trail of blood is snaking its way down my neck and on to my chin.

Somehow I have left my body. *Does that mean that I'm dying? Am I already dead?*

The terror slowly steals over me, like a coldness that spreads from my feet up to my head. A brown shape is lying in the grass, a few feet from the car. It's Kipper. His head has been wrenched into a sickening angle. The crow considers him a moment, then it flaps heavily across the grassy field towards the wooden gate. I can see the

Newsomes' farm, Mrs Eden's cottage, and, just visible over the top of the Newsomes' barn, I see the roof of our house. Now I think of my boys, and I'm desperate to get there. I need to see them. I start to move.

But I hear a voice.

'Stay here,' it says. It's a male voice – commanding and strong – and it is so loud it's as if it's speaking from inside my head.

Terrified, I turn and look for only the briefest moment.

In front of the trees behind me stands the figure of an old man wearing dirty white robes. He seems tall, and very strong. I see pale, chalky skin, and light blue eyes. There is something unearthly about the power of him, and the way he's just waiting there, all impassive, as if he knows everything I've been doing and everything I'm going to do.

'Do not leave your body,' he commands.

But his words have the opposite effect. I am so alarmed by him, and so terrified I may be prevented from seeing my boys, I flee away. I don't care about danger. I need to see my children. And I realise I *am* going to them, fast. Indeed, I am floating above the ground, travelling over the long green grass at an inhuman speed.

The gate to the field is open.

I hurry through it, and up the street. I pass the Newsomes' farm. In moments, I'm making my way towards my house. As I pass up the side of it, I look through the open window into the living room. And stop, because there they are.

There are my children.

They are sitting on the sofa. Hal's watching *Prank Patrol*. Tom's on the sofa beside him, doing a drawing on a pad of paper. It's of a dog. Tom already seems in need of some maternal attention. His hair is messy. He's got a little boyish scab on his left knee. He throws his drawing to the floor. He immediately starts a new one. It's a dog. Abruptly he throws down this drawing.

'Mum?' he calls.

Does he sense I'm here?

'Mum?' he calls again, a bit louder.

'She can't hear,' Hal tells him. 'She hasn't come back yet.'

'I think I heard her,' insists Tom. '*Mum!*' he shouts. 'Hal said I can't watch *Timmy Time*!'

'OK,' decides Hal. He hands Tom the remote. 'You watch what you want.'

Surprised, Tom takes the remote. But he doesn't seem satisfied.

'Where is Mum?' he complains. 'I'm hungry!'

Hal clicks off the TV, and looks at his brother seriously. What's he going to do?

'Tom,' he decides, 'Mum must have got held up somewhere. Let's go to the kitchen and make some toast. Then we'll call her mobile.'

'Do you know her number?' asks Tom, incredulous at this display of competence.

''Course,' answers Hal. He's not Simon's son for nothing. He's fantastically capable. 'And I know Dad's as well. It's on the fridge.'

The two boys get up and troop out of the room – the big one leading the little one.

I go round the outside of the house, so I'm ready to see them as they appear in the kitchen. Hal comes in first, with the phone to his ear. He pulls a chair from the kitchen table. He drags it over to the toaster. He climbs up. For a moment, he considers the fried chicken and the corn on the cob, but rejects them. He puts bread in the toaster. I ache with love for him.

'Hi, Dad,' he says into the phone, 'me and Tom were wondering where you are, because Mum went out to the shop but she hasn't come back yet. Can you call?' He grins. 'Also, me and Tom think the best theme tune on CBeebies is *64 Zoo Lane*. We think you could make a tune with it. 'Cept Tom thinks you should change it.' He starts singing. '"*64, 64, 64 Poo Lane!*"' He has a shy smirk on his face. He is obviously pleased with this comic theme, but he's not moved to riff on it further. ''Bye!' he says suddenly, and rings off. He puts the phone down a moment, and produces butter from the fridge. What else will he find? I'm fascinated to know what my wise, competent son is going to put on the toast. There's Philadelphia in that fridge. There's hummus.

He gets out the strawberry jam. Oh, well.

The door slams open. Tom appears. He's walking backwards. For some reason, he's dragging a paddling pool after him. He knocks over a broom, then the bin. Hal looks at him, clearly considering: should he reprimand his brother? Yes, Hal, you should! No kitchen requires a paddling pool!

The toast pops up.

The toaster is close to the window, so as Hal turns to it, he is only two feet away from me. He starts buttering carefully. He is so close that I can see each freckle on his nose. He is so close I can see that his hair is sticking up, as it always does, on the back of his head. I realise I know the smell of his head. He smells of hot Weetabix and baked apples and boy. I would do almost anything to smell that again, but I can't. I just stand on the other side of the window, unseen, feeling so much love for him it makes me weak.

'Leave them,' says a voice.

I swivel. I can see the old man in white. Unsettlingly, though it sounded as if he was right behind me, he is at least two hundred feet away. He's standing in the middle of the street, outside Mrs Eden's cottage.

'You need to come back now,' he directs.

As he summons me, I feel instantly drawn towards him. Drifting away from the kitchen window, I glance in one last time, and see Tom heading towards his toast. But then my pace picks up. In a rush of wind, I speed past the front of our house, and up the muddy road towards Mrs Eden's. But when I reach her cottage, the old man is no longer here.

'You don't have much time,' he repeats.

I look up to see that now he's back in the field, standing like a sinister sentinel in front of the crashed car. As I hurtle towards him, I feel as if I'm being summoned by a cross headmaster.

Brought to a sudden stop ten feet away, I stare up into his face. It's like staring at a dinosaur. He looks impassive, and ancient, and dangerously powerful. His pate is blotchy with freckles, and there's just a sparse covering of hair on it. His eyes are red-rimmed and pale.

'If you leave your body,' he tells me, 'time passes. And you don't have much time.'

'What's happening?' I plead.

'You tell me.'

'I've had a crash,' I begin, 'and when people have accidents, I hear, their lives flash before them. And that's happening to me, except I'm only seeing bits, and it's all in the wrong order.'

'History is interpretation,' he says. 'You remember what you wish. Our past is one we have chosen.'

'But,' I protest, 'I didn't choose any of this! I wish I could change *all* of it!'

'What did you not choose?'

'Well, I didn't choose to crash,' I start.

'And yet,' says the man, 'your car was unfit for the road, and you drove it too fast, and when you met another vehicle, you accelerated still further, and steered off the slope.'

His voice is strong and even, like the current of a wide

river. There's a chillingly persuasive logic to what he's saying.

'Thought matters,' he says. 'You have willed yourself into this situation. Can you will yourself out of it? You must become clear.'

'Who are you?' I ask.

He ignores the question.

'What else do you wish had not happened?' he asks again.

There's no ignoring that. I begin flicking through my memories, wondering what I would have wished to change. But it's like looking through your wardrobe, trying to decide which clothes you want to throw out. There are always so many you don't like; none you'd definitely want to lose.

'At college,' I begin, 'I knew a man called Hugh. He was kind and talented, but he left and he died. I always wish I'd helped him, given him some love.'

Is the man satisfied with my answer? He remains impassive.

'So,' he says, 'why didn't you?'

Why didn't I indeed? Just thinking about it makes the guilt slosh inside me like rusty liquid.

'Would you like to know?' he asks.

'Yes!'

'Would you say you need to know?'

'Yes!' I insist. 'I *need* to know!'

At this, the man purses his wrinkled lips and he blows at me. I smell an earthy smell, full of mud and mulch and the kind of air that you'd smell deep underground. I shut my eyes. His breath eases me backwards towards the car. I am driven down towards my upside-down, bleeding body, and pushed back into it, as if I'm being born all over again, except in reverse. For a moment, I once again have the feeling that I'm floating in an underground tunnel. I can hear beautiful choral music up ahead.

Chapter 4

'Open your eyes, darling,' says a voice. 'The Lady's here.'

I wake with a start and open my eyes.

I'm looking at my mum.

She looks young and pretty, though somewhat bizarre. She's wearing the green scarf from Clothkits, her hair in that tight blonde perm, and thick eye make-up in shades of orange and brown.

'Pay attention,' directs Mum. 'Here's The Lady.'

I look round slowly.

I see my brother in his buggy. He's asleep, but still dissatisfied. It looks as if, at any moment, he might wake, and if he does, he will protest his grievances very strongly.

I'm in a shoe shop.

It has the shoe-shop smell, which is a bit like hairspray and a bit like carpets just after you've Hoovered. Green boxes are piled against the wall and the shoes are standing on top of them. I also notice a pillar on which there's a mirror, and I can see myself in it. I see my messy fringe and my round all-watching eyes and my dungarees which have a rip at the knee. Now I look into the face of The Lady. She has on a brown outfit. She looks far older than any woman you would see serving in a shoe shop today. She must be in her fifties.

'What sort of shoes would she like?' says The Lady, looking at me. 'Lace-ups or sandals?'

'Sandals,' answers Mum.

'Very good,' comments The Lady. She seems pleased by that. 'I shall have to measure you. Take off your boots, please.'

The Lady is sliding over the special stool, which is padded on top with one broad sloping side. She then disappears behind the pillar, and when she reappears is proudly brandishing an even more important tool of her trade: The Measurer. As I kick off my Wellies, I begin to wake up to the thoughts of my young self. I'm thinking about Cinderella. This feels like the moment when she sees if her foot will fit the glass slipper. I've never understood why one would wear a glass slipper, especially for dancing. Wouldn't it break?

'Place your foot on this, please,' orders The Lady, in a clear sterile voice that speaks of antiseptic, of hospitals and incisions. Nevertheless, I put my foot on to The Measurer, and now – I had forgotten the exquisite pleasure of this! – The Lady carefully wraps my foot in her special tape. And then – and this is even better! – she slides down The Measurer until it kisses the top of my toe.

'She's a twelve!' declares The Lady.

'A twelve!' enthuses Mum, who sounds very pleased. 'Soon you'll be in Big Girl sizes!' she says. I don't like the sound of Big Girl sizes, but Mum does.

'I'll see what I can find,' The Lady informs us.

This comment takes me by surprise. I am used to the modern system, whereby the shoe-buyer chooses their own shoes. But in this establishment, The Lady gets that job. She disappears into her holy sanctuary: the secret back room. I am wondering: Why can't I go in there? I would surely be the best person to choose my own shoes. But, no. The Lady emerges with a box. My young self is now rabid with curiosity. I'd forgotten just what strong opinions a five-year-old girl can hold about shoes. I really really want to see what shoes I've got. But you cannot hurry The Lady. She takes off the lid and carefully uncovers the shoe, which has been swaddled in white tissue as if it's cold. And, finally, there it is . . .

The Shoe.

I practically recoil. It is quite the most disgusting one I've ever seen. It is a reddy-brown colour. It is the colour a shoe would be, had it been made of poo then wiped with ketchup. Trying to make it better, someone has clumsily punched the outline of a butterfly on the toes –

'Do you like it?' asks The Lady.

Out of politeness, I inspect the shoe. There must be someone in the world who might like it – some church-going girl who likes old-fashioned dollies and long woolly socks with patterns on. I have never been that sort of girl.

'I don't really like it,' I answer, quietly.

'Lucy,' warns Mum. 'Don't be rude.'

That seems unfair. The Lady canvassed an opinion, so it would have been ruder, surely, to have said nothing.

'Just try them on,' commands Mum.

Oh, no. I don't want to do that. Even though I'm only five, I already know Mum's habits. If The Shoe so much as touches my foot, then something very very very bad will happen. The Shoe will become mine.

'At least we'll know if it's the right size,' says Mum.

Oh, dear. This is one of her tactics. She tricks me into wearing The Shoe, and as soon as I am, she buys it. I really don't want that shoe, and I feel so angry because I know there's nothing I can do about it. I am actually about to cry.

'And in a minute we can get an ice cream,' promises Mum.

I am now urgently swallowing, in an effort to avoid crying. The Lady begins to encase my foot in the stiff flat shoe. I remember this feeling of submission so well. I can feel that the shoe will give me blisters, but there's no point telling Mum, she won't listen. Wanting to be anywhere but here, I turn and face the window. Opposite there is an empty shop, and a sign saying 'To let'. Instinctively, I add the missing letter 'i' so the sign says 'toilet'. This whole place is a toilet. People should walk off the streets so they can wee on these horrid poo shoes.

'There,' instructs The Lady. 'Just walk around the shop, and see how they feel.'

OK, thinks my young self. I shall walk, I shall say how very very bad the shoe feels, then perhaps I shall escape.

I stand.

'Off you go,' directs Mum. She is cross. The Lady is too. They both have tired cross faces and it makes me feel as if I'm swimming in a pool and can't touch the bottom. I see it. I must try to walk. Embarrassed by the scrutiny, though, I have forgotten how. When do you move your arms? It's impossible anyway, because these revolting shoes are so stiff and flat it would be easier to walk in flippers. But I walk. Give me credit, I walk. I go down to the end of the shop.

And as I arrive, I see something wonderful and surprising. How did I miss this? They are right there in a special section near the door . . . Kicker boots!!! Yes! These look like the ones Gemma has. The one I really really *love* is at the bottom of the display. It's a twelve! It's perfect. It is red, and it's got a bouncy rubber sole, and a little hole there where you can see a bit of red peeping through. This one is actually better than Gemma's. I must buy these boots and then I will run and I will swing on the swings, kicking my feet in the sky, and everyone will see the red spot peeping out like a little sun.

I run back to Mum.

I must tell my mother about the Kickers. But she is busy with The Lady.

'And that style is fifteen per cent off,' The Lady is informing her. She now turns to me. 'Did they slip?' she enquires.

'No,' I tell her. The sandals do not matter any more. I've seen what I want. 'Mum!' I explain. 'There are Kicker boots! Like Gemma has got! That's what I'd like!'

'You can't wear Kicker boots to school,' says Mum.

What? What's this? 'Why not?' I ask.

I feel as if I've just been shot with a dart.

'Don't be silly,' Mum tells me. Why is that silly? 'And these are fifteen per cent off.'

Yes! Because they're horrible! You could be paid to wear them, and no one would want them!

I sit down. And, luckily, to my profound relief, The Lady removes the sandals. It's clear she is actually on the side of the suffering child. The Lady places both shoes back in the box. The lid is put back on. My horror is subsiding. It's all going to be all right.

But then . . .

'Thank you,' says Mum, and she *takes the box. What is she doing with the box?* She takes them to the till. No! NOOO!! *Keep away from the till!* I follow after her. I could so easily cry, but I'm trying not to. I am trying to Be Grown Up.

'Mum,' I say, clearly and quietly, 'I'd really prefer the Kicker boots.'

'Well, it's your birthday next week,' she reminds me. 'We can come back then.'

'Really?' I squeak.

This sounds like another trick. I'm thinking I should have just cried.

'Are you sure?' I ask.

'I'll get these for now,' Mum tells me. 'We can't stay because Paul needs his tea, but we'll come back next week.'

I am still worried. But if Mum is telling the truth, that means I've only got to wait a few days, and then I can get the boots. But *is* she telling the truth?

'Come on, darling,' says Mum. 'I'll just pay for these. Then let's go and get a lolly.'

A lolly? Just now, it was an ice cream! A lolly is *not* the same as an ice cream! It is smaller and less filling. You never get what you want.

Still . . . a lolly is better than nothing.

'How many days till we can come back?' I ask. I need to be sure of this.

'Three,' says Mum. 'We'll come after we've taken Paul to the doctor.'

Mum leads the way out of the shop. She pushes the door, and it opens with a clunk.

Outside in the street, I brace myself for a moment. The air is hot, like the air from an oven. I shut my eyes against the glare.

When I open them again, we are not in the town centre, opposite a sign saying 'To Let'.

We are outside the doctor's.

Mum is wheeling Paul away in his buggy made from blue-and-white-striped material that looks like a deckchair. I stand on the baking pavement in the hot sunshine.

Meanwhile my confused forty-three-year-old mind is scrambling to catch up and make sense of everything. It feels like a snow globe. After a few seconds, everything settles down, and I see it . . .

Three days have actually passed.

My young self is sure of that. I know, very well indeed, that three days have passed. We have just taken Paul to the doctor's. He's got something gooey in his ears, and Mum has been given some special drops. We're now walking into town. That's good. That is excellent, in fact. I need to get to the shoe shop to try on Kicker boots so I can buy some before my birthday, which is tomorrow. The red ones are probably my favourites, but I do like the green ones too which would look *amazing* with my green party dress. Maybe I could have two pairs – a red and a green! Maybe I could wear one boot from each pair – a green foot and a red foot! That's brilliant! Why do people not do that?

I hurry after Mum.

She has stopped at the car, which is parked alongside the scalding hot pavement. I think she needs to get something out of it. She opens the door but it's so hot she actually burns her hand on the door handle and then flaps it about in the air. I have never seen a day as hot as this. There is some old bubble gum on the pavement and it has melted. I prod it with the horrible poo sandals, and it sticks on the rubber lip. I pull it, making a trapeze of pink. Then I have to scrape the sole on the pavement.

Mum is lifting Paul out of the buggy.

What is she doing?

I have to remind her. 'Mum!' I point out. 'We need to go and get the Kicker boots!'

She gives me a really cross look.

'It's my birthday tomorrow, remember!'

Now Mum gives me an even crosser look. It's as if I've invented my birthday, just to annoy her. But I stand my ground. I feel the case is very clear. We've already been to get the drops for Paul's gooey ear. It's my birthday tomorrow: why can't we get my boots?

'Come on then,' she says abruptly. 'If we're going to get those boots, let's get a move on.'

I look ahead.

Walking to the shoe shop feels like walking across a desert. We've parked next to a row of houses. They're making a little mat of shade on the pavement. But after that everything is in the sun. The cars are gleaming. The very tarmac is sweating and shimmering.

'We don't have long,' says Mum, and she walks ahead.

Mum is a very fast walker. She has already marched quite far in front. You don't have much time, I think. There's a danger Mum might change her mind. I have never needed anything more than I need those boots. I start running. I run past Mum, and then I sprint for the end of the pavement.

'*Wait!*' screams Mum – far too loud – and I stop.

Actually I was about to run out into the street, and I think that somehow Mum knows this and she's cross. Is she going to smack me? I stop obediently and I glance into the front room of the house next to me. I can see a couple kissing while watching a blond-haired man on TV. I know who that is. It's Bjorn Borg. Everywhere you go, you see him on TV. Mum reaches me. She too glances into the house a moment. Then she turns towards me and she looks absolutely furious. I see it. She *is* going to smack me. I knew it!

She swoops towards me, and she grabs my arm.

'Mum?' I ask. 'What is it?'

'Get back in the car!' she shouts.

'But what about the boots?' I remind her.

'*Back in the car!*' she screams.

I try and pull away from her. I need those boots. I do not want to be stopped, but Mum grabs my shoulder so hard she pinches the skin.

'But I need those boots!' I tell her.

'I do NOT want to talk about it!' warns Mum.

And she doesn't. I try and pull away. Instantly Mum yanks my arm as if she's trying to pull it from its socket, and she gives me a crisp smack on my forearm, which stops my escape. Mum now puts her arm between my legs and scoops me up like I'm a parcel. Before I know it, my legs are kicking in the air and my face is being squeezed into her tummy – my nose is being crushed into her stomach so I can't actually breathe, which makes me feel panicky – and the back of my head is pushing against the plastic handle of the buggy.

'*Mum!*' I shout into her stomach. 'But you *said* I could have those boots!'

It's no use though. Very quickly we're back at the car.

Mum opens the back door, and thrusts me on to the back seat. It's so hot it singes my leg. 'Ow!' I scream. 'You are *burning* my leg!'

'*Just shut up!*' screams Mum, and slams the door.

I can't believe it.

Then she comes round the other side and puts Paul in as well. As soon as he touches the back seat, he screams far louder. I watch Mum as she marches round to the front of the car. Her hair bounces as she walks. I have never seen her more cross, and it's terrifying and it's also *very unfair.* I had NOT stepped out into the road: she has got cross with me *for nothing*!

As soon as she's back in the driver's seat, I start up again.

'Mum!' I shriek. 'It is NOT fair! You *said* I could have the Kicker boots!'

'*Be quiet!*'

'But it is my birthday!' I assert. 'And you SAID . . .'

The trouble is, Mum doesn't want to talk about what she said. She doesn't want to talk at all. She silences all opposition like a seventies mum. She whacks her hand hard on my right thigh, and I'm wearing a skirt so it really hurts.

'Ow!' I yelp. That's the leg I just burned on the seat. But this smack stings far worse. It's already going red. '*Mum!*' I yell.

'I have HAD ENOUGH!' shouts my mum. 'You are a very SPOILED and GREEDY little girl!' She's shouting as if she wants to stamp each word into my head.

'But Mum . . .' I begin. I know I have to say something or I'll never get the boots. But I'm about to cry. My throat is starting to close up. I can feel the tears bursting out from behind my eyes, ready to surge down my cheeks. I try to force them back. I'm *not* going to cry. 'I *want* those boots!' I shout.

And now Mum can't take it any more. She shouts it as loud as she can. 'I WANT NEVER GETS! You're a very SPOILED and GREEDY little girl! And when we get home, you're going *straight to your room!*'

And now she's sending me to my room!

It's so unfair! But I'm *not* going to cry. I squeeze my eyes tight shut. I can hear Mum starting the car, and as she drives off with a lurch, I am swept away.

I open my eyes. The feeling of movement stops.

I am in my bedroom.

I know why, and my young self knows it too: I've been sent here, by Mum, because I got cross when she wouldn't let me have the boots I wanted, even though it's my birthday tomorrow, and she *said* I could have them. I'm still furious about that. It's not as bad as it was, but the burning sense of injustice is still there, like one of those yellow-purple patches that stay behind after a bruise stops hurting. I wish I could be helped. If I was Cinderella, a fairy godmother would have appeared about now. That's definitely what I need. '*Lucy,*' says a gentle voice in my mind, *'it's all right.'* But just hearing that doesn't make everything all right. In fact, I feel a bit dizzy and scared to be hearing strange voices, and I definitely don't see a fairy godmother.

I sniff. I'm *not* going to cry.

I look at my Fisher-Price farm, and I do not see anything there that will cheer me up, even though the Fisher-Price farmer is in his yard, and he's got his Fisher-Price camper van, and his Fisher-Price dog, who's got his little red bow tie. I love that dog. I love that camper van, and have spent a long time playing with it, but I don't want to now. When you've been sent to your room, I don't think you're allowed to play.

What are you allowed to do when you're sent to your room?

I decide that I can play, but I must not use any actual toys. So first of all I pass a bit of time by shutting each eye in turn and looking at my nose. My nose stands out of the middle of my face like a shark's fin. When I open a different eye then my nose seems to jump from one side of my face to the other.

After that I fold my hands together, and I mumble: 'Here's the church, and here's the steeple . . .'

Mum pokes her head round the door.

I quickly put my hands down, and look up at her. I can see she's not cross any more. She's wearing more make-up.

'Would you like to come downstairs?' she asks. 'You can help me with your birthday cake.'

Does this mean I'm not a spoiled and greedy little girl

any more? I need Mum to see I've changed.

I say: 'Yes.' And I follow her. We have almost reached the bottom of the stairs when Mum talks to me.

'I've made a cake mixture,' she informs me. 'You can lick out the bowl.'

This takes me by surprise.

Licking out the bowl – that sounds *very* spoiled and greedy. It also sounds like the sort of thing the dog would do. But I would like to do it. I follow her into the kitchen. In the middle of the table stands Mum's Kenwood mixer, looking as if it's tired from its work. The top is leaning back, and the whisk is lavishly coated with cake mixture. A fat globule is falling into the big white mixing bowl. I climb up on to a chair and I peer into the bowl, like a fairy-tale princess peering down a well, and straight away my mouth has gone all juicy. As Mum has implied, this is a bowl which is sorely in need of a damn good licking. But can I do it? Would that mean I'm a spoiled and greedy little girl? I'm not sure.

Either way, I can resist no longer.

First, I run my hand round the top, and I get a big fingerful of mixture. It's a bit brown, and you can see the grains of sugar. Then I lick the finger. There are a few dry specks of flour in this fingerful, but nevertheless the extraordinarily delicious taste gives me a wonderfully warm feeling inside. When I'm older, I promise, I will make cake mixture every day, and I'll never waste it by making a cake. I'll just make a nice big bowlful and then I'll lick it out. At the bottom of the bowl there are some thicker lumps. I swipe those with my finger so I've got thick mixture all the way down to the knuckle, and I plunge the whole finger into my mouth.

'Lucy!' scolds Mum. 'Use a spoon! You really are disgusting!'

I stop.

I want to swallow the mixture but I don't know if I'm allowed. I thought Mum and I were friends again, and her cross voice takes me by surprise. It's bad being shouted at in the street because you're about to run out into the road, but it's even worse when you're thinking that everything is fine and you've nothing to do but lick out a bowl. I stare for a moment, at the flowers on the wallpaper, trying not to swallow and trying not to cry. My mum puts a spoon on the table in front of me. It's the horrid old one. There's a patch in the middle of it which has gone a bit yellow. When you put it in your mouth, there's a sharp taste, like the one you get if you lick an old battery. But I don't ask Mum to change the spoon. It's clear I have no vote, and no say, and I will never get what I want. Instead I just use the spoon to scrape up the cake mixture. It leaves a metallic taste which spoils things a bit, but I carry on eating. Mum is not looking, and I can't stop myself. Slowly and carefully, I lick out the bowl, and while I do it, I am repeating in my mind 'You really are disgusting!' and 'I want never gets!', and the tears are running down my cheeks, and they're splashing into the cake mixture, and I keep eating, but I shut my eyes and gulp with the sheer humiliation of it all.

CHAPTER 5

Next thing I know, I am breathing in warm country air, and I realise: I'm back.

I feel cleansed. I feel relieved.

I can hear birds. I can smell wet mud, and tree bark, and even wild garlic. I open my eyes. I am lying on my back, on some grass, and I'm looking into the criss-cross branches of an oak tree, which are reaching up into a deep blue sky. I turn to my right. I see tall flowering nettles, and a clump of wild garlic with white flowers shaped like stars.

Then I turn to my left.

Oh.

I am on the ground, close to my crashed car.

Now I can smell the spilled petrol. Through the smashed car window, I can see my upside-down bleeding body. Blood is coming out of my mouth and it's dribbling past my nose into my hair. Flies have started to buzz round

Kipper's body. Now my pleasure at being back disappears fast. I feel sick.

I need to go and check on my boys. I stand.

I see the old man. Standing very still on the other side of the car, he is looking at me with his look of furious enquiry. Who is he? Some sort of Angel of Death come to take me away? He is blocking my way home. Dare I pass him?

'Who are you?' I ask.

Again, he ignores the question.

'What did you see?' he says.

I don't want to talk to him. I just want to go home.

'You went somewhere,' he intones. 'Where?'

'Maidstone,' I reply sullenly. 'Nineteen seventy-six. Why did you make me go there?'

'I did not make you go there,' he replies. 'You are in charge. You went there because you needed to.'

Is that true?

'How was it?' he asks.

'Hot,' I reply. 'Does this matter?'

'It matters intensely,' says the man. 'Everything has happened because you willed it. What did you learn in Maidstone?'

'My mother is an extraordinarily annoying woman,' I reply, in a sullen tone. Just talking about her has turned me into a sulky teenager again. 'She breaks her promises as if they mean nothing. As if I mean nothing. She becomes furious for no reason. She screams things such as: "I want never gets!" And then if she wants me to cheer up, she gives food.'

Is this the sort of answer he wants? What does he want? He gives me no clue whatsoever.

'And how do you think,' he says, 'that affected you?'

'I became a self-hating bulimic,' I respond, 'who thinks she can't get the things she wants.'

'Such as?'

'Such as the man she loved,' I answer. 'And if I'd given love to Hugh, I might have stopped him dying.'

The old man turns his head slightly, but doesn't alter the expression in his primordial eyes.

'You cannot change other people,' he asserts.

'But if I'd believed I deserved Hugh,' I respond, 'I might have given him love, at a point in his life when he most needed it. And that might have changed everything.'

'You must be clear,' says the man.

What must I be clear about? Why Hugh died? Was it my fault? Could I have saved him? Did I choose the wrong man when I chose Simon?

'What exactly do you want to know?' he says.

'Whether Hugh loved me,' I reply. Instantly I feel guilty about that response. Was there a better one?

'Perhaps he did,' says the man.

'Yes,' I answer, 'but it didn't happen. We never . . .' What am I trying to say? That I never made love to Hugh? Is that what this is about? Would that have changed things?

'You have a brief opportunity to see your past again,' says the man. 'But you cannot interfere. You cannot change it.'

But is that true? I saw Hugh and we kissed! That never happened in real life!

'Why can't I change the past?' I ask, and just asking it makes me feel guilty.

'You're seeing memories,' he says. 'They appear real because you know they happened, and thus you see each sight, you hear each sound. If you changed them, they would fragment and you would be nowhere.'

'So what would happen then?'

'You may die.'

But I didn't die! I kissed him, and I smelled the wine on his breath, and then I ran from that room. What would have happened if I'd stayed?

The old man is blowing softly towards me, and I can smell his somniferous breath with its taints of mud and earth and the roots of cut flowers when they've been left too long in the vase.

'Be clear,' he says. 'What do you feel you need to know?'

'I need to know why Hugh died,' I say, and with those words I feel like the Witch of the West covered in water. I'm melting back down towards the car, towards my body. But I don't want this. *I just want to see my boys.* But I can't. My eyes are closing. I am draining back into my body, like water going down a plughole. I am entering a dark underground tunnel, being buffeted by Stygian water. *No! I can't do this! I cannot take this!*

I'm gone.

Chapter 6

I'm saying it over and over: 'I can't take this! I can't take this!'

I sit still, my head slumped forward on my hands.

I sit up.

I am at a desk which is tucked into the gables of a building. In front of me is a window. Through it I can see sandstone cornicing and a stone balcony, and beyond that I see the night sky.

It takes me a moment to realise where I am . . .

I'm in my room in Oxford, the one I had for the first two terms. I feel as if I've just woken up from the most intense dream but all that has gone, like morning dew in sunshine. Now I think: what am I doing? And it's like being adrift in a boat where you hear gurglings beneath the hull: I can hear my own student thoughts.

I orient myself . . .

I've been here at Oxford a week. Around me are piles of books, mainly connected to *The Faerie Queene* by Edmund Spenser. I am writing the very first essay of my university career, and it's not going well. The books lie slumped on their spines. The room is heavy with a sense of lethargy and despair.

In front of me is the essay itself.

So far I've written my name. Lucy Potts. I've underlined that three times. I've written the title: '*Spenser's Faerie Queene. An Exploration Into* . . .' At that point the title finishes. I can't decide what aspect of *The Faerie Queene* I'm doing an exploration into. I don't feel able to decide that. I feel trapped. I'm thinking: why am I even studying English? I want to be a painter, that's what I love, but Mum told me I need a degree so that if the painting doesn't work out, I've got something to fall back on. Why am I starting my career expecting to fall back?

There's a knock at the door.

My voice comes from deep within my chest. 'Come in,' I sigh.

The door opens.

And I cannot believe how wonderful this is. I cannot imagine who I'd rather see. It's eighteen-year-old Gemma, dressed as a young society lady. There's a hint of Audrey Hepburn in *Breakfast at Tiffany's*. She's got on a black pinafore dress, which I've never seen before. Her hair is up. Her kittenish eyelashes are thickly matted with mascara. There's a hint of blusher on her cheeks, a little smile on her lips.

I can't help but smile back at her.

'Hello, darling,' I hear myself say. 'What are you doing?'

'I'm going over to the hall,' Gemma informs me. 'There's a Cheese and Wine Society evening. I'm going to seek out Richard Scott.'

'Who's Richard Scott?'

'Very handsome and brilliant director in the second year. He's taking a production up to Edinburgh in the summer. I need to be part of his plans. Why don't you come and we can woo him together? You could offer to paint some backdrops.'

'I can't. I've got this bloody essay I'm supposed to be doing.'

'Can't you leave it?'

'If my mum heard you say that,' I exclaim, 'she would kill you. The tutorial is at nine in the morning. It's got to be in an hour before that.'

'How much have you done?'

'Nothing.'

'Nothing?'

'Well, I've read *The Faerie Queene*. Quite a lot of it. And then I've read a bit of this book.' I toss a book off my desk and on to the floor before her. 'And quite a lot of this one.' I chuck another. 'And quite a lot of this one . . .'

Gemma can see I'm being petulant. She obviously doesn't want to deal with it. She really wants to get to that party.

'Well,' she says, 'if you change your mind, come along. I'll be the fascinating one in the corner.'

'OK,' I say. I feel bad that I've dampened her excitement. 'Have fun.'

She goes out, taking a little bit of hope with her.

I open up *The Faerie Queene* again. I read some lines. I might as well be reading a foreign language. The words make no impression on me at all. My student self knows what to do. I should go out, I think, and get some chocolate. That'll give me a little lift and I can get going. Then it occurs to me: what I really need is cigarettes. I can't possibly work without them. At least if I have cigarettes I can stop thinking about cigarettes and there's a chance I might write this stupid essay.

I leap up.

As I put on my jacket, I check myself out in the little mirror above my sink. The light here is dim. Even so, I can see enough. I look casually dressed but good, in jeans and a white blouse. My skin is pale and smooth and my lips are red, and I can see that I'm not svelte but the effect is luscious, voluptuous. In short, I'm attractive. I can see that now. But then I realise that, as I look into the mirror, my eighteen-year-old self is staring back with self-hatred, picking away forensically at all my faults. I have three zits. It's not surprising, I tell myself, with the amount of chocolate I've been eating. Two of the zits are small and by my hairline, but one of them, on my left cheekbone, is big. Should I . . . ? I try to squeeze it. Mistake. It's now red and swollen like a small volcano. I try to squeeze it again.

Leave it, whispers my more mature self, *it's not the kind you squeeze.*

I realise I've broken the cardinal rule: I've interfered, and the effects are bad. I feel sick and dizzy. Is this because I've changed the memory, so it's started to fragment? My eighteen-year-old self is looking round, alarmed. I am thinking: what is the *matter* with me? I'm so angry with myself that I've failed to write this stupid essay. What have I been *doing* all week? I should just sleep, then leave college in the morning. But then new determination surges in from nowhere. *No*, I think, *I'm **not** going to give in*. I wrench open the door.

Outside I smell wood polish on the stairway. My head clears slightly.

I speed off down several flights of stairs. Riding like a passenger inside my youthful body, my older self is relieved. I want to see this memory play out. I know what happens. I shall not interfere again. I shall trust, I shall let things happen. At the foot of the stairs, I burst out into the night air, and now I'm cooled and calmed. Around me sixteenth-century buildings in red brick and sandstone huddle together around neatly cut grass. Above my head the stars are glinting from the sky. Wisteria is scenting the air.

I take a deep breath, and my young self is flushed with happiness.

I still can't believe I'm at Oxford University. I think of all the famous poets and artists who might have stood in this spot. Shelley came here. And Byron and Wilde and C. S. Lewis and MacNeice and Auden and Tolkien and . . . I am not sure I'm good enough to be here, and I'll be kicked out if I can't write this essay. I must buy fags.

I hurry up the road towards the pub.

Outside the King's Arms, I stop. I have the Edward Hopper moment: I'm in the dark, looking in. It looks warm inside. The light is waxy yellow on the drinkers' faces.

I enter.

There's a ring of men around the cigarette machine. They are clearly public schoolboys. They're louder than normal students, and they've got that sneery confidence about them. One of them is leaning possessively against the machine. He's wearing a green tweed jacket and a paisley tie. I talked to him in the dinner queue three nights ago. He's called George Teazle, he's a second-year PPE student in my college. He lives on the next staircase to mine. His dad is obviously something important – chairman of a bank or something. In the course of our brief conversation, Teazle said twice: 'When my dad was working with Mrs Thatcher . . .' He's now listening to a bloke in thick cords, who's got his back turned to me.

'I don't want to spend the fucking weekend in Oxford,' thick cords is saying, 'I want to go to the country . . .'

George Teazle's eyes fix on me.

'Do you want something?' he asks.

Clearly he has status within this group. Now he's interrupted the anecdote, everyone else pauses and looks at me.

'I just want some cigarettes,' I stammer.

Man in thick cords moves aside to let me pass. I feel embarrassed that the conversation has stopped on my account, and can feel my face prickling with heat. I'm now in the middle of this ring of men. I can sense them closing in around me. I fumble in my pocket, find a couple of quid, and thrust the coins in the machine. I scan quickly to see what brands are on offer. The Marlboros are out. I don't care. So are the Silk Cuts. There are Camels though. I like Camels. I associate them with the school trip to France I once took. I smoked loads and flirted with bloke after bloke, and it was glorious. I yank at the little drawer and try to pull out some Camels.

It won't open.

'You need more money,' says George Teazle. 'They put the price up to two pounds twenty.'

Now I'm even more embarrassed. I check my pockets stupidly, but I know I have nothing more. The men are waiting. I'm sensing them eyeing me up from behind, and my very buttocks are blushing with embarrassment. Having entered their circle, I don't want to leave without achieving my aim. Besides, I really want those cigarettes.

'You need another twenty pee,' says Teazle slowly.

I want to say: Yes, I'm not stupid, I do realise that, thank you.

Instead I ask: 'Do you have twenty pence?'

George Teazle doesn't even check his pockets.

'No,' he says. 'Sorry.'

'I'll pay you back obviously.'

'Listen,' he says, 'I've got a packet of Silk Cut someone left in my room. If you're coming back now, I'll give them to you.'

I don't want to go back to George Teazle's room. But I'm desperate to escape from this situation.

'Oh,' I say. 'Thanks.'

Of course, I realise I've created a further problem. How long am I supposed to wait while George Teazle finishes his drink? He's got a pint of ale with two inches left in it. He lifts it to his mouth. As he tips back his head, I can see his bottom lip fastened to the underside of the glass like a small wet slug. His Adam's apple bobs up and down twice. Then he puts the glass on the counter.

'Right,' he says with a faint twinkle in his eye. 'Let's go.'

I flash him a polite smile.

As we move off, the group turn. 'Nice work, Teazy,' says one of the blokes.

Oh, God. Is this supposed to be some sort of seduction scene?

As we leave the pub, Teazle opens the door for me. Say what you want about these public schoolboys, they do have good manners. Out on the street, he turns to me courteously.

'What are you up to tonight?'

'It's my first tutorial tomorrow,' I say. 'I'm supposed to be writing my essay. I can't do it.'

'Why not?'

'I just think all my ideas are bad.'

'They probably aren't,' he says quickly. He doesn't want to be drawn into the conversation. I think he feels embarrassed by my openness.

'I feel that everyone else is so clever and I'm not,' I say.

He sort of rolls his eyes in response. I decide to change the subject.

'Sorry to drag you away,' I say.

'That's OK.'

'Was it an important occasion?'

'No.' He says the word 'no' more poshly than anyone I've ever heard. He pronounces it 'nee'. 'It was just a bunch of schoolmates meeting up. You know what it's like.'

Actually I really don't.

I know only one person at Oxford – Gemma, who's determined to become the next Theatrical Sensation. When she and I walk around, we feel giddy with triumph and excitement. We're certain that, at any moment, everything will disappear as our clothes return to rags and our footmen back to mice. I don't explain this to George Teazle. I can't see him being up on Cinderella. In fact, conversation falters. Not knowing what else to do, I study my surroundings desperately. Through a window, I see a student with red hair who's boiling a kettle. I note a pigeon watching us from its perch on a gargoyle.

Once back in college, we climb up to his room on the first floor. It's far larger than mine. It's typical college accommodation: a square living room with dark wooden panelling, two doors leading off it to the bedrooms. There's no decoration apart from a framed photograph of a house at Eton College, and two Giotto prints. For the first time, I think I could like George Teazle. It's hard not to like someone who likes Giotto. I love the way the pictures are somehow sublime, and yet childish. Teazle finds the cigarettes in a drawer, and passes them over.

'Have one here if you like,' he says. 'I might have one myself.'

I figure it'll only take five minutes to smoke a cigarette, and it seems rude not to.

'OK,' I say, and pass one to him.

'Cheers.'

I sit down on his sofa. It's uncomfortable, and covered with an Indian throw. Teazle is rooting for a light in a desk. He finds one. He lights his own fag. Immediately the room starts to fill with Silk Cut smoke, which always seems somehow bluer and more chemically than other cigarettes.

'There you go,' he says. And lobs over the lighter.

He busies himself in the corner. On a tray he has a couple of tumblers and a bottle of whisky. He's like an old man, with his tweed jacket and his paisley tie. Who the hell has whisky in his room?

'This is quite special,' he announces. 'Why don't you just have a small one? It could loosen the mind.'

'All right,' I say.

He comes over with the whisky and sits beside me on the sofa. He flicks his ash on to a marble ashtray on the coffee table in front of him.

'Cheers,' he says, and we chink glasses. I hate chinking glasses. It feels so fake and stupid. But George Teazle has a hospitable twinkle in his eyes. I sip the whisky. It's like liquid fire. As it reaches my chest, it spreads warmth.

Crouching within my eighteen-year-old body, I've been lulled by the whole scene. But the whisky seems to rouse me to my senses. *What the hell am I doing?* I think. I realise it . . . Something bad is about to happen. I am about to make an enemy of George Teazle, and that's unwise. In years to come, he runs a hedge fund that puts him on the *Sunday Times* Rich List. In his late-thirties, he achieves notoriety when he buys an Edvard Munch reckoned to be the most expensive painting ever bought in a private sale, but apart from that George Teazle is one of those powerful men who work silently and in the darkness, like a snake. I want my young self to get out, but how would I tell her that? I cannot interfere. I can't white out now. I need to see what happens next.

'Don't worry about your essay,' says George Teazle. 'You shouldn't be unconfident.'

'Thank you,' I say.

'You're very good-looking, for a start,' he says.

'Thank you,' I say again.

I find that I'm staring with surprise into his eyes. What else should I say?

'I don't think I am good-looking actually,' I admit. 'But if I were, would that preclude me from being unconfident?'

'You're one hell of a lot better-looking than most students,' he states. Is that a compliment to me, or an insult to the Sisterhood of Female Students? I stare into George Teazle's face. I don't know what else to do. He's actually not bad-looking himself. He just has something cold and reptilian in his manner, which doesn't exactly lift a girl's spirits. Now he's reaching his face towards mine, as if he's peering at some dirt on my cheek. What is he doing? Is he inspecting my zit?

Then he kisses me.

Oh, Lord, I'm kissing George Teazle!

The kissing is not too unpleasant. He has placed his wet lips against mine. It doesn't feel too awful. It feels like he's being kind. Despite my revulsion, I feel a little happiness. Isn't it always nice to be kissed? I'm beautiful! I'm being kissed! Then his mouth opens and his tongue slithers out like a lizard from under a rock; Oh, God, what do I do? Above all, I feel embarrassed. Treacherously – and this really disgusts me – I feel briefly aroused.

Then Teazle touches my left breast.

Instinctively I push him away. Hard. I've forgotten, though, that I'm clutching the whisky glass and my tumbler hits his and they smash.

'What the fuck did you do that for?' he challenges, quite loudly.

'I'm sorry!' I burble. 'I'm really sorry! Do you want me to clean that up?'

There are a couple of big chunks of glass on the floor. I kneel down and pick them up.

'What the fuck did you do that for?' he demands again. 'These glasses are antique.'

He puts one polished brogue on my shoulder and pushes. I stumble back on to his coffee table, and the ashtray falls to the floor.

'Don't push me with your foot!' I shout.

I am still holding the broken glass in my hand. I feel a momentary spasm of rage. I chuck it at the wall, next to the framed picture of Eton College.

'You'd better fucking clear that up!' George Teazle warns.

Had I? Is he going to make me? I want to leave.

Just then the door opens, and a face appears.

'Hi,' says a very big and handsome man with a wonderfully smooth, even voice.

Watching within my eighteen-year-old self, I feel an intense rush of pleasure to see him. But I say nothing. I barely breathe. I don't want anything to change now.

'Is everything OK in here?' asks the man politely.

'Yup,' says Teazle.

The man's eyes flick to me inquisitively. I say nothing.

'I thought I heard some smashing and shouting,' says the newcomer.

'We're fine,' asserts Teazle.

The man's eyes go from him to me. Suddenly his face fills with warmth.

'Oh,' he says, 'just the person I need to see. I promised I'd pass you that book as soon as I'd finished with it!'

I'm about to say 'What?' at this transparent lie. Then I realise that this man has correctly assessed the situation. He is trying to help.

'Great!' I reply.

'If you come with me,' he suggests, 'I'll give it to you now.'

'Thanks.'

On auto-pilot, I quickly go over to him. In the doorway, I turn back to George Teazle. He's looking angry and shifty.

'Thanks for the drink,' I say. I don't want him to hate me.

The door shuts safely behind us. I'm back on the stairway. It has dark wooden panelling and dim lighting. I look into the face of my rescuer. I couldn't imagine anyone better suited to the role. He's very tall and broad. He also looks immensely kind.

'Are you OK?' he whispers.

'Yes,' I say. 'Thank you.'

'What happened?'

'Oh, he . . . tried to kiss me,' I said. 'Then he grabbed my breast.'

At this a cold look comes into the handsome man's eyes.

'What happened then?' he prompts.

'I pushed him off. Broke two glasses. Then he shoved me into the table with his foot.'

My rescuer smirks a little. 'But apart from that,' he says, 'he was a perfect gentleman.'

'Yes!' I say. For some reason I feel an overwhelming desire to laugh. I often do when I'm in trouble.

'Why did you even go in there?'

'He offered me some cigarettes,' I say. 'Oh, shit . . . I left them in there!'

'Want to go back in?' asks the big guy.

Now we're both stifling giggles.

'God!' I whisper. 'There is no chance on earth I'd go back in there!'

'It's OK,' the guy says. 'I have some in my room.' And pushes open the door opposite us. In the doorway, he turns to me. 'Of course,' he says, 'that's exactly what Teazle just said to lure you into his.'

In fact it hadn't occurred to me to doubt this guy. He's got a wonderfully relaxed manner. Somehow I'd trust him with my life.

'Actually,' I say, 'I'd love a cigarette.'

'Sounds like you need one!' he answers, opening the door.

I follow him in. There's a packet of red Marlboros lying on a sofa.

'Here,' he says.

I take one.

'By the way,' he says, holding out his hand, 'I'm Hugh Ashby.'

We shake hands, and that moment of touching him is wonderful. It's like drinking something cool on a hot day.

'I'm Lucy Potts,' I say.

His palm feels large and warm. I find myself relaxing despite the unpleasant scene with Teazle. I look around the room, which is covered in windsurfing pictures. Men with blond hair are leaping off waves amongst cascades of water.

'Are you a keen windsurfer?' I enquire.

'God, no!' Hugh smiles. 'That side belongs to my room mate. He worships some man called Robby Nash. Apparently he's quite good. This is my side . . .'

He waves to the other half of the room, which is piled with the most eclectic array of books. They're about architecture, art, and quite a few are on music. He has only one picture, which shows a twinkly-eyed man with a balding head and witty eyes. Underneath the picture are two words written in beautiful script: '*Très Perdu.*'

'Who's that?' I ask.

Hugh smiles at the picture fondly. 'Erik Satie.'

'How was he at windsurfing?'

'Not so good.' Hugh smiles. 'But tremendous at composing melancholic piano music.'

His gaze falls softly on my face.

'Are you sure you're all right?' he asks.

'Yes,' I reply. 'Thank you. I'm over Teazle. Though I was actually feeling a bit lost anyway. I'm supposed to be doing my first essay for tomorrow, and I just haven't an idea how to start.'

'What's it on?'

'Spenser's *Faerie Queene.*'

'Have you read any of it?'

'Quite a bit, yes. It's mainly about knights.'

'What do they do?'

'They quest. In Spenser, a knight is never happy unless he's questing. It's like he's looking for his other half. When he finds his damsel, then he is "parfait hole".'

'Is that a quotation?'

'Yes,' I reply. 'It means "perfect hole". It struck me as a pun, because having found their other halves, then the knights will be perfectly whole, but they'd always have a perfect hole – that yearning inside that every questing knight feels. I liked that contradiction.'

Hugh looks calmly into my eyes a moment as if considering something.

'You realise, don't you,' he says, 'that you've just given the thesis for a perfect essay?'

'Really?'

'It's all in that quotation, "parfait hole". I'd take a Freudian approach: how the knights are looking for love, which suggests they're seeking the union and completeness which, allegedly, we all had as children. A good argument. You just need to scatter around a couple of eclectic quotations and you're on course for a first-class essay. I suggest you go with Plato, that bit in the *Republic* which describes how, in the beginning, all beings were hermaphrodites. They had four legs and four arms and they had two sexes – male and female. They were separated by the gods, which is why after that people must roam around looking for their other half.'

'You're good,' I comment. 'But I still need to quote from the poem, and I can't do that without re-reading it.'

'That's the first rule about studying literature,' pronounces Hugh, '*don't* read the text. It takes far too long. I propose your entire essay should consist of the different places where Spenser uses the words "hole" and "parfait". You'll be giving it a restrained palette, like Matisse using just two colours.'

This is so strange. He's discussing literature, with reference to painting. It's as if he already knows all about what interests me.

'I do like Matisse's sense of colour,' I agree.

'Who doesn't?' says Hugh.

'Are you a painter?' I ask.

'No! No no no. I lack the talent. But my mum's a painter.'

'So am I!' I say.

'Really?' The information seems important to him. The moment feels loaded. 'I'd love to see some of your work.'

'Well, you can. But not now. I really need to write about *The Faerie Queene*. How am I going to find all the instances of the word "hole"?'

'Easy,' says Hugh, and peers out of the window. 'The library is still open. Let's pop in and nick the Spenser Concordance.'

'What's a Concordance?'

'It's a book which lists the different words used by each major writer, giving instances where they appear.'

'What?' I say. 'Who the hell would make one of those?'

'We're in a university,' explains Hugh. 'By definition we're surrounded by people with way too much time on their hands. Come on. Let's find four instances of the word "hole", and four of "parfait". I'm sure they'll all be used in slightly different ways, about which you can hold forth, on your theme. That'll give you eight paragraphs which is more than enough. I propose you should then sit down, and just write as fast as you can. Take those fags. You'll need them.'

'Thank you,' I say.

We leave the room together and head down to the library.

'By the way,' I say, 'are you studying literature?'

'No,' he says. 'PPE. Mum wanted me to get a degree that could lead to making money.'

'Wow,' I say. 'You seem to know how to write a great essay!'

'I'm a jack-of-all trades,' he explains, 'master of none.'

We're at the bottom of the stairs now. The night air feels cool and peaceful. I touch Hugh Ashby lightly on the arm.

'Thanks again for rescuing me from Teazle,' I say. 'Ugh . . . he was reptilian!' I wrinkle my nose at the horror of it.

'Hey,' says Hugh, 'you're OK now!'

He has his hand on my shoulder. Somehow I end up hugging him. His big frame is hard but fantastically comforting. There's also a friendly smell of pub wafting off him.

'Thank you,' I say. 'You're an angel.'

'A big wingless angel,' says Hugh.

'Who smells slightly of booze.'

'Perhaps that's normal for angels,' he says. 'They probably love a quick pint.'

Companionable now, we walk across the quad towards the library. When we reach it, he turns to me.

'Oh, by the way,' he says, 'my room mate and I are on the First Year Committee. We're having a party in a couple of weeks' time, at which I must make a little speech to break the ice. Will you come?'

I smile up at him. I realise he's surely invited other girls to the First Years' Party, but I am the one he's inviting now, and I like it. I want to hear all his invitations, up to the one where he says, 'Would you like to be my wife?'

'Can I bring my friend Gemma Weakes,' I ask, 'who's not in the college?'

'What's she like?' asks Hugh.

'Brilliant,' I answer. 'Amazing.'

'Then she must surely come,' he decrees, and for a moment we both forget to say anything. We just stare into each other's eyes with such naked longing it's faintly embarrassing. The lighting on his face is exquisite. On the right-hand side, his cheekbone is lit by the soft yellow glow coming through the library windows. To my left there's an old-fashioned lantern-style lamp on a metal post. It's casting a bluer light, which is illuminating the left side of his manly brow and also the upper edge of his top lip, which has an irresistibly sexy curve to it, which makes you long to draw, or indeed kiss.

'Are you getting that?' enquires Hugh, breathing in. 'I can smell jasmine somewhere, but I can't see it.'

I know I should get a move on. There's still that essay to write, and I want to find the Concordance before the library shuts. But for a moment, I don't want to go anywhere. I shut my eyes. I breathe in slowly. I see that Hugh is right. Somewhere nearby there is a jasmine plant. I can't see it but I can smell it.

Actually it doesn't even smell like jasmine.

It smells of roses – which is a sharper smell somehow. I smell the roses. Eyes shut, breathing in, I have the strange sensation that I'm being moved, feet forward. My eyelids are gleaming orange. Is bright light shining on them?

I open them.

The scene has changed.

I'm at the edge of New College gardens. To my left and behind me pink roses are growing up the wall. The base of each petal is yellowy-orange, like a flame. The tips are a rich pink. In front of me is a flowery flame of a different kind. It's The Amazing Gemma Weakes. She's wearing a plain white dress, looking like a twenties flapper, and she's making a note of something in her Filofax. I admire her long kittenish eyelashes, her beautiful rather square jaw.

To my right, there is a little grassy bank leading up to a wide green lawn.

The First Years' Party is about to start. People are here, but they're not yet in a party mood. I'm overlooking a couple of hundred first-year undergraduates who are clumped together on the grass, as if assembling for a fire drill.

'We should go down and start mixing,' I suggest, although I feel very hesitant about it.

'Yeah,' says Gemma. 'But I'm trying to work out who I'd want to talk to.'

We both survey the group. At the edge of it there are two quiet academic-looking girls chatting together. They're wearing college tracksuits and are nodding at each other politely. Two tall burly men walk by them. They're rowers, stalking the crowd like great stags. Two other girls are walking up the slope towards us, clearly public-school types. The one on the left wears a floaty Indian top.

'I've got some *rerrly* good charas,' she informs her friend.

Whenever I talk to the public-school kids, they seem to discuss 'charas'. I know it's some form of dope, but what kind exactly? Dope that went to Rugby and has a home in the country?

'Can you see your friend Hugh?' asks Gemma.

My eyes have been busily seeking him out, but I can't see him anywhere.

'I cannot wait to meet him,' says Gemma, placing a hand on my arm. 'Everyone else seems to have done already.'

'Really?'

'Yes.' Gemma smiles. 'He is by a distance the most discussed student. If I tell anyone I've been visiting your college, they always say: "Have you met Hugh Ashby?" I find I'm collecting information about him.'

'What have you heard?'

'That he was brought up on a Greek island. Was a swimming champion. Apparently he did the best history A-level in the whole country, and he's got a half-brother at St John's. And his dad is famous, of course.'

'What?' I exclaim. 'I haven't heard that. Who is his dad?'

'He was a pop star, and he's got a title and a massive house in Hertfordshire. Apparently Hugh is having his nineteenth birthday party there, and everyone wants to go, but he can't give out more invitations. I know Richard Scott's going,' says Gemma, flashing me a very mischievous look. 'By the way, are we supposed to have brought drink to this party?'

'I dunno!' I reply. 'I can't get any money. The bank machine is already spitting my card out like it's disgusting.'

'Mine too! What are we going to do?'

'I don't know! I enquired about barwork at Pizza Express. But they pay less than three quid an hour.'

To my right, in the courtyard, a door slams open. A man marches out. He looks like he's in *The Blues Brothers*. He's wearing a black suit and black sunglasses and a serious expression. He's holding a bass drum, which he hits – bom bom bom bom – portentously. Behind him comes another man, identically dressed in black. As a forty-three year old I recognise this man instantly, and am amused to see him looking so young and serious. In fact, I feel overjoyed to see him. Marching out into the party, holding an electric guitar and a little portable amp, he's playing the same bass note again and again and again. Behind them is a third man. This one is considerably bigger, and he is dressed like Lawrence of Arabia and seems to be having more fun than his friends. He's doing a strange sideways walk, like he's Lawrence of Arabia in an Egyptian frieze.

It's Hugh.

He quickly grabs the attention of the crowd.

Women break off mid-anecdote and watch him, with looks of fond affection. I notice the historian who, in later life, becomes an economics expert on *Newsnight*. He's looking at Hugh with open admiration. *This is more like it*, his excited expression seems to say, *now something will happen*. The three men parade right through the crowd and over to a bench. Hugh climbs on to it. The instruments cut out. There's a ripple of applause, and he addresses the multitude.

'Hallo!' he says exuberantly. 'Welcome to the First Years' Party! I think we're going to have a magnificent three years together.'

As Hugh talks, Gemma and I come down the slope to hear better. We've reached the back of the crowd. I am watching Hugh over someone's shoulder. He looks wonderful. Far behind him stands a dark green pine, deep in shadow, but Hugh is picked out by a shaft of yellow evening sunlight, and looks very handsome and very happy.

'I have a game we could play,' he's saying, 'which is a fun way of breaking the ice. It works like this. Each man must shut his eyes. Ladies . . . if you find any man cheating, slap him!'

Most men shut their eyes. I hear a couple of slaps, and some giggles.

'Now, ladies,' commands Hugh, 'walk five steps into the crowd. Ladies . . . march!'

I part from Gemma and we mingle. Meanwhile the drummer is drumming and Simon is strumming while Hugh is saying: 'One, two, three, four, five!' We're all obeying. Some of the girls are taking exaggerated high steps.

'Now, ladies,' says Hugh, 'grab the arm of the closest man. It may be one you've never met.'

I grab a guy called Rob Steele, who in later life tries to pick me up in Soho House. He's a lawyer. He has a rugby shirt and prematurely receding hair. He has his eyes shut, but he's smiling a lovely amused smile.

'Ladies,' says Hugh, 'put your mouth to his ear.'

I do. Rob Steele's ear is rather large, but it has an attractive manly smell, like hot biscuits. 'And tell him a secret. Now.'

What shall I say? I check Rob Steele isn't peeking. 'Yesterday I ate three Twixes and a Bounty,' I whisper, 'then I threw them up.' Actually I've been doing that sort of thing for a few years. Admitting it, I feel a little pinch of shame lifting off me.

'Good!' says Hugh. 'Now take five steps again, and find someone else. One, two, three, four, five.'

I leave Rob Steele and melt away into the crowd. I take five steps and find myself before Mark de Vere, a gangly man with long hair and twinkly glasses. In my second year, we will share a brief pleasant friendship. He has Indian drapes hanging from his ceiling and he burns incense.

'Whisper a new secret,' says Hugh.

What else am I hiding? I think of something. I don't know if it's a secret. But it feels very important, and I've never told it to anyone.

'My dad left home on my sixth birthday,' I whisper. 'And I can't remember what he looks like.'

'Good!' says Hugh. 'Now melt into the crowd, girls. And then shut your eyes.'

I do. I see why the boys didn't cheat. It's an act of trust to keep your eyes shut in public.

'And, boys,' orders Hugh, 'take five steps, find a girl and tell her a secret.'

I wait expectantly. Will someone whisper to me? I'm intensely curious to hear what they'll say.

I can sense a man next to me. His mouth is warming my right ear. 'I cheated in my A-levels,' he confesses, 'I don't deserve to be here.'

I want to say: I *so* know the feeling, but I don't. I stay silent as a sphinx.

'Boys,' commands Hugh, 'five more steps, find another girl, and tell her a secret.'

I keep my eyes shut.

Someone else arrives. The voice is camp, unmistakable. It's Simon Bell, the only out gay man in our year. He will go on to become a Big Noise in Planet 24. In my left ear, he whispers: 'I want to fuck Hugh Ashby so much, I think I could die.'

I laugh at that. I know the feeling. I fancy that half the people in this crowd positively yearn to fuck Hugh Ashby.

'And now, ladies,' says the much-fancied Hugh, 'open your eyes.'

I do. As I open them, the world seems impossibly beautiful. The flowers at the edge of the garden seem gorgeously bright, and all around me on the fresh, green lawn, men and women are opening their eyes and they're smiling at each other. Even better, I'm looking straight at Hugh Ashby, and he gives me a smile of extraordinary intimacy and warmth. Oh my God, I think, he actually does like me!

'And now,' he says, 'everyone, walk round the party, and, out loud, tell people the secrets you've heard. Of course they won't know whose secrets you're telling. Go!'

I walk up to a man. I've no idea who he is. He's wearing red corduroys. I would never normally approach a man in red cords.

'I cheated in my A-levels,' I tell him.

'I had an operation to reduce my breasts,' he informs me.

We look into each other's eyes and laugh. It's a delicious moment of complicity.

'Now move on,' commands Hugh, 'and when you see someone, tell them a secret. Of course,' he adds, 'you might want to sneak out one of your own.'

I'd already thought of that. I step in front of a tall, stooped man. He has long hair and a drooping back. He's a human stick insect.

'I once killed a cat,' he tells me happily.

'I want to fuck Hugh Ashby,' I tell him. It doesn't matter what I say. All around me, people are cheerfully spilling secrets. It's a wonderful feeling. I feel loud and exultant. I have never felt more free.

'And now!' shouts Hugh Ashby, over the noise, 'walk around *shouting* out secrets!'

I do. Everyone is walking around and they're smiling and shouting. You can't hear what anyone's saying, so I just go for it. 'I love Hugh Ashby!' I shout to the first person I see. I know I don't, but it feels like a delightfully daring thing to say. 'I love Hugh Ashby!' I shout to the second. 'I want to be fucked by Hugh Ashby!' I yell to the whole wide world. As I shout it, I'm worried that Hugh himself might hear. But he can't. It doesn't matter what

I shout. We're all shouting so no one can hear. Nothing matters. We all feel utterly free and utterly bonded. This is such a great idea! We're all looking at the magnificent Hugh Ashby, and wondering what he's going to say next.

'And now,' he decrees, raising one hand, 'everyone must dance!'

At that, music comes on. It's 'Dancing Queen' by Abba. Sure, that song is the biggest cliché-ed floor-filler in the world, and there's a good reason why: it always works! Everyone starts to dance. At first Hugh is dancing on his bench, but he soon leaps off on to the grass. I head towards him. As I weave past my fellow partygoers I see King of Homos Simon Bell, who gives me a camp wink. When I reach Hugh, he's twirling a girl. I know her a bit. She's called Agatha Winscombe, a ridiculous girl in the English department who's unnaturally obsessed with the Brontës. Hugh treats her with the sort of courtesy due to a goddess. They dance for a minute or so and I stand watching them, feeling like a courtier, waiting to seize my moment.

'I'm going to get a drink!' she says, and disappears.

I lunge in. I want to get his attention before anyone else does.

'Hugh,' I say, 'that was the most wonderful game.'

'Thank you, Lucy Potts,' he says. He looks at me very gallantly and his smile is as warm as the sun on the Caribbean Sea. 'I thought it would help to bond everyone.'

'It has!' I say. 'Look at them. They're ecstatic!'

'I'm so glad,' he says.

I'm looking up into his big beautiful face.

I feel a sudden desire to ask him to invite me to his birthday party, but realise that would be stupid. And, pausing too long, I lose the chance to broach any subject. Other people are descending on him. One of them is Gemma. She's wiggling at the waist like a worm on a hook. For some reason, she's wearing red plastic devil's horns. She puts them on me. She cuts in on Hugh.

'Hello,' she says.

'This is my friend,' I say, 'Gemma Weakes.'

'The Amazing Gemma Weakes,' says Hugh, 'it's a pleasure to meet you!'

He smiles at her gallantly. This is, I realise, an insight into his particular charm. He's like a king, assembling his court. Enjoying Hugh's regal gaze, she basks like a flower in the sun. She only has a moment of it. Someone else arrives.

'Hey, Hughsie!' says the guy.

'Evening, Cocky!' says Hugh.

'Lucy Potts,' he announces, 'The Amazing Gemma Weakes, this is my room mate, Cocky Cockburn. He's studying PPE, he's a very keen windsurfer, and a most brilliant DJ.'

I turn to the man.

He's the one who was playing the guitar. My young self notes that he's quite good-looking. The newcomer is almost the same height as me, with regular features and very big, friendly-looking eyes. He has a wide voluptuous mouth, long sideburns, and is wearing a baseball cap. He looks amiable, albeit self-conscious. My younger self is not too interested in his arrival, but my older self drinks in every detail of him. I note how trim he looks. His t-shirt shows off his pert pectorals, and he looks slightly tanned and extremely healthy.

'Easy!' says the man, shaking my hand.

'Do you have a DJ name?' I ask.

'Yeah, man!' he replies. (Did he just call me 'man'?) 'They call me DJ Monster!'

'What?' exclaims Hugh. 'You've never said that before! You're called DJ Monster?'

'Yeah, man,' he says. 'Half of Woking know me as DJ Monster. And the other half know me as The Awesome Mr Monster.'

'Did you DJ in your year off?' I ask him.

'No!' says The Awesome Mr Monster, sounding slightly less Awesome. 'Just in the school holidays.'

He smiles bashfully at me. He's obviously slightly ridiculous, but very sweet. If I hadn't just met Hugh – it occurs to me – I'd probably be attracted to his friend. I'm sensing there could be a place for him in my life. Hugh is clearly Prince Charming, but perhaps his room mate could be Buttons.

'But why do they call you DJ Monster?' I ask.

'Well . . .' he begins. He is putting on such a peculiar accent, he sounds slightly Jamaican. 'Before I was The Monster, I was known as *Simone.*' He says that with a French accent.

'And what,' I ask, 'actually is your real name?'

'Well,' he says. 'It's just . . . Simon.'

I can't help but repeat it.

It's Simon, I whisper, *your future husband.*

I don't know why I talked like that. There wasn't even any need for it. I'm really angry with myself. I'm vowing that I really really won't interrupt again. But the damage has already been done. The memory is fragmenting. I feel faint. Sounds grow muffled. My vision is bleaching out.

'Well, it's lovely to meet you!' I manage.

'I'm sure I'll see you again!' says Simon, and his voice seems to be floating in from another realm.

I turn away from the boys, and stagger a few yards to a drinks table. I sense I must bring myself back to the here and now. But how? At one end of the table there is a big bucket, filled with cold water and beers. I feel a strange desire and give in to it.

I hold my breath, shut my eyes and plunge my head into the water.

The cold steadies me.

But still I feel strange. It's not just my head that feels wet. It feels like my whole body is diving into water. There's that moment of tension as the muscles seize up – *Oh my God*, they seem to say, *we're cold*! – but then, a moment later, my whole body is suffused with the ecstatic bliss of release.

I open my eyes. I am wearing goggles.

I am underwater, in a pool. It's glorious. In fact,

conditions are as perfect as a girl could imagine. The pool is large and turquoise-tiled, the water is dappled with bright sunlight, and it's all fizzy with bubbles.

For a moment I just glide.

I feel rinsed clean. I feel that, whatever was troubling me just moments ago, now isn't. I'm sure there *was* something, but it has faded away. And then I realise that, to either side of me, there are people frenziedly swimming.

And I wake up to my new actuality, and realise what's going on.

I'm in a race.

I'm still in my first term as a student, and I'm in the Cuppers Swimming Gala. It's the fifty metres butterfly and I want to win. I'm an excellent swimmer. It's one event where the fleshier girl has an advantage. I set off at speed for the other end. I burst from the water, and as I do I fly my arms forward, and as they hit the surface they lead me through a perfect butterfly wiggle, and then I power them through the water as fast as I can. Six more rapid strokes and I've overtaken the swimmer to my right. This is good. I'm doing well. But I can see there are a couple of others still ahead. I'm tiring. But I must catch them. I must catch them. I fly my arms forward, I wiggle my body. But I'm tiring. I'm tiring. I barely have the strength to lift my arms from the water . . .

As I hit the end of the pool, my chest and arms and legs are burning with exhaustion.

I pull off my goggles and hat and leap from the water like it's scalding lava. I stand at the poolside gulping in great lungfuls of air. I put my hands on my thighs and lean forward and pant.

When I straighten up, I see that men are parading past, ready for their swim.

One of them wears a red dressing gown and a white rubber cap. He is giving me a look of quite extraordinary sauciness. Oh, God, it's Hugh Ashby. It's Hugh Ashby, and I'm standing on the poolside in a swimsuit with my cake-eating physique open to view! Horrified, I hurry over to the banks of red plastic seats on which a couple of hundred undergraduates are sitting.

Amongst them is The Amazing Gemma Weakes.

Typically, she's absurdly over-dressed for a trip to the pool. She looks like Isabelle Adjani in *Subway*. Her glossy brown hair has been backcombed for added lift, and she has on thick black eyeliner and is wearing a white blouse with the collar turned up, and pearls. As she passes me a towel her expression is pure Gemma – it's sparkling with amusement, but somehow supercilious.

'Well done, darling,' she says, 'you came fourth. I think you'd have made third if you'd started a bit quicker. What happened to you?'

She peers at me attentively. Her gaze seems to go right to the back of my eyes, as if she's seeing me, my older self, hiding inside. I would so love to bring Gemma into my confidence. I want to tell her that I know, logically, we're both eighteen and in our first term at college. But at the same time, I know that I am forty-three, and I've been in an accident, and I'm revisiting this memory, but

I don't know why, and I feel very scared. I also want to tell her I can't believe that she's here with me now, because I can't imagine anyone I'd rather see. But that sounds mad, and I'm not allowed to interfere, so I say none of it. But somehow my young self has felt this maelstrom of thought. I feel unbalanced and bereft for reasons I don't understand. I think I could cry.

'All right, love,' drawls Gemma. 'It's only a student swimming race.'

I wrap the towel round me, and sit down next to her.

'You OK?' she asks. Her tone is classic Gemma. She sounds like a big sister. She's giving me sympathy, but there's a slight undercurrent at the same time: look, she's also saying, don't make such a fuss.

'Yup.' I sniff. 'I just feel embarrassed about wandering around in my swimming costume.'

'Babe, you're at a swimming pool!'

'But I feel fat!'

'Look,' says Gemma, 'you're more Marilyn Monroe than Audrey Hepburn, granted, and perhaps you'll become fat one day. You probably will, with the amount of chocolate you put away. At the moment, you are luscious and womanly and you have breasts that are being ogled by the entire room.'

I give her a grateful smile. 'OK. But listen . . . I'm cold. I need to go and shower.'

'Let's just see the start of the next race,' says Gemma.

I look around. The place seems to have filled up.

'How come there are so many people here?' I ask.

'Well,' says Gemma, 'I wanted to see you swim. But I have an added motive, and I suspect I share it with many of the girls here.'

'And it is?'

'Hugh Ashby,' she says. 'I want to see if he really is as good as everyone says. I also want to grab the chance to see him in a pair of Speedos.'

'Yup,' I say.

She's right, of course. Gemma is always right.

People have continued to talk about Hugh Ashby. I don't think every story about him is true, but we're about to test the veracity of one of them right now. Hugh Ashby is about to swim. Appropriately enough, he has the middle lane. He's a man who effortlessly assumes the spotlight. Still in his dressing gown, he climbs on to the starting block, and there is some good-natured cheering from the ranks behind us. Hugh smiles over at us, and then he does some joke muscleman poses as if he's a Victorian strong-man. That causes a ripple of laughter. He acknowledges the laughter with a funny wave, swivelling his hand from the wrist like the Queen Mum, waving from a carriage. That's what makes him so alluring, I realise. He seems completely without malice, and he acts, at all times, as if he's having fun.

I look down the row of competitors and there's another man I hadn't noticed till now.

Simon.

He's at the end of the line, looking nervous. His body is lean and muscled. He has a shy smattering of hair between his pectorals. He looks very good actually. His washboard stomach looks hard and bumpy. He looks like a male model but, alas, lacks Hugh's charisma and star power. His self-conscious anxiety is palpable from here. Looking at his younger self brings out maternal feelings in my older self. I have a sudden desire to go over and give him a hug. *It's all right,* I'd say. *It doesn't matter how hard you try, Hugh is going to streak out in front. And no one is even looking at you anyway. They're watching him.* But I don't. I shan't interfere. I know I'm seeing all this for a reason, and I'm determined to work out what it is. In the meantime, I'm watching Hugh myself. He is a cake, swollen in the oven. He is a roller-coaster, about to begin its descent. He's at the very peak of his perfection. It would be a waste not to look at him.

'On your marks . . .' commands the starter.

Deftly, Hugh Ashby removes the gown and drops it on the floor, and the watchers make a sound I've never heard a crowd make, before or since. As they see the wonder of Ashby's physique – the sculpture of his stomach muscles, the plump fleshiness of his pectorals – all the watching girls give a collective sigh of desire. *It's true,* I realise. *I did fancy him. He's a magnificent beast.* I think: *I must stop thinking.*

'Get set . . .' says the starter.

Hugh bends. He places his feet in diving position. He braces. We have a brief moment to admire the muscles of his back, the twitching sinews of his shoulders. Then . . .

The starter button sounds.

BEEEEEP.

The swimmers burst into the air, and I, and all the other two hundred spectators, crane forward to watch. We are so focused, so attentive, it's as if time is slowing down. The swimmers are springing into the air in slow-motion. This is a good picture, my eighteen-year-old self thinks. Watching it all from the perspective of a forty-three-year-old artist, I agree. *This is a wonderful picture,* I think. *Just look at this. Look at the light, look at the power, just **look** at the movement.*

And then it's as if the film freezes completely, and the colour fades out of it.

I'm no longer at a swimming pool.

I'm just looking at a black-and-white photograph, taken from the side, showing some young men diving into a pool.

My young self smiles at the image fondly.

To the right of the picture I can clearly make out Simon. He is already slightly behind, and he's not diving well. His arms are bent and his head is up, as if he's bracing himself for the terrible effort ahead. To his left and slightly behind him are two more swimmers. You can't see their faces. You can just see their reaching arms, their taut bodies. And to the left side of the picture is the lead swimmer.

And that's Hugh.

He's half a foot higher than the other divers, and he's

bounding into the air like a great racehorse soaring over a fence. His thick muscled arms are reaching out straight in front of him. His dive is perfect, except for the head. He's looking up, as if staring out at the wonderful prospect before him, and he's faintly smiling.

The photo is in the back of *Cherwell,* the university newspaper.

I am reading a copy in my college Porters' Lodge. The paper's discarded on the little window seat overlooking the quad. I know what I have to do. I must rip the picture out. Then I must paint it. I could capture the sparkle of the water. I could capture the mysterious smirk on Hugh's face, which makes him look as if he's seeing the future and he likes what he sees. It is a wonderful image. I couldn't imagine one I'd rather paint. But then a critical voice kicks in. I think: what would happen if Hugh found out you'd painted him? (It'd be embarrassing.) And would it be a good subject anyway? (It's so obvious! It's crassly commercial!)

Watching my thoughts as a forty-three year old, I am struck by the sudden change of heart.

My desire to paint the picture was like a tiny seedling, which was then frozen by the harsh North Wind of my own disapproval. It was almost brutal. I realise I've done that all my life. I've placed an Ice Queen in my own head, and she has frozen everything with her cold breath. I'm glad to have noticed that. I'm also fascinated by how the divers froze in mid-air, as they turned into a picture. *I did that*, I reflect. I was told that I cannot change the past, but

I am certainly controlling the way I look at it. What else can I do? What are the rules of this experience? All at once I feel excited.

Skipping down the steps from the Lodge, I almost bump into The Awesome Mr Monster, who's jogging out in some big bouncy trainers.

'Lucy Potts!' he says, in his sweet but self-conscious voice.

'Hello, Simon,' I purr. I feel very easy with him. It's partly because he so obviously fancies me. I really don't fancy him though. He's got another baseball cap on today. This one is much squarer and it tells of an ensemble called A Tribe Called Quest.

'Off running?' I enquire.

'I'm supposed to be going to a lecture,' he tells me cheerfully. 'But it starts in eight minutes. I'm gonna have to *move*!'

Simon doesn't move, however. He smiles at me, and I find myself smiling back. He seems to want to talk some more.

'How's Hugh?' I ask.

'Well . . .' he begins. 'Well, he's . . . I'm not sure he'd want me to say.'

Of course that gets my interest. 'Why?'

'Well, he's . . . he got into a fight.'

'*He got into a fight!*'

'Yes.'

'Why?'

'Actually,' whispers Simon, leaning in, 'it was to do with that guy who molested you.'

'George Teazle?' I whisper. Instinctively I look around to check no one's listening. I fear Teazle could have spies. 'He didn't really molest me.'

'Yeah, well . . .'

'Is Hugh OK?'

'Er . . . yeah. Well, he is now.'

'Shall I go and see him?'

'Erm . . . he might not answer the door. He's not left the room in three days. I'm a bit worried about him actually. But . . .' Simon considers a moment. 'I reckon he'd like you to call, so . . . why don't you take my key? Let yourself in, then just hide it above the doorframe on the landing.'

'OK.' I take the key. 'Thanks, Simon.'

'Listen, don't tell him I gave it to you.' Then Simon thinks. 'Oh. I guess he'll work it out.' His grin spreads over his wide mouth. He looks unusually doggy. 'Erm . . . listen. I've got to move!'

'OK.'

'Laters!' he says, then turns and sprints off with hilarious speed. He looks like a Staffordshire Bull Terrier racing to catch a Frisbee. My young self looks at him with fondness, and, yes, a touch of derision. It's actually amazing, given how obsessed he is with being stylish, that he can get it so badly wrong. Who the hell else would sprint off with such bustling speed? That's not cool. My older self, however, just admires his energy. I think: he's so like Tom. I feel very fond of the man who will one day marry me. I do actually love him, I realise. I can't believe I'm being allowed to see him again like this.

One of my dons walks by. My young self is embarrassed to be caught staring.

I realise I should hurry to Hugh's room. But I need to stop off at my own first. I should check I look OK.

A blink later, I'm wearing my best jeans, my hair is brushed, and I'm knocking on his door.

There's no answer.

There's a little card in the nameplate reading: Simon Cockburn and Hugh Ashby. I put Simon's key in the lock, but I am uncomfortable about using it. I knock again. Then I hear movement in George Teazle's room. I really don't want to see him. So I quickly unlock the door and slide the key on the doorframe.

And I go in.

Hugh is sitting on the sofa reading a book. He's wearing jeans, a shirt and a dressing gown. He has a small bruise under his right eye, but, aside from that, the most notable thing is how upbeat he looks. As I enter, he doesn't move but looks at me, astonished.

'Lucy Potts!' he says in greeting.

'Hugh!' I beam. 'Are you OK?'

'Absolutely fine, yes!' he answers. 'Are *you* OK?'

'Yes! Yes!' He is waiting for an explanation of why I'm here. How do I put this? 'Listen,' I begin, 'Simon lent me his key. He . . . He said you had a fight with George Teazle.'

'Oh,' says Hugh, waving his hands bashfully, 'I did *not* fight him. I . . .'

'I think we should report him.'

'No no no NO! Listen. It was entirely my fault! I was drunk! It was very stupid.'

'What happened?' I ask.

Meanwhile I sit down on the armchair opposite him.

'I was drunk and . . . basically I decided to gatecrash the Bullingdon Club.'

'What's the Bullingdon Club?'

'It's a posh dining society. It's supposed to be an honour to be asked to join. They hold lavish dinners in secret locations. And I heard they were having one upstairs at the Lion Hotel. So I decided to gatecrash.'

'Was it easy?'

'Fairly. Though it was on the second floor, and I could only get there by climbing a drainpipe.'

'That doesn't sound safe!'

'Yeah. Like I say . . . it was stupid.'

'You could have really hurt yourself!'

'I know . . . I didn't care at the time.'

'So what happened?'

As Hugh talks, I begin mentally sketching him. He looks so damn interesting from this angle. His black eye contrasts with his courteous manner and Noël Coward dressing gown. Plus he's sitting in front of a massive picture of a wave. I could call my picture *The Gentleman At Sea*.

'I . . . climbed up,' he explains. 'They'd left a window open, and smoke was wafting out, and the sound of well-bred men at play. Which, I must say, stopped very gratifyingly the moment I climbed in through the window.'

'What did you say to them?' I ask.

Hugh has got a surprisingly heavy brow. It's what makes him look so masculine

'I said: "Hello . . . I always wondered how to get into the Bullingdon Club. And now I know . . . you just need to climb in through a window!"'

'What did they say to that?'

'Not much. There was a bit of a silence. Then one of them – Toby Wheatley – said: "Aren't you Lord Bobby's boy?"'

'Who is Lord Bobby?' I ask.

At this Hugh looks very shifty.

'He's . . . well, he's sort of my dad.'

'Sort of . . . how do you mean? Who is he?'

At this point, Hugh explains.

My young self is enthralled. I *have* actually found out about his dad. In fact, I've observed his famous long flowing hair, in black-and-white photographs which also include Mick Jagger and Princess Margaret. He was an actual lord who became singer/songwriter for a band, and made a stupendous amount of money, and then retired from music to be a painter. The older me is completely uninterested in Hugh's dad. I know him to be a terrible painter and a narcissistic bully who dies, nine years in the future, leading to an unseemly court case waged between his eldest son and last wife. I am more interested to hear how Hugh describes the man who's caused most of his problems.

'Have you heard of him at all?' he asks bashfully.

'No!' I say.

I feel a bit shy of admitting I've been reading up about Hugh's father. Besides, I want to flush out the maximum information.

'Well, he's . . .' Hugh tries. I've never seen him like this. He seems uneasy. 'He . . . He . . . I can't even say it.'

'Go on.'

'He . . . He believes in polygamy, OK? So he has a number of mistresses. Fifty-four, so far. He does a painting of each one. And he met my mum at some arty party around nineteen seventy. She became Mistress Number Nine. Had a brief affair with him. Got pregnant. He was quite clear that he didn't want her to have the kid. Me. But she did.'

'Did you ever live with him?'

'For a few months, when I was six.'

'What an arsehole!'

'No no no! He's . . . he's fine! He's a good man really, he's . . . he's helped Mum out with money. And he's paying me an allowance now. He's also going to host a nineteenth birthday party for me. He's all right.'

'Well, he's your dad, so let's be grateful for him.'

'Exactly.'

'Without him, there'd be no you.'

'Quite.'

'So are you a lord too?' I smirk, amused by this thought.

'No. I'm illegitimate, but he's still my dad, which is the sort of thing that would impress the sort of person who's a member of the Bullingdon Club. And in fact one of them said: "Well, give that man a drink." So I took it. Feeling a bit like Judas with his thirty pieces of silver. I didn't really know what to do then.'

'What were you planning to do when you climbed in?' I ask.

'I was drunk. I had no plan. So I just sipped my wine and looked round the room. They were all wearing women's wigs, for some reason.'

'Women's wigs?'

'Yes! Don't ask me why. I looked round, and saw George Teazle. I said: "Hi, George . . . nice hair. Did you buy it, or did you take it from someone?" He said: "What do you mean?" I said: "I wondered if you saw some poor woman walking along, then you just scalped her." He said: "I think you should go, you're pissed." I said: "Well, I do have that excuse. You didn't. When you molested Lucy Potts." He said: "Who's Lucy Potts?" That really annoyed me. I don't think he was faking it. I don't think he'd registered your name. I said: "The woman whose tit you grabbed before kicking her." He said: "I didn't fucking kick her. And I didn't 'grab her tit' either." "OK. Maybe you have a problem with manners," I said. "Just so you know . . . it's not really done to grab someone – whether by the breast or anywhere else – then, when they object, to push them with your foot."

'At that point there was silence. Then Howard Latham spoke up. Do you know him? He's a Rowing Blue. Imagine a very posh giant, with all the brains of a slightly nasty ten year old. He said: "I think you should go." So I said: "I think *you* should, 'cos you take up way too much space, a bit like Belgium . . . Although you're less offensive than Teazle, who has, as Lucy Potts points out, a sort of reptilian quality."'

'I forgot I said that.'

'By now I was enjoying myself. I thought I'd stand there insulting them all one by one. But Teazle said: "I'm going to go and get security." He got up and walked towards the door. For some reason I got really angry then. Do you know who George Teazle's dad is?'

'Not really.'

'He's the chairman of a bank that has just sponsored a huge dam in Indonesia. A multi-million-pound project. Massively environmentally damaging. Displaced about a hundred thousand people from their homes. It was all part of a deal whereby the British sold something like 20 billion pounds worth of arms, and obviously it won't be George Teazle who'll be firing the weapons, but at some point he'll be spending the cash. People like that disgust me. So I said: "Teazle, why don't you have the guts to do your own dirty work?" He didn't want to stand around debating with me. He went for the door. Whereupon I climbed up on the table. I tried to step over it to get to him, but Latham blocked me. So I gave him a gay slap in the face. Which was sort of silly. Sort of funny. Then he hit me, very hard. Next thing I knew, I was being carried into a taxi. It brought me here and I had to pay for it.'

Hugh stops talking. For some reason he smirks at me. His default setting is levity.

'Hugh,' I say, smiling. 'Basically you got yourself into a fight because you were protecting my honour.'

'I'd love to make out I was some sort of knight errant. But I was also very pissed.'

'It was still very kind of you, though unnecessary and rather strange. I've only talked to you twice before today.'

'I know.'

'And George Teazle – he was a bit unpleasant, but I've had worse. I spent my teenage years in Ashford.'

'I'm sure.'

'Why did you take it so seriously?'

'I . . . It just really annoyed me.'

'I can see that. But why?'

He looks at me very seriously. For a moment it seems as if he's about to say something important. But then . . .

'I don't know,' he says.

We grin at each other. I want him to explain more.

'Next time you decide to get into a fight on my behalf,' I say pertly, 'will you consult me first?'

'I shall,' says Hugh. 'I tell you what: I'll warn you, and you can come and watch.'

He pauses, and looks searchingly into the back of my eyes.

'Not that I intend to pick any more fights with anyone,' he assures me. 'I was just drunk.'

My older self is thinking: he's determined to be nice about everyone. That is his trouble. The younger me is just thinking: I'm pretty damn sure he likes me. Should I invite him out for a drink? Then I'm thinking: I haven't said anything for several seconds. I should get out of here, before I mess things up.

'All the same,' I say, getting up, 'thanks.'

He smiles. I smile.

'Goodbye,' I breathe.

And I float from the room, light as a butterfly in sunshine. I think I'll have hundreds more opportunities to drop in on him here, so I can flirt and hear of his adventures. I think the present will stretch on for ever. But that's the trouble, realises my older self. We think the present will always be with us, like a loyal dog who walks by our side. But it won't. I also realise I'm thinking too much. I'm not actually noticing the present myself, and that's possibly why it's disappearing. I'm out in the stairway outside Hugh's room. I can't see anything at all. I'm holding the door handle, but the door itself has gone, and so has the card with his name on it, and so has he.

CHAPTER 7

A blink later, I've just walked past Balliol.

To my left there are some tall iron gates, and behind them there's a huge garden, flowing away like a great green sea.

I'm so happy.

My young self has just found out that there's a life-drawing class at the Ruskin I can go to, even though I'm not an art student. This afternoon I sat there for two very happy hours, sketching a naked woman. The model was in her forties, I'd say, and plump, but nevertheless she showed off her rounded body with a wonderful lack of self-consciousness, and I traced my pencil in sensuous whorls that imitated the generous pliancy of her flesh. I loved her. I loved drawing her. Walking back down towards college, I'm swinging my arms and feeling so joyful I could skip. Turning up New College Lane, I see something that makes me happier still.

Hugh is coming out of the newsagent's.

He hasn't seen me. I love to watch people unobserved. I creep up on him, as if I'm on safari and watching a big panther beside a watering hole. He is dressed ridiculously. He's got on a blue velvet jacket. It's buttoned, and for reasons I cannot fathom he's sewed badges up one sleeve. His hair is messy and tousled and brushed in a side parting, so he looks old-fashioned but gorgeous all at once. He's standing on the steps outside the newsagent's, eating one of the pies they sell in Broad Street and looking about with an expression of immense satisfaction. Now he sees me.

'Lucy Potts!' he says in his glorious velvet voice. 'You seem to be bursting with pleasure!'

'Thank you,' I coo. 'What's with the outfit?'

'I'm dressed as Erik Satie,' declares Hugh. 'He described himself as The Velvet Gentleman.'

'I see!' I remark, and we twinkle at each other. 'And what about the badges?'

'Those are cub badges!'

'Did you take them from a cub?'

'I earned them,' says Hugh, 'when I was a cub myself.'

'And then you sewed them on to your jacket?'

'When a cub has earned badges, he likes to show them off.'

'You're ridiculous!'

'I try.' He smiles.

The conversation is interrupted by an old red camper van making its way noisily up the street. I know that van. Early in our marriage, we take it on a holiday to Exmoor.

It pulls to a halt, and The Awesome Mr Monster leaps out. He's wearing a baseball cap, of course; also trainers, a t-shirt, and khaki combat trousers. They have massive pockets. He could probably store a whole toolbox in those trousers, and, from the looks of things, he has.

'Easy!' he calls.

'Hello, Simon,' I say.

'Do you like my new wheels?' he says, and gestures proudly at the van. 'I'm calling her Cassady the Camper Van.'

'Very nice,' I comment. 'What's she for?'

'Everything!' he enthuses. 'I'm gonna use her to transport my DJ-ing equipment. I'm gonna take her to festivals. I'm thinking I might even use her for college balls.'

'How?'

'Catering!' says Simon.

'Can you cook?'

'Definitely! I can do Cajun food. Spicy rice. Chicken jambalaya. Anything.'

'So where are you going now?'

'We're driving to my dad's house,' Hugh informs me. 'He's throwing a party for me, which we need to discuss. Want to come?'

My greatest ambition is to attend this party. I am looking for any excuse to get there. And besides, I'd happily accompany Hugh anywhere.

'Sure,' I say. 'I'm not doing anything special.'

'Wicked!' says Simon, and opens the door to the van. 'I gotta make two things absolutely clear,' he says.

'What?'

'There ain't no point asking Hugh if you can come to the party,' Simon tells me. 'Everyone asks him that, and his dad ain't letting him have any more guests.'

As Simon says this, I don't glance at Hugh. I'm struggling to hide my disappointment. I want to go to his party, the way Cinderella wanted to go to that ball.

'All right,' I say. 'And what's the other thing?'

'In this van,' says Simon, 'I am in charge of the tunes.'

My older self is thinking: no, really! My younger self is less cynical. I don't care what the conditions are. I just want to go in that van.

I say: 'Absolutely fine by me.'

With that, Simon guns the motor.

It's now four o'clock, but being November, it's getting dark. It's a wonderful evening though. The sky is a fresh light blue, the sun a wistful yellow, and we're eight miles outside Oxford. Leaning to my right, I can just see a couple of dreaming spires in the wing mirror. Before us looms that steep hill, with the proud beech tree on top, which I always imagine as the very spot where *Watership Down* occurred. I feel great. The road is empty, and I'm alone on it, in a van with my new favourite men – Hugh and Simon, Batman and Robin. Robin is driving. Batman and I are crammed together on the front seat, and our thighs are touching. That's partly because my thighs are so damn wide, but – who cares? – my leg is softly touching Hugh Ashby's and I can feel his body warmth.

Hugh is rolling a thin elegant joint, and asking about Gemma.

She's putting on a play in a few weeks' time – an Acid House production of *The Bacchae*. She's invited agents from ICM, William Morris, all the big agencies. The agents don't seem to fit with the spirit of an Acid House *Bacchae*, argues Hugh. Why must everything be a means to an end? He feels bemused that our fellow students are already thinking about their careers, as if playtime were already over, as if they were all little companies that must speedily find their niche in the market. 'Everyone is thinking about their future,' says Hugh, 'but what about the present?'

What about the present indeed? I reflect. It seems such an unexpected opportunity to find myself sitting beside him, but there's a dissatisfaction about him that I've not seen before. He says he wants to stop studying PPE because he's realised he hates economics – the science of it, and its effects. '*Give a man a fish,*' he says, '*he eats for one day. Teach a man to corner the market in fish, be grateful for the small acts of philanthropy he does on our behalf.*'

'Who said that?' I ask.

'Sam Lipsyte.'

Something about the name Sam Lipsyte bothers me. Why is that?

Simon begins to enthuse about economics. He likes the way it's about rules for predicting how people will behave.

He finds that interesting, he says. Hugh has completed his joint, and offers it to me with a courteous smile, as if he were offering me a fine wine.

Wordlessly, I take it, and he lights.

The first drag immediately sands down the edges of the world. It makes me feel safe as a cat by an oven. It makes our journey feel like an adventure. Actually we're off the motorway now, and heading along a smaller road beside some parkland.

'If you could go back to one time,' asks Hugh, 'and one place, where would it be?'

'Mediaeval Florence,' I answer.

'But when?'

'I'd go before Michelangelo and Leonardo. (Imagine the competition!) I'd go to about 1420. The town wasn't big then, just a few thousand people, predominantly artists, living in little houses along the river. I'd seek out Masaccio, and I'd help him till I'd learned all his tricks and techniques.'

Hugh smiles wistfully at this. Another part of his charm. If you say something to him, he doesn't just listen. He inhabits what you're saying.

'Who's Masaccio?' asks Simon. 'Was he a footballer?'

'He was a painter,' I say, 'who painted saints and angels, but made them look real. People say it was because he understood perspective. I think it was because he really saw them.'

'He also died when he was twenty-six,' adds Hugh, 'in mysterious circumstances.'

'Yeah. I'd probably save him,' I say.

'How?' asks Hugh.

'Sex,' I answer.

'How do you know Masaccio was handsome?'

'If you paint like that, you don't need to be,' I answer. 'And I'd keep shagging him every time danger came, which would be a lot, and I'd save him with sex.'

Hugh giggles. Simon looks a bit wistful.

'Where would you go?' I ask Hugh.

'Thank you for asking,' he says. 'I've put a lot of thought into this.'

'And?'

'Well, it couldn't be the twentieth century.'

'Why?'

'It's a scabby, diseased time.'

'Why?'

'Living in this century,' says Hugh cheerfully. 'Is like living in a fairground. Everything is getting noisier, louder, and you know the place is run by opportunists who just want to fleece you. The things I like are simple – butter melting on to toast, the feeling of cool water spreading down my chest on a hot day – but you can't enjoy them when you're next to a fairground.'

'Do you really think that?' I ask.

'Sure,' he says. 'The Berlin Wall came down. Everyone was pleased. I'm not. It feels like the death of a seductive idea – that people could be equal. Is there really no alternative to capitalism? Capitalism is a million people, all lined up along the shore, all trying to get into a boat which will take six people, and which will sink, a mile from shore. What's so great about capitalism? I don't believe in growth; I believe in shrinkage.'

'So when would you go back to?' I ask.

Hugh pauses. His pale eyes stare ahead. 'The time that I've set my party,' he says. 'Paris, 1888.'

'Why then?'

''Cos you've got Cézanne, Gauguin, Manet, Monet. You've got Van Gogh three years from the end, seeing the world with a vividness and colour never matched before or since. Painting is just before the intellectual abstractions of Picasso. Music is just after the drunk grandiloquence of Wagner, just before the noisy confusions of Stravinsky. It's the time of Debussy and Ravel and Fauré, a time of elegant simplicity.'

'Why 1888 in particular?'

'Well you've got a twenty-two-year-old Erik Satie, who'd been dismissed by his piano teachers as "worthless" and "the laziest student who ever lived", and one night he sits down and composes *Gymnopédie One*, which I find one of the great cultural wonders of all time. How had no one found those notes before? I don't know, but he did, and the tune is so simple, and yet so unbearably moving. It's the embodiment of: "If music be the food of love, play on;/ Give me excess of it, that, surfeiting, / The appetite may sicken, and so die. / That strain again! It had a dying fall . . ."'

I have a momentary fear he's going to quote the whole play.

'Of course, it wouldn't be a great time to be a female painter,' I comment.

'No,' agrees Hugh. 'The women only got to be models, but maybe they enjoyed that?' he says, giving me an uncertain look. 'OK. I take that back. I won't argue that. But it's hardly a great time to be a female painter now. If you want to be an artist today, you have to be a photogenic showman who's prepared to do stunts. Ultimately you have to be a model.'

'You think so?'

'If you want to be a success, in this world, which is one big shouting contest, you'd better take your clothes off, and do it in new interesting ways, while you're still young.'

I smile ruefully.

'Maybe,' I comment. I turn to Simon then, noticing that his nose is slightly squashed, making him look like a boxer. 'When would you go back to, Mr Monster?'

'July the first,' he answers without hesitation.

'Why?'

'Prince played the NEC, and I missed it. I like that guy. He's cheeky.'

I smile at Simon's simple relish for the now. He's gifted with happiness. I want to ask him more.

But conversation's arrested. We're arriving.

Simon turns the camper van right. We go through an arched gatehouse – sandy-coloured limestone, very pretty. Also there's a room above the arch, which I always find thrilling for reasons I can't really explain. We go under the archway, and suddenly we can see a drive slowly undulating down a hill, past an exquisitely beautiful copse of trees arranged in a round clump. The road then passes beside a wide glittering pond, past the crumbling stone tower of a Victorian folly, then up to the most spectacular Tudor palace I've ever seen. It's four storeys high. It has battlements. Wings. A portico. Tall elegant windows. I must go to this party, I think. I *must*. And ultimately I must get married here, and Lord Bobby can do the music, and Hugh and I can leave by boat, across the stately expanse of water.

I get out of the van first, and march towards the portico.

'Lucy,' calls Hugh. 'The main entrance is just for tourists.'

We go round to a side entrance. This is far less grand. It's down some steps and round the back. Hugh rings on the door, and it is opened by a frowsty woman who is wearing a white linen top. She has dyed black hair, thick make-up, and an exuberant, rather kindly manner.

'Huuuuuuuugh, my darling,' she slurs, and gives him a kiss.

She's obviously some form of stepmother.

'Hello,' she says. 'I'm Franka.' (Is that a name?)

We're shown into a long darkened corridor. It's lined with really shit portraits done with masses of heavy impasto.

'And these,' says Stepmum proudly, 'are all Bobby's.'

'They're really good,' says Simon kindly. It's clearly the expected response.

'They show every one of his fifty-four mistresses,' she says. It occurs to me Hugh didn't show me his mum. Maybe it's not a version of her he wants to acknowledge. At the end of the corridor, Franka pauses. 'Look,' she says proudly, 'there I am.'

The weird thing is that hers isn't the last picture. There's another one after her. Franka pauses a moment so we can all admire her portrait. The drafting has been done in a semi-naïve style. I'm not sure if this is deliberate or because Lord Bobby can't really draw. The paint itself looks clotted.

'How does he get the impasto so thick?' I ask.

'Ah,' says Franka, delighted – I am clearly asking the right question – 'he puts sawdust in it! A technique he invented himself.'

'Very original,' I remark.

Luckily the art-appreciation session is over. She knocks on a door tentatively. The Great Artist is obviously within.

'Come in,' calls a man's voice.

We go into a very large living room. You wouldn't know it was in a palace, though it is certainly a bigger room than you'd find in a three-bedroomed semi in Ashford. There are sofas laden with books and papers, and a table down at the far end. Half of this is covered with books, the other is laid for dinner. A head sticks out of a door. It's a man in his sixties with long grey hair. He's obviously just been taking a shower. The long hair is wet; his freckled shoulders naked.

'Hello!' he calls.

The voice doesn't fit with the hippy appearance. He sounds like a posh teacher. He looks at me for a moment, his experienced Lothario's eyes seeming to take me in. I feel that he's assessing me for the position of possible Mistress Number Fifty-five.

'Won't be a moment . . . just finishing in here. Do sit down. Franka will give you a drink.'

It takes him a suspiciously long time to emerge and I hear a familiar sound. I think he's blow-drying the famous long grey hair. Ten minutes later he comes to join us. I can see he has a certain poise, a blustery charm. It's not remotely in Hugh's league, but it's there.

Franka doesn't join us for dinner.

As a mistress, maybe she's not invited. Who knows? She serves it, then goes. It's surprisingly badly cooked fare – some sort of meat pie, served with cabbage and mash – and we eat it crowded together round half the table. While eating, we mainly discuss Hugh's party. Bobby enthuses about the various people who are coming. 'Everyone loves the theme,' he tells us. '*Tatler* want to do a spread on it, and there're quite a few gallery people coming. How's it all going your end?'

'Simon will be DJ-ing,' Hugh tells his father.

'Oh, good,' enthuses Bobby.

'And the invitations went out ages ago. I've had RSVPs

from almost all of them. I've had RSVPs from all the Reserve List too. In fact, I wanted to ask you about that. . . A hundred guests wasn't very many, and of course I'd love to invite more of my new friends from college.' Hugh smiles at me. 'Lucy, for example.'

He looks pleadingly at his dad. I'm assuming that good manners alone will make the old boy say: 'Of course she should come!' But rather to my surprise, he says: 'Well, I was *very* clear about this, Hugh. You can only have a hundred guests. We simply don't have the funds to cater for more. Plus the insurance won't allow it.'

Bobby's tone is more abrupt than I was expecting. I feel stung. Hugh, however, stays absolutely calm. If he's at all flustered, he hides it well.

'I quite understand,' he concedes. 'But I know we were going to have two hundred guests in all. Is it possible that any of your guests can't come?'

'Erm . . .' says Bobby, looking around rather petulantly. 'No! I'm sorry. I said that a hundred would be your lot. I've done what I can!'

'I know!' says Hugh. 'And thank you *very* much for that.'

I look hard at Hugh, whose behaviour around his father is subtly odd. He could be auditioning for a position as a diplomat. He's painfully polite. Defeated. I am too. The young me is wallowing in self-pity. I'm thinking: I cannot go to this party. It's not an event for people like me. It's for people who are in the Bullingdon, or who have houses in the country.

My older self can't take any more.

Don't be so fucking meek, I whisper suddenly. *You* must *go to this party.*

Then I realise I've broken the rule again. I've interfered. Why have I done that? I really don't want to fade away from here. I need to stay. If I'm going to learn why Hugh killed himself, then surely this is important. I concentrate furiously on the here and now. See each sight, I tell myself, smell each smell . . . The periphery of my vision is fading away, but I focus intently on Lord Bobby's face. His eyebrows are grey and whiskery. The skin underneath them is pink and I can see tiny flakes of dry skin. I have just put a mouthful of food in my mouth. It's boiled cabbage. I notice there's gravy on it, which must have spilled from the pie we're eating. I concentrate on that gravy. Is there a trace of nutmeg in it?

Gradually my vision clears.

I've done it, I think. I've stopped the scene from fading. Is my young self growing used to the promptings in her ear? They seem to bother her less. Besides, I know that I *did* go to the party, though in the strangest circumstances.

'Now,' says Bobby, suddenly brightening, 'how are you getting on with finding the burlesque artiste?'

'Oh,' says Hugh. 'I thought that was more your line of thing?'

'No!' splutters Bobby. 'We were quite clear about this. It was something *you* were supposed to arrange.'

'Do you think we need a burlesque artiste?' asks Hugh.

'It's basically a stripper. I'm not sure I'm comfortable with that. I wouldn't say it's something I want.'

'Well, it's art,' pronounces his father. 'And the woman won't be stripping, she'll be doing a performance while wearing a mask. Whoever it is can remain anonymous, so it's hardly asking too much of them. I thought we could put up a little platform extending over the fountain. The photographic possibilities will be sensational!'

Hugh still seems uncertain.

'So you want me to find someone who'll take their clothes off in the pond,' he comments. I think he's being sarcastic, but Bobby doesn't read it that way.

'Yes!' he says enthusiastically. His eyes are popping. 'Frankly I'm surprised that you, of all people, should baulk at this. It never ceases to amaze me how squeamish the English are about sex. The party's theme is Gilded Youth, a *Fin-de-siècle* Celebration. It was your idea, Hugh! It's supposed to be Le Chat Noir – cabaret, Toulouse-Lautrec, Montmartre.'

'And how much have we budgeted for this . . . burlesque?'

'I don't know,' answers Bobby. 'A couple of hundred. We can probably extend it to five hundred.'

Say you'll do it, I whisper.

'I'll do it for five hundred,' my younger self says. 'Provided you tell no one it's me.'

All three men turn to me.

'Are you sure you want to do this?' asks Hugh, looking horrified.

'Yes!' I affirm.

'Oh, good!' says Bobby. He looks excited. 'That'll be tremendous!'

Oh, shit.

What the hell have I just said?

My older self is terrified that I've altered events, but have I? I went to that party anyway, and I did do the act, but the truth is I never knew quite how it came about. The offer was a mad impulse that came from nowhere. *Did it come from me? Can a person from the future affect a person in the present?* Either way this latest interruption has had a bad effect on my younger self. I'm thinking: what is *happening* to me? I'm scared I am going to finish up in some white-tiled ward. I'm telling myself: the party isn't till the summer term. I'll probably find a way to pull out. I won't have to do it, will I? *Will I?*

My mind floats away from this scene. It drifts out of the window like a moth, till it's outside in the dark, looking in through the window at myself, sitting with this unlikely threesome of men – the old one with his long grey hair, and his handsome son with his mask of courtesy, and the other one with the square jaw, who's politely trying to balance his cabbage on the back of his fork.

I have drifted off. I'm gone.

CHAPTER 8

The sick, lurching feeling has returned.

I feel as if I'm still drifting in an underground tunnel. I feel I'm moving faster, through buffeting waters. Up ahead I hear singing. I should go towards it.

NO!!!

I open my eyes again. I'm walking up a dimly lit staircase.

Gemma's bottom is leading the way.

She is looking like Acid House Gemma. She has her hair up in Tank Girl-type bunches. She has on a white vest, showing off her athletic shoulders, plus trainers and black combat trousers. They are baggy on the leg, but – and of course this is no accident – tight around the muscular shape of Gemma's bottom. It must be conceded that she has one of the world's greatest bottoms. Statues should be made of it – and they certainly would be if Gemma had anything to do with it. She is already wiggling it as we make our way up. She turns to me.

It takes me by surprise. My God, she is so beautiful!

When I think of Gemma, I think of her sparkle, her relentless ambition. But at this point she's not a member of the Groucho. She doesn't have a publicist. She's young. She's feminine. She wears thick black eyeliner and has painted a red flower on her cheek.

'So, darling,' she says, 'the doors actually open at ten, but I need to get there for nine to set it up with the rest of the team. Simon says we should have a quick spliff in his room, and then we'll go.'

What are we doing? I'm still confused.

Then it comes back to me . . . Gemma is currently obsessed with dancing. She thinks she's great at it, and she's putting on a series of club nights with The Awesome Mr Monster.

'Where is it tonight?' I ask.

'It's over at the Poly,' she says. 'In their hall. You can come with us now if you need a lift.'

'I want to finish a drawing,' I say. 'I'll come later.'

She's reached the door of Simon and Hugh's room. I look at it a moment. It has black paint and a new card in the nameplate. The old one has been replaced. It now reads: 'Mr Ashby and DJ Monster'. From inside I can hear the sound of Parliament. George Clinton is talking about the 'Mothership Connection' in a voice that's full of honey. I can also hear laughter. But all I'm thinking is: I'm about to see Hugh. I haven't seen him all term. I heard he's barely left his room. Every time I walk past, I look up here, and, when I see his light, I feel a little pang.

'By the way,' says Gemma, 'do you want an E?'

'An E?' I ask.

'We're all having one,' she tells me. 'That's partly why we're meeting first. We're going to take it now, so we're coming up when we get there. Do you want one?'

I am not sure I want to take an E. Taking one feels like the opportunity to enter a secret realm, and of course I feel jealous of everyone who takes Es. They always look so blissed out as they wander round chewing gum and hugging each other. But I guess I'm a touch squarer than everyone else. I've read the newspapers. I've read about the ones who die through dehydration. Also about the ones who die through drinking twenty litres of water. No matter how high I get, I don't think I'll ever try outdrinking a camel. I'm more bothered by the other reports – the ones that tell of the depression that comes after the serotonin high wears off.

'I'll decide later,' I say.

'OK,' says Gemma lightly. She's not bothered either way. She just wants to get into the room.

We both enter.

The room has changed considerably. There are far more pictures for a start. The wave picture has gone. Shame. I liked that. Now Simon's interest in windsurfing has been replaced by his new enthusiasm for paragliding (pictures of men hovering over mountain tops). But the wind-sports section is overshadowed by his keen embrace of pop icons

(Prince, The Cramps, The Smiths). The sofa has been pushed forward to allow more room for his DJ decks.

And the room is considerably busier.

There are at least twelve people in it and they all seem strikingly trendy and confident. Dressed in clubber gear – trainers, t-shirts, hats – they are sitting and drinking. There's a hubbub of excited chatter. To my forty-three-year-old self, it feels like a privilege to be in a room full of students. I feel as if I'm surrounded by rare animals – pandas perhaps. Simon is manning the decks, and enjoying it. He's skipped the music on to something with a funky beat. I don't know what it is but Simon does and he's delighted to hear it again.

He's changed too.

He still wears a baseball cap, of course, but now he wears it with the peak at the back. He's stubbly and his jeans look new and slightly flared. He's wearing a white t-shirt which is tight enough that I can see his shoulder muscles as he lifts his arms to the ceiling. He's finding his style, thinks the younger me. He hasn't found it yet, but he's looking. He reaches a part of the song that he especially loves and he grins and bobs, still punching the air. The older me thinks he looks very happy and free and feels glad for him.

He looks over at me.

He's not expecting to see me, and it takes him a moment to recognise me. But when he does he grins, and I feel good. All the same, I don't want to go over to him. Where is Hugh? I'm scared he'll have found all this too much for him, and have crept away into a quiet corner like a wounded animal. I'm actually scared he's left college altogether, and that's why we're partying in his rooms. I'm only here because I want to see him. Where is he?

Then, looking to the left, I see him sitting at the end of a sofa.

He is talking to someone on his left and rolling a joint on a record cover on his lap. He looks very handsome and radiant. Instantly my heart fills with love for him again. But straight away I'm nervous. Can I go straight over? Should I be a bit less obvious? Should I give it a bit of time? Then I notice that Gemma is now in the middle of the room, talking to a girl sitting on the opposite sofa. Gemma's bottom is parked almost in Hugh's face. That's no accident. She's practically proffering that bum like an ice cream. I have to talk to him before she does. But I don't want to barge in on him. He looks happy. He deserves to be happy.

I'm thinking all this when Hugh looks up. He sees me, and beams.

'Lucy Potts!' he calls, and I'm instantly relieved.

I go over to him. There's nowhere to sit, so I kneel on the floor like a worshipper. As I settle myself down, he grins still more. Wow, he looks joyful!

'*Hel*-lo,' he says.

'Hello,' I whisper. 'I've not seen you in ages.'

'No,' he agrees.

'I heard you hadn't left your room in a month?'

'That's not quite true,' Hugh says. 'I've been out for two tutorials, a haircut, and a trip to the kebab van. But generally, for excitement, I find I don't need to leave this place.'

Someone says something to Simon, who looks at his watch. Then he turns off the decks.

'Er, guys,' he announces. 'Tammy says there's a mini-bus waiting for us outside. We should go.'

There are cheers and a couple of 'Woo-hoos!' Everyone gets up. Gemma leans over me.

'Hi, Hugh,' she says, and kisses him.

'Hello, gorgeous,' he replies.

She turns to me.

'So for the first couple of hours,' she says, 'I'll mainly be hovering around near the door. But there's a little VIP bit at the back. From about eleven you'll be able to find me there.'

'OK,' I tell her. 'I'll come as soon as I'm done.'

'Coolio,' says Gemma, and gives me a kiss. She doesn't want to miss the lift. She hurries out.

The room empties quickly after that and I find myself getting ready to go also. The last two to leave hold the door for me. I turn round and see that Hugh is the immovable object in all this. He is still sitting where he was on the sofa.

I linger in the doorway.

'You not going?' I ask.

'Ooh, no,' he says. 'I shouldn't like to.'

'Don't you want to see everyone?'

'I've seen them. And enjoyed them. Now I need a bit of time to digest it all.'

'What are you going to do?'

'Listen to music. I've moved away from 1888. I've begun exploring the start of the nineteenth century.'

'Really?' I say.

I feel instantly at ease with him. I feel we're carrying on where we left off only recently.

'Do you know, I think it's possible that Beethoven's piano music is just slightly more beautiful than Chopin's. I'm trying to decide. Meanwhile,' he says, holding up his joint, which is long and elegantly rolled, 'I thought I'd tuck into this. Would you like to join me?'

I know that most students smoke weed, but I still feel uneasy about seeing Hugh doing it. Alone on that sofa, he looks a bit Late Period Nick Drake. On the other hand, I would really like to sit there with him.

'I'd love to join you,' I say. Let's be honest, there is nothing I'd rather do on this earth.

I go over. He passes me the joint. 'Here you go,' he says. 'You light it.'

I sit down beside him. He passes over one of those old-fashioned lighters that's fastened to a heavy stone. As he fires it up, his hands shake slightly. My handsome giant is showing vulnerability. What's the matter with him? I take the first warm drag of his joint. It's strong. Immediately I feel more receptive. Colours are brighter. Sounds are more significant.

Hugh is busying himself with Simon's decks.

'It's not always easy living with The Awesome Mr Monster,' he explains, 'but you do get a cracking sound system. Right. This is Beethoven, the slow second piano movement of the Emperor Concerto.' He has the record out of its cover already. 'It's strikingly similar to Chopin's Number One. Or you could say that much of Chopin's oeuvre came from his attempt to surpass the second movement of Beethoven's Emperor. I see it as a straight fight: Chopin versus Beethoven in a contest to make The Most Beautiful Piece Of Piano Music Of All Time.'

I'm loving this. It feels so special to be with Hugh again.

'And who wins?' I ask.

'Well, Beethoven has the advantage,' decrees Hugh. 'He came first, so Chopin, however sublime, can only be a copy, or variation, on the master. Plus, he's Beethoven.'

He puts on the record. Places the needle carefully. The violins glide in.

'Before they bring out the piano,' comments Hugh, looking at me with a wonderfully passionate expression, 'both composers concentrate on strings. In Chopin's case they are almost deliberately boring, so that you're all the more stunned by its exquisite beauty when the piano comes in. Beethoven does the same but, being Beethoven, he makes the strings more big and epic. You sense him commanding that the whole of Vienna must stop and listen because he is about to play a tune.'

As ever, Hugh is describing the effect produced exactly. I've never heard someone talk more accurately. The music proceeds to a very measured beat. Beethoven is indeed willing Vienna to a halt. Horses are slowing. Carriages are stationary. Beethoven's ordering us to listen.

And I do.

Meanwhile Hugh is staring thoughtfully at the record going round and round. He reaches out for a glass which is on the right-hand side of the decks. It looks like lemonade inside it. He drinks absent-mindedly. I'm aware of how delicate he really is, how delicate all this is. I want to savour every detail. As I inhale on Hugh's joint, I notice the tiny crackle it makes. I notice that the smoke is slightly more yellow at the tip. Meanwhile, my young self is rapidly calculating how I'm going to get over to him so as to kiss him. I realise it's obvious: I could share the joint with him. That's what I should be doing.

I go over and stand beside him. He turns and looks at me.

'Any second now,' he says, taking the joint dreamily, 'the piano finally comes in.'

He stares into my eyes, with a contented expression in his. It looks as if he's finally proving a point he's spent all his life trying to make. Both of us are holding our breath. He's warned me that this is going to be good – I am about to hear Candidate One in the contest to decide The Most Beautiful Piece Of Piano Music Of All Time – but even so the music catches me unawares. As the piano comes in, I feel as if an angelic cat is slowly walking up my spine.

I also realise I'm still staring into Hugh's eyes.

My left arm brushes against his and the contact makes my bare skin tingle. I'm looking up into his face. It is turned towards me and several inches higher than mine, but it feels somehow as if I am over him. I feel as if I have to tense my neck, because it is a physical effort to prevent my lips from sinking softly on to his. His mouth is parted and he has a far-away look in his eyes. Never in my life have I wanted to kiss someone more than I do at this moment.

He turns his head down.

I tilt my head up.

I look reverently into his eyes. He leans in slightly. It's obvious we're going to do it. I turn my body. He turns his. His eyes close slowly like a cat's. His lips look very full and very soft. His left hand reaches up and touches my right ear. I tilt my face further forward. I approach closer. My hand is touching his beautiful cheek. I shut my eyes, I press my lips to his, and stop in ecstatic bliss. We kiss.

I pull back gently and open my eyes. His open too – sleepily, drunkenly.

'I love you,' he says.

'I love you,' I answer.

I say it a bit quicker than he does. He seems filled with bliss; I'm a touch polite.

'I *love* you,' he says. He sounds astonished by what he's feeling.

'I love you,' I say.

I really mean it now. The feeling of love is rising from my stomach like a gossamer balloon filled with warm air.

'I *love* you,' he says, with emphasis now.

'I love you,' I say.

I didn't know it was possible to love this much. I feel I've stripped away all pretence. I'm at the core of my feelings, and every bit of them loves him.

'Oh my God,' he says, with a sleepy smile on his lips. 'We're so fucked.'

'What?!' I moan.

'Did you take an E?' he asks.

Oh my God! *He's on E!* He didn't mean what he just said!

'Yes,' I say, feeling the balloon puncturing inside my chest. 'I took it about twenty minutes ago.'

(I've never done E. Do the effects start in twenty minutes?)

'Oh,' he remarks. 'You're just joining me then.'

'Yes,' I agree. 'I'm just joining you.'

But I'm not. I've never taken E. Not now. Not ever.

My young self has rarely felt so crushed. I just said I love him because I love him. He said it because he's drugged. I feel like such an idiot! Witches are shrieking in my head: 'Lucy! You *idiot*! What *have* you done?!' I feel like a schoolgirl with a crush! I sit, frozen, staring at him. I'm hoping he can't see too much of the disappointment in my eyes.

The door opens. I move away from him guiltily.

It's Simon. The Awesome Mr Monster is wearing a black hooded top I've never seen, and he has sunglasses perched on his baseball cap. He looks surprised. He also looks concerned. It's obvious he knows what was just going on, and he's hurt. I feel terrible, as if I'm betraying him.

'Simon!' says Hugh. 'Are you OK?'

'Er . . . Yuh!' says Simon, a bit too definitely.

'Did you forget something?'

Simon doesn't know what to say. 'Er . . . To be honest,' he says, 'I realised I hadn't said goodnight to you, and I wanted to check you'll be OK.'

'Oh,' says Hugh, touched by that. 'Thank you.'

'But I see you're fine,' says Simon hurriedly. 'Better go,' he says, but again stops in the doorway. 'Erm,' he says, then looks at me. 'Goodnight, Lucy!' he calls. Then stops again. 'Or . . . do you want a lift?'

'Er . . . yes!' I reply. I'm thinking: if I'd taken an E, I'd probably be wanting to go to the party. But also I just want to get away. 'Why not?' I say.

'The minibus is outside the Porters' Lodge,' he says.

'I'll be along in two minutes,' I say. 'I'll just fetch something from my room.'

'Right,' says Simon. He can tell I want to be left alone with Hugh and it makes him uncomfortable. 'Have a good evening, Hugh. Laters!'

He bolts out of the door.

I'm now desperate to get away. I'm scared I could cry. I feel exposed.

'Right!' I say. I'm sounding like Simon myself. Over-emphatic. 'I'd better get off!'

'Right,' says Hugh. He looks surprised. He looks sad.

I hurry to the door.

'Listen,' I say, turning at the last minute, 'I'll see you soon.'

'Yes,' agrees Hugh. 'See you soon.'

He looks very lonely, and his eyes have an awful plead-ing look like a dog that's been hit. Suddenly I don't like the sound of it: leaving him all alone, drugged. But it wasn't me who gave him the fucking E! Why did he do that? I feel really annoyed with him. I also feel mortified by what I just did. I feel I was tricked into giving him my love.

'Will you be OK?' I ask.

'Yes!' he states. 'I'll struggle on without you. I always do.'

I'm not sure what to make of that. I'm desperate to get away. I give him an idiotic smile, and duck out the door. It swings shut with a bang, and I look for a moment at that card: 'Mr Ashby and DJ Monster'. Safe on the other side, I stand gripping the door handle. I breathe in slowly, and the feeling of mortification blows over me like a cold wind.

I shut my eyes.

I have that strange feeling again. I'm being washed down the same tunnel, and this time I'm going a lot further. I'm buffeting against subterranean walls. Elsewhere time is passing. Clocks tick, leaves grow, a million people die, and many more are born . . .

Up ahead, I can hear angelic singing.

Stop! I think.

I wake with a start.

I'm in my room in Isis House. The clock says 5 a.m. Dawn.

People say that the dawn is the best part of the day. And so it *is*, if you really enjoy lying awake listing reasons why you should kill yourself. My thoughts are a gurgling tumult. I'm worrying about Hugh's party in two weeks' time. I haven't seen him since last term when I kissed him when he was on E, then fled. But I still feel committed to his party. I know it's happening. Gemma has got a proper invitation to go with Richard Scott, even though she hasn't slept with him in two months. I'm still supposed to be stripping, but I don't have a 'burlesque' outfit, and I've not yet worked out how to strip. I saw some done on telly. Channel 4 have been very generous with the amount they show their late-night gentlemen viewers. The stuff I've seen always seems to involve skinny girls who dangle like bats from poles. I'm not sure why that's sexy. I am also sure I could never do it. Why did I make the offer? For weeks now, I've seen the ordeal looming up on me, like a car in slow motion skidding into a crash. Why haven't I pulled out?

My older self is listening carefully to the tumult of these thoughts.

I'm scanning them, of course, for any mention of Hugh. During his second term at college he ceased emerging from his room and disappeared from college life for a while – which, if anything, made him all the more talked about. I disappeared too. At the end of the term, Gemma got the chance to take on Isis House – a much-desired property by the river – and we moved in together. We learned to cook. We learned to love walking.

That's what my young self decides to do now. I dress quickly and go outside.

Walking has an aimlessness about it which always calms the mind, and this morning is particularly fine. The first rays are filtering between the trees and cutting through the slight mist. The light is waking the river. Clouds of flies have taken to the air. A solitary rat flops into the water. Geese are flying up and down in little squadrons. They are landing on the surface with a splash. I always enjoy that. I go over the Folly Bridge, then past the pub, and climb round the gate into Christ Church Meadow. A swan is strutting self-importantly along the riverbank. I head up towards Christ Church. This is always a majestic sight. The top of the cathedral is visible above a sandstone building, at the end of a glorious wide avenue of vast towering plane trees. In the middle of it, a lone man is jogging towards me. He has on a blue tracksuit, a baseball cap, and a big broad grin. The grin gets wider as he draws nearer.

By the time he's reached me, it's as bright as the morning sun.

'Luuuuuuuuucy Potts!' says Simon, in the slightly strange Jamaican accent he adopts for greetings.

'Hello, Simon,' I say. 'What are you doing?'

'I'm in the Third Eight,' he says. Imagine being in the Third Eight! Why would you bother? 'We're training at six. I'm just having a quick jog-a-nog to limber up.'

He rests his hand on my shoulder while he stretches out his quadriceps. He's got very long dark eyelashes. They sweep up as he examines my face. His presence is like fresh-baked bread. It's the sound of sheep in a field. I feel safe. I feel calmed.

'How are you getting on,' he says, talking with uncharacteristic quietness, 'with the old . . . stripping thing?'

'Ugh!' I remark. 'Simon, I can't believe I got into that!'

'Are you sure you want to do it?'

'Well . . . no! But I really want to go to Hugh's party. I think it could be good for me in some way.'

'How?' enquires Simon, not entirely convinced.

'Well, it's not stripping as such. It's burlesque, which is an art form.'

'Yes . . .'

'And I'll be over a fountain, in front of a Tudor house. It'll be an experience. And I was thinking it might be . . . liberating somehow.'

'OK. Why?'

'You see, I have been self-conscious about my body for much of my life, and I feel that, if I can do this, I'll be shedding something.'

'Well, respect to you for your artistic integrity and your commitment to adventure,' says Simon. He gives me one of his self-conscious frowns. 'But . . . basically . . . who's helping you with it?'

'What do you mean?'

'Have you got, like, a manager or producer?'

I don't really know where he's going with this.

'Why do I need a manager?'

'Basically . . . have you got music, an outfit, all that?'

Now he's stressing me out. 'No!'

'Can I help?' he offers.

'Simon, I can't see you as a stripper.'

'Nah nah nah! Just . . . well . . . basically . . . I went down to London a couple of nights ago and saw my older brother. We always meet every May the seventeenth, 'cos it's the anniversary of our middle brother's death.'

'You had a brother who died?' I ask.

'Yeah, man!' says Simon. 'Leukaemia.'

Simon seems to be the most buoyantly cheerful person I've ever met. It's strange to think his life has been touched by tragedy. 'And . . . are you OK about it?'

'Yeah yeah yeah!' says Simon, dismissing my fears with a wave of his hand. 'I got all his clothes! Including his cowboy outfit! I was the coolest cowboy in Woking! Anyway . . . so I met up with my other brother. And he – I've gotta explain this – he does location scouting for adverts, and he wanted us to go to a strip club.' Simon smirks bashfully. 'Hey, I only went to keep him company! Anyway . . . basically . . . I had a chat with one of the artistes – the best one actually – who was called Natasha Von Strinkel.'

'What was she like?'

'I must say, she was good.'

'But what was she *like*? Did she dangle from a pole? Was she fast and athletic?'

'Nah nah nah! She was slow and . . . Listen, I had a talk with her afterwards. I told her about you. I asked for tips.'

I can't believe this! Simon is certainly strange. He's also the most touchingly helpful man I've ever met!

'What did she say?' I ask.

'She said: "It's all just an act,"' says Simon, giving a decent imitation of Natasha Von Strinkel's louche cockney accent. '"I think to myself that one glimpse of my body is worth ten million pounds. Then I look at the audience and I think: do they deserve it? Then I think: fuck 'em, I'll do it anyway. 'Cos *I* fancy it . . . "'

Simon grins at me. He seems proud of the way he just reproduced Von Strinkel's voice.

'And where did she get her music,' I ask, 'and her clothes?'

'I asked all that. She wore stockings, and black frilly stuff she got from a place called Fetish on the Charing Cross Road. Then she wore a dress and a fur coat she got from charity shops. And the music she used was *kicking*. I definitely think you should use that. It was a sax piece by Johnny Hodges, called "I Got It Bad And That Ain't Good". But I think she had some funny version with a bit of a beat to it.'

'Where am I going to get that?'

'I'll get it, no problem!'

'Are you sure?'

'Yeah, man! No probs . . . I can put some drums on it and mess it up a bit.'

'Really?'

'I'm a DJ! It's no problem. And anyway, I'm pretty much the promoter of the evening, 'cos I've promoted before, and 'cos I'm Hugh's room mate.' I have no idea why he is giving me such a lengthy explanation. 'But basically I'll help you – manage your bit, whatever . . . erm . . .'

I want to say: Why do you have to be 'the manager'? Why do you need a title? I don't. I just say: 'Thank you, Simon. I'd love your help.'

'Wicked! Natasha gave me her number as well, which I can pass on. If you want to ask her anything, or go and see her, or whatever.'

'You got Natasha Von Strinkel's number?'

'Yeah, man!' says Simon a bit smugly. It occurs to me that Natasha Von Strinkel probably thought she was giving *him* her number. Or that's definitely what he wants me to think. He swings his little knapsack off his back, and takes a card out of the front pocket. It says 'Natasha Von Strinkel', and shows a black-and-white photograph of a very alluring woman. She has thick eyeliner, and the ghost of a smile on her dark lipsticked lips. 'There you go,' says Simon proudly. 'Call her if you like.'

'Simon,' I say. He looks at me expectantly. 'Thank you so much!'

For a tiny moment he gives me a scared look. He looks boyish and lost. But the moment passes. Suddenly he's Jean-Paul Belmondo once again.

'OK!' he says, and reaches forward and pecks a little kiss on my cheek. Straight afterwards he becomes embarrassed by his own temerity. 'Wicked!' he declares. 'I gotta go! *I gotta row!*' And he nods a bit, and blushes, and then turns and runs off towards the river. I can't help but laugh. He even runs in a cheerful way. He somehow jogs from foot to foot. Simon, thinks my young self, you are one of the strangest men I've ever met. You're also one of the sweetest, and I think you've just saved me.

My older self is less pointed in my feelings. *Simon*, I think, *I love you*. I stand for a long while, watching him run off down the broad avenue of mighty plane trees. Behind him the dawn is lighting the sky a fresh, pale wash. *Actually,* I think, *it's not just you I love. It's life.* The scene feels unimaginably precious. For a moment, I imagine it as a painting by Turner. The sky, rendered in oils, is orange and blue, and somehow you know a tempest is coming, and the whole canvas just throbs with significance . . . Is that how I should paint it? Then I see it as a scene on a Ming vase. The wide avenue is in white. The trees are blue, so is the jogging man . . . I see it in my own style then – in oils, fairly realistic, but with the outlines a little clearer and the colours enhanced, the way they are when the sun shines after a storm. Painted orangey-red, in the light blue sky, I see a title: *The Right Man Runs Off.* That could be the title, I think. Simon has now reached the river and he turns and jogs down towards the boat houses. Or maybe the title should be *It's not just you I love. It's life.* And then from nowhere a wave of emotion rises up my chest, and, as it hits the top, I gulp and shut my eyes.

CHAPTER 9

I have the sense, once again, that I'm moving.

I open my eyes, and see that I am.

I'm in the front of Simon's camper van, and we're just coming to a stop in the most extraordinarily beautiful spot. Left of frame – as it were – is a grassy bank, which slopes down from the great ornamental pond set in its stone basin over which I shall be performing. The camper van is going to function as a green room. It is parked on a wide path of yellow sand, which points like an arrow to two tall yew trees. These are lit by white light, coming from the left. Between the trees there is a large replica of Michelangelo's David, whose pouting face is turned to the right where there is a tree, covered in white flowers which curl upwards like angels' wings.

Simon gets out of the van and walks down the path towards David. When he reaches him, he taps his bottom.

He looks back at me and grins. I smile back, but don't move. In my mind, I'm running over my act, one last time. It's pretty much nicked from Natasha Von Strinkel, who Simon and I did go and see. I shall be doing her moves. I pretty much copied her outfit. I have also given myself a similarly exotic name.

It will work like this . . .

At 9.30 Lord Bobby will stand on the steps in front of his house and give a little speech of welcome. He will introduce Hugh, who will say a few words and then introduce me as 'Countess Svetlana Moujinsky, who has come all the way from St Petersburg'. Simon will play music. The crowd will turn. And I shall walk out on to a wooden stage erected over the ornamental pond. I shall remove my clothes and dance, after which the party shall be said truly to have begun.

It's now 9.14.

The two hundred guests are just arriving, dressed in black tails and top hats and velvet dresses worn with long satin gloves. Simon and I are amongst them. To our left, wide stone steps lead up to the majestic façade of the Tudor house. To our right glitters the wide pond with the ominous wooden platform suspended over it. Above us, the sky has darkened to indigo and the first stars are peeping out, eager to see the festivities. To the left of the pond there is a gigantic marquee, which has been rigged up with lights and a sound system to be played later by The Awesome Mr Monster. But, for now, music is played by a small ensemble of gaunt troubadours, dressed in black, who are stationed at one end of the wide staircase. A drummer is providing rhythm, an accordion is wheezing a gypsy gig, a clarinet is providing sweetness and melody, and a double bass is twang twang twanging, to give bassness and earthiness and sex. So the atmosphere is very fresh and quick, as the guests take their first sips of the special Chat Noir Cocktail. Who knows what is in it? Dark and velvety, it is rumoured to contain absinthe. It is certainly delicious, producing shudders and a feeling of warmth as it goes down.

Everyone is happy.

But I'm not. I am dressed as Countess Svetlana Moujinsky, but I don't feel like her. I feel like Lucy Potts, wearing some rag-tag clothes I bought from charity shops. I'm wearing, under my white fur coat, a thin satin skirt – dark bottle green – fishnet stockings, and a basque. I've got gloves, a hat, and some peacock feathers. I nicked the peacock feathers bit from Natasha Von Strinkel. The idea is to hold them just high enough to conceal the crack between my buttocks, and then – just before departing – to drop them so as to treat the audience to a last ten-million-pound glimpse of bottom. I've also got a Venetian-style cat mask, which I'm not wearing. That's in my pocket. I keep squeezing it nervously. Losing my mask – that is one of the many things that currently terrifies me. Simon seems nervous too. He's dressed in an outfit he hired – a black tail suit worn with a top hat. He looks good. I lean towards him.

'I can't take this waiting around,' I whisper.

'No,' agrees Simon. 'But I don't think Countess Moujinsky would let anyone see her before a show.'

'That would be letting them have a few million pounds' worth for free,' I agree, smiling.

'Shall we go back to the camper van,' whispers Simon, his eyes twinkling with intimacy, 'and have a cheeky line of coke?'

That surprises me.

'Have you got some?' I ask.

'A little.'

'I've never known you buy coke before!'

'I ain't sure I'm gonna get it again,' he says. 'I hear it's quite more-ish. But I figured that if we didn't have some tonight, then when would we?'

I smile at him.

'So shall we go back to the van,' he says, 'and try it?'

'I think that might be wise,' I agree, and we hurry away from the crowd feeling naughty and bonded. We scamper round the pond and find Cassady the Camper Van waiting patiently for us down the slope. I'm wearing a spectacular pair of satin high heels – £8 from Oxfam. I take them off to walk down the slope and the short grass feels wet against my feet. Simon is already on board. He's lighting a couple of candles. That's very Simon: he always likes to set the atmosphere – he has a mild obsession with candles. We sit at the back, where there's a little Formica table on to which he tips out cocaine from a folded sheet of magazine paper.

'Who did you buy this off?' I ask.

'A friend of my brother's,' says Simon, chopping out the powder with a phone card. 'I feel that I'm your manager for this special occasion, and I thought you might like some.'

'Thank you, Simon,' I say. 'You think of everything.'

'How you feeling?'

'Very nervous,' I say, barely able to meet his gaze.

He holds the glance for a moment.

'You look like ten million pounds,' he says.

'I feel like five quid,' I say.

Simon smiles.

'See if that helps,' he says.

He passes me a rolled-up note, and I close one nostril and hoover up the line as elegantly as I can. It tastes like chalk and dirty money. But I can feel it form a magic sludge in the back of my throat, which seems to do good things to me. Loud piano chords sound in my head. My lack of confidence melts away. I'm suddenly seeing each detail, and everything is sharp, everything is beautiful – the faint wisp of smoke from Simon's candle, his wide flat cheekbones, his thick black eyelashes and eagerly attentive eyes.

Simon has a line too. In his dark brown iris, I can see candlelight shimmering.

We both smile. Suddenly I have a desperate urge to confess *everything* to Simon: that I know he loves me, and I'm terribly grateful, but I don't want to respond because I am desperately in love with Hugh, though somehow I fear our love will never come to pass. But I don't.

Simon takes a flask out of his pocket and passes that over.

I take a quick hit from that too. It's brandy. As it hits the back of my throat it seems to chivvy the cocaine further into action. Then the alcohol spreads to my chest and I feel drunk. I feel the drugs are melting the veil between my separate selves. I know that Simon and I are no longer nineteen-year-old students, who are naughtily taking drugs together. I'm intensely aware that we are forty-three-year-old adults, and we've married, and I've been blaming him for making my life drab. The thought is painful and immensely confusing. I want to apologise, but I feel already as if reality is about to fracture and I could slide away from this moment. *That must not happen,* I think. *That must not happen.* Because then I will never find out about Hugh, and I will be unable to prevent him from leaving college, and then everything will go wrong. *But how am I to stop him leaving college?* As I ponder that confusing prospect, I realise I'm feeling faint. Reality is fragmenting. *Stop thinking,* I tell myself. *Be here. Be still. See each sight, hear each sound . . .*

'Are you all right?' says Simon.

'Yes,' I say quickly.

'Good,' he says. ''Cos it's nine twenty-eight. We should both get into position.'

'Yes,' I agree.

Feeling like a condemned prisoner being led to the

gallows, I climb out of the camper van. I notice a frayed piece of rubber on the step. I notice how the freshly cut grass is slightly bouncy under my feet. I bend forward and stretch for a moment. A terrifying thought hits me then – something I never pondered during all my rehearsals. *What am I supposed to do at the end?*

Natasha Von Strinkel didn't have that problem. She just dodged behind a curtain. I'll have walked forty feet down a platform built over a pond. There will be no curtain. I'll just have to walk back again. And what should I do with the peacock feathers while I do? Can I really keep wafting them all that way? And where the fuck – for that matter – *are* my peacock feathers? I haven't seen them since we left college this afternoon!

'You're going to need these, babe,' says a voice behind me. I turn. Simon is holding out the feathers.

'Thanks,' I say.

Once again, I have a strange desire to apologise to him for everything. I don't. I just take those peacock feathers with trembling hands. As planned, I tucked them into my garters.

'I'm gonna go up to the sound desk,' says Simon. 'I think you need to get into position.'

'Yes,' I say, and my stomach drops away. Why am I doing this?

'Lucy,' says Simon. 'You look wicked. Have fun, yeah?'

'Thanks, Simon.'

He checks his watch. He realises he's only got a minute to leg it to the sound desk and scampers up the bank, and

I see him jogging off in his bobbing Staff bull terrier run. With shaking hands, I put on my mask.

I take a deep breath.

I can smell the pond beneath the platform, the moss and cool water. I hear the guests laughing and talking. I walk up the slope, almost feeling like Countess Svetlana Moujinsky, and cross the few yards of cobbles to the edge of the raised pond. None of the crowd notice me. I sit quietly on the wall. Across the other side of the black water, everyone is looking at Hugh's dad, who's standing at the top of the steps making a speech. I can only hear the odd word – '*extremely* proud . . .' '*wonderful* occasion' – but I can make out the tone of his voice: staccato, high-pitched – a voice that seems to jab like a sharp elbow. I'm distracted anyway. My heart is beating so loudly I can actually hear it. Bobby builds up to a climax: '*Very* happy birthday!'

And Hugh walks up the steps and turns to face his guests.

He looks gallant and dignified and handsome as a hero. The two hundred guests erupt in a rousing chorus of 'Happy Birthday'. Hugh smiles while they sing, looking so proud and grateful it makes me bleed inside. As the cheers fade, he starts to talk. Compared to his dad's, his voice is deeper, steadier. His voice is chocolate melting into the ears of his guests who laugh appreciatively. He speaks some more. They laugh again. I wish I could hear what he's saying. There's a huge laugh now and a round of applause. Then another laugh, and some whistling. Then there's a longer stretch of quieter talk, but, towards the end, he cranks up the volume and there's a massive laugh. Now he is declaiming like an actor: 'All the way from St Petersburg in Russia . . .' Oh, fuck. Oh, shit. Now it's my turn. 'Countess Svetlana Moujinsky!' With that, Hugh makes an extravagant gesture with one arm, and everyone turns to look at me.

I stand on the wooden platform.

I wait.

I feel very glad of the mask suddenly. Behind it, no one can see where I'm looking. The crowd spreads out around the circumference of the pond. I see them jostle a little to get a better view. Necks strain upwards. They look like a bunch of geese, waiting for food.

Fuck 'em, I think.

And at that moment the piano intro starts, and, slowly as a spider advancing on a fly, with a faint sway of my hips, I walk downstage. I sense everyone watching expectantly. They are absolutely silent. The music, however, has reached the end of the piano intro. The sax is about to kick in. This is where Natasha removed the coat. I haven't reached the end of the platform. I'm fucked.

But then the piano starts again. I realise that Simon has repeated the intro. Thank you, Simon.

Reaching the end of the platform, I look down at the two hundred guests. *Know that one glimpse of your body is worth ten million pounds. Wonder if they're worth it,* I tell myself. Then the sax comes in, slow and mighty, like a wave building out at sea. The music is very loud. It echoes off the walls of the five-hundred-year-old house. It seems to come up through the soles of my feet, undulating up my body, making my hips move in a slow spiral. I look at Hugh. He's staring intently. I look at the crowd. I think, you fuckers are not worth it. But I'll do it for my own amusement.

I unbutton the fur coat.

I shrug one shoulder, letting the coat slide gently down my arm and fall to the stage. Everyone is watching, electrified. Even the girls. *Take off more,* they're saying. *Please please please take off more.* Slowly, angling my waist slightly, I turn my back on them. I reach one hand languorously above my head. As I tug the glove from it, I pretend that the other hand is Hugh's and he's finally doing what I've always wanted him to do: he's undressing me.

As I settle into the act, I cease worrying about the crowd.

Nerves fade. I just listen to the music. I take my time. I – dare I say it? – enjoy myself. I discover that stripping requires an ability I've had all my life: you must be able to see yourself from outside, so you can judge the pictures you're making. My consciousness is barely in my body at all. It is fluttering around in the night air like a bat. It is watching critically as Countess Moujinsky turns her white back to the crowd, and drops her bra to the floor. It watches as Moujinsky turns herself to face the crowd once again, with her hands over her breasts. Keeping her fingers on them for as long as possible, she lifts her shoulders up . . . up . . . and as she finally slides her fingers off her breasts and releases them, her arms are in the air, and she is a huge fleshy flower beautifully unfurling. It watches as Moujinsky turns her back to the crowd again, and inches the pants down. Those pants are a theatre curtain which is slowly descending, *exposing* the picture. But Moujinsky doesn't let the audience see her buttocks. The Countess would *never* do that. She covers the whole display with a peacock feather. She steps out of the pants, leaving them on the wooden boards . . .

And now I'm back in my body.

I can feel the night air caressing the sides of my hips. I am aware of everything I've just done.

The music is reaching an end. The finale of the act seems to be swooping closer quicker than I expected. I know that, as the sound fades to silence, I must hit a pose. And I do. I turn my back to them again, and as Johnny Hodges blasts his last, I finally fling the peacock feathers high into the water, bringing my arms up above my head and standing in complete nakedness.

The music has stopped. So have I. I stand there frozen for one two three four seconds. The spell is broken.

Behind me the crowd burst into applause.

But what do I do now? Suddenly it's obvious.

I dive like a swallow into the water. That clearly surprises them. As I come up, I can hear the applause grow even louder. I hear screams. I think perhaps I can hear people leaping into the water themselves. But I'm not sure. I swim butterfly. It seems more elegant. I'm aware too of the tantalising glimpses of buttocks it affords, as I rise like a dolphin from the water. Five strokes and I have swum to the side. I can hear them still cheering. A man is running over with a towel.

It's Simon. His dear lovely face is positively beaming with pride. I rise out of the water into his dry towel. How did he find a bloody towel so fast?

'Countess Svetlana Moujinsky,' he says, 'you have done well.'

He presses the towel round me, and we hurry down the bank to the waiting camper van.

Simon discreetly leaves me alone.

I towel my hair. I dress in my other party clothes. I am sitting on the step of the camper van smoking when the first squall of mortification hits me. *What the fuck did I just do?* I think. I see myself gyrating clumsily up on that platform. My fat body flails around. My breasts are white and floppy like blancmanges. What the fuck did I just do? *And why?* Maybe it's the shock of having dived into that cold water. Maybe the coke is just wearing off, and in place of the glow of confidence there's the ache of shame. Anyway, I feel so chagrined, I lie back and shut my eyes. I also feel really cold. My whole body starts to shiver. I hug my arms around myself and wish I were dead. I can hear someone arriving. I think it's Simon. I don't open my eyes. I don't want to see anyone, and I don't want to be seen myself.

Then I feel lips pressed against mine. They are soft. They are very warm. I open my eyes.

'Hello, Sleeping Beauty!' he says.

It's Hugh, with all his manly strength and his eyes twinkling with irony. I feel life returning to the system. I sit up.

'Lucy,' he says, 'that was quite spectacular. Everyone is excited! Did you see? Quite a few of the guests jumped in too. Of course, everyone wants to know who you are. I haven't told though. I will not tell!'

I slide to my feet

'Are you OK?' he asks.

'Well . . . I was just suffering a quick squall of shame!'

'You're so like me,' he remarks. 'But you shouldn't be ashamed. You were unutterably spectacular! Here, I fetched your clothes. And I brought you a drink.'

He passes me a cocktail glass.

'I don't think I can drink that! Can I get something hot?'

'Yes, of course. Let's go and get it right away!'

'I don't want to see anyone else yet. Can we keep away from them?'

'Sure. Here, just . . . can you dry your hair a bit more?' He passes me the towel. 'Then maybe you can wear this hat?'

He passes over a hat. He also takes my hand. His touch is warm and life-giving.

'Come on,' he says, 'we can go round the side of the garden, and then through the back way into the kitchen.'

He leads me up the slope.

The kitchen is a great vaulted place, with bustling cooks and polished chrome and waiters in black tie picking up trays. Hugh is the prince of this domain, though, and we're immediately given a mug of Ribena laced with whisky. It revives me perfectly. Coming out of the kitchen, I see we're at the back of the formal part of the house. There's a smell of wood and polish. I can see vast formal portraits of Hugh's ancestors. They stare down coolly from horses. They peer from under perruques. I can see straight through to the front door, the tourist entrance. The guests we encounter all seem to be possessed by wild excitement. Two men walk into a side room, holding drinks, smoking. A couple come in at the main entrance.

'Oh my God,' declares the girl, looking round, squealing with excitement. 'This is fantastic!'

She spots the giant staircase and runs up it.

'Are they allowed up the stairs?' I ask Hugh.

'It's not my home,' he says. 'I don't know what anyone's allowed.'

A man appears in the doorway. He's talking to a woman, nodding sympathetically. He's very tall, with a long, stooping frame.

'Shit,' says Hugh, 'it's my brother.'

'Your brother?' I ask.

I see a tall man, with a hawkish nose. He looks like he's working hard at being serious. He has pronounced wrinkles between his eyebrows.

'Well . . . half-brother,' says Hugh. 'I don't want to see any of my family. Let's move.'

He clutches my arm, and we disappear. We go through a heavy mahogany door, and find ourselves in a gallery which seems to run the entire length of the house.

'Hugh,' I say, 'I'd really love to see your bedroom.'

Is that too forward?

'Oh,' he says. 'OK. The bedrooms are on the top floor.'

He nods, and points. There's another staircase in a tower. It doesn't make sense, this house. It's like several houses all crammed together. A house designed by Piranesi.

'How come the bedrooms are on the top floor?' I ask.

'Well, the proper family aren't on the top floor,' says Hugh.

The wording seems peculiar. '*The proper family?*' I ask.

'You know what I mean.' He seems very uncomfortable. He sets off up the stairs two at a time. It looks as if he's fleeing from something.

I've never seen a bedroom in a palace before.

It's surprisingly like a normal bedroom. It's just much bigger, with oppressive dark brown panelling, and a huge bed which has posts at the corners and some clothes laid out on it. I'm instinctively drawn to the far end of the room where there are windows with leaded panes in diamond patterns. I peer out. To the left, I can see the vast expanse of the garden – two miles of valley, including a lake – sweeping off into the distance. To the right, I can see the party. There's light, and people moving around, and the pond, and a huge tent from which happy, jaunty music is blasting out. The light from outside catches the underside of Hugh's cheekbones.

'Was it wonderful to live here?' I ask.

For a brief moment he stiffens slightly. Then, after a pause, he says: 'Well, I moved here from Oswestry.'

'What was in Oswestry?'

'Rain, mud, and Welsh people, who all hated me because they thought I was posh. Even though I lived in a caravan at the edge of a wet farm that stank of shit.'

I say: 'Really?' My hand reaches for his, but loses confidence before arrival.

'We didn't have any money at all. And that's why we were so excited to move here. I was six. I didn't care that it was a five-hundred-year-old palace. I was just impressed that they had baths. They had baths, and cooks, and paintings, and corridors so long you could ride a scooter down them.'

'And what was he like then – your dad?'

'Oh . . . the sad thing was I really loved him,' says Hugh. 'You forget what lovely things dads are, don't you?'

'Well, I can't remember my dad at all!'

'Can't you?' Hugh is giving me his enquiring look. 'Have you tried?'

I sense he is trying to shift the focus back on to me, to stop me from asking about him. I'm not having it.

'And what were the rest of the family like?' I ask.

'It can't have been easy for them,' he says, and nods again. Why does he keep doing that? 'As far as they were concerned, this was their home.'

'So what was it like living here?'

'It . . .' Hugh starts. But then stops. 'Do you mind if we don't talk about this any more?'

'Why?'

'The past is a bad place.'

'Is it?'

'After this we moved to Greece, and one day we wanted to build an extension so I could have my own bedroom, and we dug up an old cesspit in the garden. We dug through layers and layers of old shit mixed with mud and broken glass, and at the bottom there was this huge frog. He looked a little bit like my dad actually. He was massive and he had these big angry bulging eyes . . . That's what the past is like. You dig up layers and layers of shit, and at the bottom is an old amphibian who wants to kill you. Do you know what I mean?'

I touch him on the arm.

'I know exactly what you mean,' I reply. 'But I don't think everyone feels like that. I also feel you have to kiss that frog and make him go. Or he'll lurk there for the rest of your days.'

Hugh gives me a sunny smile.

'Nicely put,' he says. 'But I'm not kissing a frog. I'm not even kissing my dad. Though I'm sure you're right.'

I am getting used to his tactics now. He's trying to change the subject by showering me with praise. I'm not having it.

'Let's go to the party!' he suggests.

He turns and heads out of the room. I follow him.

'So what were the family like?' I repeat.

The question stops him in the doorway. Why am I taunting him with difficult questions? It's not classic courtship. Why don't I just kiss him?

'The family were . . . sweet enough,' says Hugh, and nods again as if he's trying to convince himself. 'But as far as they were concerned, I was the interloper who never left. So inevitably they would say things like: "Dad, Hugh has taken my bike!"'

'I don't get it! Did they not know you were their brother?'

'*I* didn't know I was their brother till I was fourteen, which was when Mum told me the Great Secret, so no, I don't think they knew. I thought that Bobby was just a rich and rather eccentric friend who'd taken us in. I think he tried to be nice. I remember when it was my birthday, he said: "Hugh, what would you like for your birthday?" Of course now I think: that's not a good question. If you love a child, you *know* what they want. You don't put the responsibility on them for their own gift, particularly if they don't feel they're worthy of one anyway.'

'Did you not feel you were worthy of a gift?'

'No! Ask any adopted child, or any stepchild living in a house where they're not sure they're welcome: they don't feel worthy of anything.'

'Really?'

'Can we get out of here?' he says suddenly.

And walks away.

I hurry after him. He's striding off down a long dark corridor, and I'm scampering to keep up. I'm desperate to understand. This feels so important, I need to keep the conversation going.

'What gift did you choose?' I ask.

'That's the point!' he says, still striding onwards. 'I couldn't think of one. I was up in my bedroom thinking about it, when it hit me: a light sabre! It was nineteen seventy-seven. Of course I wanted a light sabre! I'd never wanted anything so much. If I had a light sabre, I thought, I would flash it before me and lay waste to my enemies. God, I wanted one! So I got out of bed and came running down here, down this very corridor. My mum had a room up here as well. We were up with the servants. It was that bedroom right there. And I ran to it, and I remember I didn't even knock . . .'

As Hugh tells the story, he's reached the door in question. He puts his hand on the door handle.

'I just burst right in,' he explains, 'and I shouted: "A light sabre! That's what I want!" And there was Mum.'

As Hugh says this, his voice trails away. He looks really haunted, and then he turns and heads back for the stairs.

'And,' I prompt, 'what was she doing?'

'Oh, she was . . . you know . . . paying the rent.'

He starts bounding down the stairs.

'What do you mean?' I ask.

We're halfway down the first flight. Hugh stops and turns back to face me. I've never seen him like this. He looks furious.

'She was leaning over her bed, with her arse out, and he – that tall prick with the long hair – was pumping her from behind, but really *stabbing* her with his cock. I think he may even have had her hair in his fist. Mum had this pained expression on her face. She looked like a pig being slaughtered. Of course, it may just have been routine sex, but it looked like he was really hurting her. And he turned to me. "What do you *want*?" he called out furiously, and I said a bit pathetically: "A light sabre! That's what I want! For my birthday!"'

With this, Hugh stops talking. I've never seen him like this before, so broken and desperate. I put my arms around him but it's like hugging a shop dummy. He's stiff and totally unresponsive. After a few seconds, I pull away. I am desperate to get that smile back on his face.

'So,' I say hopefully, 'did you get that light sabre?'

'Yes, I did!' replies Hugh. 'I took it off to Oswestry when we went for a visit. It was just a long tube of plastic, with a light bulb at one end. And this Welsh kid called Gareth rolled a marble down it, and it smashed.'

Hugh seems to have got himself together now. He resumes walking down the stairs.

'So then we went off to Greece. There was a very small school there and I didn't ask for anything, especially light sabres. I just did what I was told, and the school regarded me as some sort of miracle child because I could read, and loving the praise of the teachers, I worked really really hard. And that's how, years later, I ended up at Oxford . . . and what a consolation prize that's proved.'

We've now reached the bottom of the stairs. We're in danger of being swept back into the party. He pauses. 'On the downside,' he says, 'I'm now studying a subject I despise. But on the upside, I've met you.'

He's standing on the ground floor. I'm still on the bottom step. Unusually, his face is just below mine, and he looks wonderfully handsome, and his eyes are gazing up at me, sadder and more beseeching than those of a lost Labrador puppy, standing in the rain. So I cup my hands round his wonderful wide handsome face.

'Hugh,' I say, 'it's OK. You're big now, and strong.'

And I press my lips to his. His are very soft and warm. God, I love him. I'm going to save him. I'm going to make everything all right. I kiss him again, but then we're disturbed.

The door opens.

'Libby!' declares an excited voice. 'Here she is!'

I turn to see Hugh's dad. The Frog King is springing towards us, and his eyebrows are thick and bristly and his eyes are bulging and his cheeks are pink with lascivious excitement.

'The girl of the hour!' he exclaims. 'That was absolutely marvellous! Everyone thought so!'

I'm thinking: my identity was meant to be a secret, you dick! Will you stop shouting about it?

'Thank you so much,' I say.

'The whole party is filled with art people!' splutters Bobby. 'There's already a lot of talk about doing another event at the Chelsea Arts Club. You've simply *got* to do it again!'

'I'm not sure about that,' I say. 'I only did it this once, as an experience, and because I really wanted to go to Hugh's party!'

'Oh, I quite understand,' says Bobby, although he's actually missing the subtext of what I'm saying, which is: why couldn't I come to this party without stripping, you dick? 'I'd be more than willing to double the fee,' he says, and then starts stammering in a geriatric way which I find particularly obscene. 'I . . . I . . . think we agreed a couple of hundred for tonight.'

'We didn't actually,' I remind him. 'We settled on five hundred.'

'Right,' he says. 'Well, let's say, if you do it again at Chelsea, the fee could be eight hundred.'

I'm looking up into his popping eyes. For some reason I'm really angry that he said my fee was two hundred. I think he was still trying, even at this late stage, to get me for a knockdown rate. It occurs to me then: he's mean. Maybe you have to be mean to be a polygamist. You can only give out love in small quantities, so that you've got enough to go round.

'Dad,' says Hugh, failing to keep a note of anger out of his voice, 'Lucy is not a stripper. She's an artist and a friend, who agreed to do this once as an experience. It's not a matter of offering more money – though you did just try to halve it for tonight.'

'I did *not* try to halve her fee for tonight,' insists his father, outraged. 'I've just offered her eight hundred pounds, so you *can't* accuse me of meanness.'

'Lucy,' says Hugh, 'let's go.' He puts his arm around me, and tries to walk past his father.

'*Don't* just walk away when I'm talking to you!' orders Bobby. He's really angry now. Stung by the command, Hugh turns back. I glance at him. There's something about his manner that is very familiar to me: it's that of someone who is used to being hit or shouted at. He's disengaged. Eerily calm. Under the surface, though, I can see that he's livid.

But his dad can't. Or maybe he doesn't care.

'I find your behaviour jolly rude,' he warns. 'I'm putting on this party, for your benefit, and . . .'

'It's not really my party, though, is it?' counters Hugh calmly. 'Or it wouldn't have one hundred of *your* guests. And I would have been able to invite Lucy, who's pretty much my only real friend here. And by the way, Lucy is her name.'

'I know she's called Lucy!'

'When you arrived you called her Libby!'

'That was a bloody accident!'

'No, it wasn't,' continues Hugh. 'You didn't care what she was called. You just saw some tits and an arse you wanted to see again.'

'Fuck you!' spits Bobby.

'Fuck you,' says Hugh, very calmly. 'You dirty, selfish fucker.'

'Take that back,' orders his dad, 'straight away!'

'I will not,' insists Hugh. He's even calmer now. His voice is so steady he could be voicing an advert for sherry. But his dad is red with rage.

'Take it back,' he threatens, leaning in, 'or I will cut off your allowance straight away. And if I do that, you'll struggle to stay at college. Though frankly I'm not sure anyone would care. Your tutors say you're barely working on your subject. Alfie says you gatecrashed the Bullingdon Club and started a fight. He says George Teazle was furious. What sort of way is that to behave? That's not radical. That's just loutish!'

Both Hugh and I say nothing as his father launches into his verbal assault. I'm actually curious to see what other incidents he will bring up. But for a moment it seems he has run out of bile.

'Are you going to apologise to me?' he demands.

'Not a chance,' says Hugh.

'Then I shall stop your allowance,' his father declares, with a twitching note of triumph.

'I don't care,' Hugh tells him. 'I don't want anything from you. I've got quite enough already. I have half your genes. Which is a thought I find frankly sickening.'

'Get out of this house straight away!'

'Don't worry,' answers Hugh. 'Nothing would induce me to stay!'

And he puts his arm around me, very protectively – as if I'm the one who's been under attack – and we turn and we walk back through the kitchen. The staff see something's up. It's as if we're a funeral cortege. They fall silent as we pass. Hugh has to let go of me as we walk out of the narrow kitchen door. But then he puts his arm back round me as we go out into the cool night.

In silence we walk around the fringes of the party, careful to keep out of sight of everyone else. Hugh is still bristling with anger as we walk through a formal garden, in which tall grasses wave from behind box hedges. We go round to the camper van where – thank God! – we find Simon. He's just walking up the slope towards us. He can see at once something's wrong.

'What's the matter?' he asks.

'Simon,' says Hugh, 'what's the chance of you driving us out of here? I'd really like to leave.'

'OK, boss,' says Simon.

So we get into the van. Hugh sits in the back as if he's the child, and Simon and I are in front, like the adults.

'It's a shame,' says Simon. 'I was looking forward to playing my tunes!'

'You can stay if you want,' says Hugh. 'I don't want to ruin the party for you, Simon, or for any of the guests. I just very much don't want to be at it myself.'

'It's OK,' says Simon. 'We're here for you, bruv.'

'Thank you, Simon,' says Hugh. 'And thank you, Lucy. I wasn't intending to speak to my father again, but I shall do so once only – to make damn sure he pays your fee.'

'Thank you,' I say.

Hugh doesn't say anything more. I glance back at him, but he doesn't look at me. He's staring over at the statue of David, sad-faced. I turn to Simon, who seems oddly jolly. He raises his eyebrows as if he's amused. Simon really hero-worships Hugh. He feels flattered to be the one who's whisking him away. Simon revs the noisy engine and, as we surge backwards far too fast, I see the statue of David reversing into the distance. I shut my eyes.

CHAPTER 10

All is still.

I have that heavy, sodden feeling you get when you let the water out of the bath but then just lie there in the tub, like a beached seal. I realise it . . . I just had my chance, all over again, to stop Hugh before he left college. And I blew it. Why did I do that? With my eyes shut, I lie still. I don't want to move.

'Lucy,' says a deep, calm voice. 'Where have you been?'

I open my eyes. I'm back at the crash, lying on the grass. I'm staring up into the oak tree and the blue sky, or I would be if there weren't a very old, very tall man, looking down intently at me, like some kind of ancient surgeon.

'What did you see?' he asks.

'Hugh,' I explain. I want to cry. 'I saw it all, from the moment I met him to the moment we left his party, after which he left college and disappeared from our lives.'

'Did you not see him after that?'

'I saw him one last time at college. He came to a party at our house, very late, and fell asleep on my bed. I woke up and found him, and . . .' My voice trails away. 'And I didn't kiss him' is what I want to say. '. . . We just drank tea and talked a bit. And the next morning he left college.'

'Could you not have seen him after that?' asks the man evenly.

'Not for a long time. No one knew where he was.'

'Could you not find him?'

'No!' I insist.

And it's true! I remember it . . . Hugh had left no address, and this was the early nineties. There was no internet, no mobile phone. We tried to find him. I wrote letters to his mother. Simon did the same. We even wrote to his father. For a time, we thought the college had an address for him and might give it to us. We left messages with doctors. We wrote to the Erik Satie Society. Nothing! Hugh didn't want to be found! What could we do?

'And where was he all that time?' asks the old man.

'It turned out he was in a flat in Putney.'

'Why does this man bother you?'

'Because he died! And I was in a position to help him and I didn't. If I'd known what was . . . going to happen, I wouldn't have chosen . . .'

My words trail off. I don't know what I'm saying.

'Would you not have chosen the man you did choose?'

That's an awful thing to say! I would never say that I would not have chosen Simon. I love him! I love my boys!

'I wish I'd done things differently,' I say. 'I might have helped Hugh at the time he most needed it, and then perhaps he would still be alive and . . .'

'Would you have chosen Simon?' the old man intones again.

'I didn't choose!' I say. 'That's the *point*! I feel I've never chosen any of this! I feel my whole life has just come at me like a storm, and I can't *see* anything or *feel* anything . . .'

'So you need to feel that you've chosen your life – that you're in control?'

'Yes!' I plead. I feel I have as much control as a dog, who's being held down on the vet's table.

'Say it,' he says.

'What?'

'I need to feel in control.'

'I need to feel in control,' I repeat.

But what does this mean? What is going to happen now? I feel I'm drifting off again.

'Where are you sending me?' I ask.

'I'm not sending you anywhere,' he says.

'What do you mean?'

But I get no answer. The man just smiles a thin smile. Then he purses his blue lips and blows towards me, and I smell his breath with its trace of mud and lacy skeletons and bones. It affects me like anaesthetic. I shut my eyes, already moving.

Bang.

I open my eyes.

I'm looking at a large front door. Its dirty glass panel is strengthened with chicken wire, and the wall to the right of it has been decorated with Sellotaped pieces of paper. The top one reads: 'Flat 5e, Potts and Weakes'. As soon as I see that, my spirits plunge.

I think I know where I am: I'm twenty-two, and I'm in Manor House.

I turn round slowly, and I see some bins. Yup. The smell of kebab is on the wind. The sound of traffic is roaring from behind. There's no doubt about it: I'm in Manor House. As with many of London's worst corners – Burnt Oak, Wood Green, Shepherd's Bush – the fine rural name is misleading. There are no Manors in Manor House, and if there ever were, they were crushed to make room for the Seven Sisters Road. Why, oh why, am I here? If ever there were an unweeded, neglected corner of my memory, it would be Manor House.

I start to tune in to my thoughts.

They are not cheery. My thoughts are a defeated trickle which wind through garbage and discarded supermarket trolleys. They are in fact full of resentment that I left college five months ago, all set to shoot into the epicentre of London life like some kind of artistically talented smart bomb, and ended up living in Manor House, Flat 5e – aka 'The Dog Basket'. I'm spending my nights doing barwork, and my days painting in a dark, poky bedroom with walls covered in woodchip wallpaper.

Looking down, I realise I've carried some things out of the door: two plastic bin bags filled with dirty laundry. I grip a bag in each hand and set off. Soon I am making my way past the various bus stops. That is one thing you can say about Flat 5e, aka 'The Dog Basket': it has excellent transport facilities. It has no less than three bus stops immediately outside, and, after only thirty yards, you come to Manor House tube station. I pass the stairs to the tube. I pass the pie shop, which always has a crowd of men clustering outside, eager for pies.

I can see the launderette ahead of me, on the other side of the Seven Sisters Road. The traffic signal is showing a green man. The six lanes of traffic are halted. I hurry across the northbound lane, and make it to the island in the middle. Of course I should stop there, the green man is now flashing. But I don't want to be stranded in the middle of Seven Sisters Road so I decide to sprint across the southbound side. In moments I am halfway across, within smelling distance of the launderette. A comforting fug of detergent has come out to welcome me, when disaster strikes.

I step on a battered saveloy that has been dropped in the road. My front heel skids on it, and I perform a power lunge in the middle of the road. As I stumble my hands rip open one of the black plastic bags, which disgorges laundry. I manage to grab a few items – one of Gemma's bras, a t-shirt I bought in Corfu – but by now a dirty white van is bearing down on me, beeping. Abandoning the discarded clothes I scarper for the pavement. I reach it just as the van roars past. I turn and see a pair of black socks being run over by its wheels. As the van revs away the socks are clinging to its undercarriage, like prisoners making their escape.

I swear loudly, and then, gathering up the remains of my load, I make it into the launderette. Apart from Gemma it's empty, though you can sense the woman who runs it, lurking somewhere behind the sign that says: 'cup of detergent cost's 50p'. Gemma has headphones on.

'The whites are nearly finished,' she announces, far too loudly, 'but I'm afraid you'll have to take them home. I'm already late for my meetings.'

I am annoyed by that. I've had enough trouble with just two bags of washing. There's no way I'm taking home three. Gemma smells my irritation immediately, and takes her headphones off, ready to defend herself. Now I want to pacify her.

'What are your meetings for?' I ask, as kindly as possible.

'Audition for the London Dungeon,' she says, giving me a look like she's calculating whether I'm going to attack her. 'Then I'm meeting a costume designer who might work on my short film.'

'Great,' I say, with a note of bitterness.

'What's the matter?' she says.

'I don't mind being poor,' I explain. 'But I'm fed up with the way it uses up so much time. I resent spending an afternoon in the launderette. I resent working in my bedroom, painting over the same stupid canvas that shows the same dark dismal view.'

And the reason I'm working in my bedroom – as we both know – is that she's filled the living room with stuff needed for her short film. Shall I say that?

'I need to get out!' I say. 'I need space! I need light!'

'I thought,' she says, standing up, 'that the studio you saw in Clerkenwell was perfect?'

'It is perfect,' I say. 'In that it's big enough. It's got great light. And it's part of a complex of creative people I really like. But it's also eighty quid a week. I can't even afford the rent of the bloody Dog Basket! There's no way I can afford eighty quid a week on top.'

'OK,' says Gemma. She doesn't have time for this. 'Listen, I just talked to Simon on the phone.'

'Has he seen Hugh?'

'Apparently,' says Gemma.

'Any news?'

'Not much. That's the thing about someone with ME: not much activity to report.'

'Is Simon going to tell us Hugh's address?'

Hearing this question, my older self remembers this ongoing subplot, which was like a sore in my consciousness for a while . . . It was Simon, inevitably, who finally tracked Hugh down and started to visit him. But Hugh made him promise that he'd keep the address secret. He was ashamed of it, apparently. He was also ashamed of what had become of him. That was one reason he'd stayed hidden, he said. Gemma gives a more cynical one, however. She claims Simon is keeping Hugh from me, because he's in love with me himself.

'Hugh has still not divulged his address,' says Gemma. 'But Simon has been promoted. He's now in a department called Internal Auditing. Apparently he's going to be earning a hundred and fifty grand a year.'

'Bloody hell! Doesn't that mean he'll be making, every month, more than I'd make from a year of barwork?'

'I don't know, will he? I do know he wants to take us out for dinner next Wednesday in the Tiroler Hut in Bayswater.'

I'm not that keen to see Simon. Since we've all been in London, we've already seen him about six times. He invited us to his flat only last weekend, though only Gemma went.

'What's the Tiroler Hut?' I ask.

'Apparently it's London's only Austrian themed-restaurant. They have Wiener Schnitzel. And they also have a man with a monkey who plays the accordion.'

'Who plays the accordion? Man or monkey?'

'We'll find out next week,' says Gemma, and smiles mysteriously. What is she so happy about? She gets up and gathers her laundry. Then she drops it. 'And Hugh's going to be there!'

The news hits me like a bombshell. At first I'm in shock. I've got used to thinking of him, tucked up in a flat somewhere anonymous in London. I feel almost panicky at the thought of seeing him again. I'm hit by a blast of differing emotions. I feel excited. I feel unready. I feel scared.

Gemma grins at me.

'Look at you,' she says, shaking her head. 'You're still so in love with him!'

'No, I'm not,' I plead. (Is this love? I feel as if I've just contracted the 'flu. I urgently need to sit down.) 'But why is . . .'

'Why is what?'

'Why is Hugh coming out, and . . .'

'. . . why is Simon arranging for you to meet Hugh,' prompts Gemma, 'if he loves you himself?'

'Yes!'

'Well, I don't know,' says Gemma, in her mock-supercilious drawl. 'I'm just an actress. I don't understand why people do what they do. I merely understand how they'd look. But I'd guess Simon is offering you Hugh, because he thinks it's the only way he'll get to see you. And to Hugh, he's offering you – the much-fancied Lucy Potts – because it's the only way to coax him out of the house.'

I lean back against the dryer. I feel hot, and a bit weak.

Gemma is pulling her clothes out of the dryer and dumping them into a blue IKEA bag. I feel very troubled by her analysis of the situation. I think she's right, and it makes me feel uneasy for Simon. I think he does love me. I know he does actually. He's said as much, on a couple of occasions. But I realise he's happy to sacrifice what he wants if there's a chance he could help Hugh. That's really noble of him.

'Good old Simon,' I remark.

'Yeah,' says Gemma. She's now mincing past rather pertly towards the door in a cloud of Coco Chanel perfume. (Gemma believes you can stint on accommodation and food; you must never stint on scent.) 'The man's a fucking saint, and, quite frankly, the second he gets over his obsession with you, I'll pounce on him like a panther.'

'Will you?' I ask. Normally Gemma is attracted to people in the film industry. She's someone who instinctively mixes business with pleasure. 'Wouldn't that be like pouncing on your own brother?'

'Not really,' she drawls, turning at the door to give me one of her Marlene Dietrich-style heavy-lidded vamp looks, 'because I don't have a brother, and even if I did, I'd probably pounce on him . . . if he had a hundred and fifty grand a year, and he looked like Simon.'

I snort at this. I'm amused that Gemma is presenting herself as a sex panther, who goes in for incest. It's surprising, even for her. I'm actually curious to know what she'll say next. But she says nothing. She just pushes open the launderette door. Emerging on to the Seven Sisters Road, she lowers her Jackie O glasses and surveys the passing traffic, as if they were racehorses parading at Epsom. It's a gloriously Gemma performance.

''Bye, darling,' she calls, and doing a little wave of her fingers she walks out of view.

She disappears for a moment, and then I catch sight of her through the window – making her way across the busy road with her laundry. No one pays any attention to her as she passes. Why would they? She's only twenty-two. She's not yet kissed James Bond. She's not yet appeared in forty-six episodes of *Dragon Hunter,* playing the girlfriend of the Dragon Hunter. She's just a good-looking girl

– over-dressed, and over-scented – who's click-clacking across the Seven Sisters Road in her cork-bottomed wedges. But, looking at her from the perspective of a forty-three-year-old woman, I know who she is. And I feel truly honoured to have just seen her.

But my twenty-two-year-old self thinks none of this. Why should I? I just think: I am going to see Hugh again.

I am over the shock of it now. I feel relieved and warm, as if I've just eaten my Christmas lunch and I've still got several presents to open. I lean back against the dryer, and, for a brief contented moment, shut my eyes.

Did I just shut my eyes?

I am sitting next to Hugh.

All four of us are sitting in a side booth in the Tiroler Hut, which turns out to be a darkened basement restaurant with black-and-white pictures of Austrian mountains, a throng of happy diners, and – as promised – a man with a monkey, who's playing the accordion. Hugh is sitting to my left and his right hand is resting on the bench next to me. It's hidden beneath the table. I'm feeling so adolescent, I'm thinking I could reach down and squeeze it. I've been thinking that for the last twenty minutes, I've hardly listened to what anyone's been saying.

My thoughts have been in turmoil all evening.

We all met in the pub opposite the Tiroler Hut. Gemma and I arrived together. We came in, and first of all I saw

Simon. He was sitting at the edge of the pub, with a bald man wearing a coat with a fur collar. Dressed in a dark blue Paul Smith suit and wearing highly polished, square-toed shoes, Simon leaped to his feet. He was being particularly doggy, he was eager and grinning and he was wagging his tail and he was kissing us.

It took me a moment to realise that the bald man was Hugh.

My first response was a feeling of betrayal. For three years, I've been in love with the witty Adonis in my head. Somehow he'd been transformed into this disappointing figure, who didn't even get up when he saw me. His face was puffy and he'd shaved his head, but that didn't disguise the fact that he was going slightly bald. Hugh knew what I was thinking. He had a guilty, haunted look. You could tell Gemma was horrified by the change too. 'Gosh!' she murmured. But she's an actress. She then threw her arms round him, and after that we were all so keen to cover up our first reaction, we all starting talking at once. I made a toast to 'Old friends, and new beginnings.' Simon made a toast to Gemma (she got the job at the London Dungeon). Then we all toasted Simon's elevation to the world of Internal Auditing, and he explained what it was, and somehow he then segued into telling us, at some length, about why he liked Jackie Chan, repeating lines from the trailer of his latest film, about which he is childishly excited.

Hugh hardly spoke. It didn't seem to matter. He did however let slip his address, and I instantly memorised it: 181a Felsham Road. Mostly, he just sat drinking and nodding and looking so damn pleased to see us, and so proud and full of wonder at everything we've been doing, that I felt grateful and loving towards him, and that's when I started wanting to hold his hand.

'And what have you been doing?' Gemma asks him, at length.

'I have made a very full analysis,' begins Hugh, with a trace of his old wit, 'of the daytime TV schedules. I've read the papers. I've got depressed.'

'Why?' asks Gemma. She's obviously bristling with suggested therapies and different approaches.

'You can't read the papers,' he says, with his incongruous air of cheer, 'and not get depressed. The world is polluted and over-populated, and yet everyone just talks about the economy. I feel as if I've been invited to a house in which there's some ailing old dog called The Economy with whom everyone is strangely obsessed. "How's The Economy?" everyone is asking, and the news is never good. Occasionally The Economy seems to rally briefly. It has a little sniff around the garden. But then The Economy returns to its normal position – flat on its back, groaning. Let The Economy die, I say! Let's talk about something else!'

We all laugh. I think we're delighted to hear Hugh make a joke, even if it is one that climaxes in death. His little performance seems to take something out of him, though. He pours himself another glass of wine. In less than an hour the four of us have finished four bottles, most of which has gone into Hugh. I feel so protective towards him, I can't resist any longer. I place my hand on his. He turns it upwards and gives mine a friendly squeeze. His hand feels so big and warm. It's a huge comforting duvet of a hand.

He turns to me.

'But, Lucy,' he asks, 'what are you painting?'

As he asks the question, he peers into my eyes as if he really wants to know. The last of my unease dissolves. It's always like this. Talking with Hugh opens up a whole world in my head, where anything can happen. I tell him how I've been painting the view out of my bedroom. It's a homage to the famous pre-Raphaelite picture, *Hampstead from My Window.*

'Is it any good?' Hugh enquires, and removes his hand from mine while he takes out another cigarette.

'It's been good, six or seven times,' I answer. 'The trouble is, I can't decide on the focus. At first the picture captured the Seven Sisters Road on the left and Finsbury Park on the right. It was showing something about the divide between town and country. I emphasised that . . . Then I got more interested in the window in the foreground. I drew in flakes of paint, beads of rain on the windowpane . . .'

'Why can't you do six or seven different paintings?' asks Hugh. 'Wouldn't that be the basis for a good exhibition, which would say something about the subjectivity of perception?'

'That theme's been covered,' I explain. 'And I don't want to give up on this painting 'til I'm satisfied with it, because canvases are expensive.'

'How much do they cost?' asks Simon.

'About twenty-five quid.'

'That's not much,' he remarks.

'Some weeks I earn a hundred and eighty quid,' I reply. 'There's rent, food, bills . . . To me, twenty-five quid is a lot.'

Gemma comes to my aid. 'I totally understand. I want to get new head shots,' she explains. 'I know this brilliant photographer, but I don't have three hundred quid for a session.'

'I'll pay it,' offers Simon. Gemma is stunned by that. 'Please, let me pay it.'

Gemma has no qualms about it. 'Simon,' she says, 'you're on!'

'I just want you to thank me when you win your Oscar.'

Gemma beams. 'My darling,' she vows, 'I will.'

She kisses him on the cheek.

'And Lucy,' says Simon, and immediately starts blushing and putting on his self-conscious frown, 'I think I can help you too . . . Erm . . . Basically I'm buying a big house off Highbury New Park – it's a bigger house than I need for the moment, but it's an investment – and, er, basically, it's got a big light-filled basement that I don't need. I was thinking . . . why don't you use it as a studio?'

I'm amazed by that, but could I possibly accept this offer?

'Wow,' I begin, 'that would be, could be . . . amazing.'

A shy smile starts to spread over his face. It gives me a pang. Simon looks the way Tom did, when I told him we were going to Disneyland. He gets out some estate agent's details. It's a beautiful house, which costs 450 grand. The 'basement' is probably the best room in the house. It stretches the entire length of the building. It has large windows at both ends. There's a photo of it. You can see through the windows into the garden. The idea of moving from a bedroom studio in the Dog Basket, and into this large, light room – that's like moving out of a hot sticky day, and diving in the sea. I would love to paint here. But Hugh is back in my life. It feels like the wrong moment to give a commitment to Simon.

'This is too much,' I tell him.

'I won't be using it!' he declares.

'But I'm sure you could think of a million things to do with it,' says the young me, while the old one is thinking . . . don't I know it? He must be itching to fill this with paragliding equipment, or his records.

'Tell you what,' says Simon, in his manly deal-striking business manner, 'think of me as your manager. Give me ten per cent of the proceeds from any paintings you sell, having painted them in that room.'

I haven't yet sold a painting, as Simon well knows, so this 'offer' is mere flattery.

Hugh has got to his feet.

Somehow I had forgotten he's so tall. Standing up, he loses his air of puffiness. Upright, he looks like a champion swimmer again. Where is he going? He's left his coat, but taken his cigarettes. He disappears round a pillar. For a moment I've lost him. I'm briefly distracted by the man with the accordion, accompanying four others who are singing 'Stayin' Alive' by the Bee Gees. It's an unwise choice. They don't sound like they're women's men. They sound like Pinky and Perky.

Simon is looking over at his friend.

'Where's Hugh going?' he says.

'I'm amazed he's here at all,' says Gemma. I've just noticed she's wearing my jacket. 'How did you manage to get him out?'

'I picked him up in my car,' says Simon. 'I promised him Lucy would be here, and that he could drink up to three bottles of wine.'

'I think he's managed that,' says Gemma, flicking a Marlboro Light into a foil ashtray. 'Maybe he's just going for a pee.'

'Maybe he's asking to sing,' says Simon, unconvinced.

'I wanna sing in a minute,' says Gemma.

We all look at Hugh suspiciously. I think we're assuming he won't just walk out. Hugh is eccentric, and he's got ME, but he's always polite. He wouldn't get up and go, would he? Gemma turns to Simon, and lifts her glass a little drunkenly. 'Thanks again for the offer of the head shots. Congratulations on joining the Internal Audio team.'

'Internal Auditing,' says Simon. 'It's actually a very prestigious department. I want to stay there three years, and then I want to go into Renewable Energy.'

I'm not really listening to them.

Hugh is walking up the stairs. He's leaving.

Focus, I think, but I say nothing. *Follow him.*

Somehow my youthful self is taking the advice. I'm getting up from the table. I'm gripping it with my hand. I'm concentrating on the foil ashtray which holds a nest of Hugh's cigarettes. Gemma looks up, concerned, as I move. I lurch drunkenly past the man with the squeezebox. The sound grows queasily louder. Then, gathering resolve, I dash across the restaurant as if I'm about to be sick. On the way I notice each grey floor tile. As I sprint up the stairs I notice the scuffed linoleum strip attached to each step. In moments I'm out of the door, and it's OK. The worst is past. Reality is returning. I've conquered it. I'm seeing more clearly now. I'm in Bayswater and it's got that distinctive smell that London has after rain – the scent of wet dust and damp bins. Across the road, I see the lit window of a pub.

That'll be where he is.

I don't even check the road. I bolt for the pub. To my right, a black cab hits his horn. I don't care. As I leap on to the pavement, I cross a wet *Metro* newspaper. *Metro*? Surely that's not right. I think Hugh died before the advent of *Metro*. *I must not think that*. I must not think. I concentrate on the pub. It's a classic old-style one. It has a big bar in the middle of the room, which is lined with glasses, ashtrays, and severely gaunt old men. And to the left, sitting quietly in a booth by the wall, looking very handsome and slightly sad, is Hugh.

He eyes me as I come over.

I'm now used to the way he's changed. I'm used to the shaved head. My feelings about his appearance have altered completely. Even unwell and unhappy, I find him disquietingly attractive. He slides his drink over to me as I sit down opposite.

'Whisky and ginger?' he offers.

'Thank you,' I say.

I sip it. I feel the sweetness of the ginger on my tongue. I feel the flush of warmth as the alcohol spreads into my chest. It's OK, I think. I've made it, and I'm with Hugh. I know he's ill, but his mere presence gives me a profound sense of peace. I greedily take in every detail of him. His skin has deep pock marks, which somehow make him even more handsome. I'm willing to forgive the flaws. I love him. His big hand is on the table. It is shaking slightly. I want to put my hand on it. I want to stop him shaking.

'So,' he says, 'how *are* you?'

This is very Hugh of him. We've just been together, but he behaves as if none of that counted, because we weren't alone.

'Oh,' I say, 'all right.'

'So what are you going to paint next?'

'I don't know,' I say. 'What is an artist supposed to paint?'

'There is only one thing an artist is supposed to paint,' says Hugh. 'And that's the images they see when they dream.'

'Who said that?' I ask.

'I think it was Ruskin,' he says. 'But it could have been Rolf Harris. I get them mixed up. I may even have coined it myself.'

'But isn't painting a bit . . . useless,' I plead, 'as a job?'

'Lucy,' says Hugh, 'the world is full of jobs that are useless, and most of them are actively harmful. That's where the money is – at the very edge of morality. Sell off a bit of innocence, trash a bit of landscape, make yourself some cash. And no one cares as the world is raped and pillaged like a whore in wartime. Everyone's in too much of a hurry. But what's a painter? A painter is someone who *looks*, someone who says: I think this is beautiful or interesting, and, as a homage, I'm going to recreate it. What could be more celebratory than that? What could be more sacred? Anyway, you're really good at painting. By the next time you see me, would you tell me what picture you're going to do?'

'Yes,' I say. I see we've just made a date to meet again. 'Shall I visit your flat?'

'No one would be more welcome,' he replies.

Everything is OK. I shall be seeing him again. I place my hand on his.

'So,' he says, studying me seriously, 'are you going to take up Simon's kind offer?'

'I'm not sure,' I admit.

'He's offering you a studio that takes up a whole floor of his house. It's a good offer!'

'Yes!' I agree.

For some reason, both of us are smirking. We're trying not to laugh.

'So what's the problem?' he says.

'Well,' I confess, 'there may be strings attached.'

'There may,' agrees Hugh.

'And one of those strings may be attached to Simon.'

For some reason Hugh's mouth is twitching with amusement, but at the same time he's got a tear in the corner of his eye. I can't help myself.

'I wish *you* had a house in Highbury with a free floor,' I say.

His smile fades.

'But I don't,' he says. 'I've got a small flat in Putney, and it's filled with books and pizza boxes.'

'Why did you go?' I ask suddenly.

'I just . . . fancied a drink.'

'You can get a drink in the restaurant.'

'Yeah, but . . . Nurse Simon was looking worried every time I filled my glass.'

'He thinks you drink too much.'

'Not much he can do about that.'

'But, Hugh, why do you drink?'

'Well, I . . .' He takes a deep breath. The tear detaches itself and runs down his cheek. 'I'm just waiting for the spark from heaven to fall. Do you know what I mean?'

'But . . . can't you find the spark without necking three bottles?'

'It's hard, Lucy.'

'Why?'

'Well, look at you all.'

'What?'

'You've all found your place.'

'Have we?'

'Simon is doing his Internal Auditing. I don't know what that is, but Cocky does, and he seems filled with purpose. He's also got a well-cut suit and some shiny shoes, and that seems to please him. Fair enough. He's Cocky Cockburn, the man with the Midas touch. He likes money. And you and Gemma are living in Manor House. Now, I have never been to Manor House. I have a strict rule never to venture further east than Highbury Corner. One has to have limits. But you sound happy there.'

'Do we?' I ask.

'You do,' he says, and as he does, his voice goes high and squeaky. 'Meanwhile, I'm in Putney, trying not to drink before midday.'

His voice shakes. He's crying properly. I look at him, astonished.

'But,' I begin, 'why don't you stop?'

'I could stop drinking,' he says. 'But I might still find I'm not that interesting. And that I'm lost.'

He's such a big man, and he's always seemed so confident and certain. I don't know how to handle him like this.

'Well, let's do something,' I enthuse. 'We need to find you a place. Let's get you a job!'

'What could I do?'

'Something in the arts?' I say.

'I'm not like you,' he says. 'I don't have the creative spark.'

'But you do!' I say. 'You talk about art more accurately

and more eloquently than anyone I've ever met. You could be a critic.'

'A scavenger on art,' he says.

'That's such a negative thing to say!' I protest. 'Criticism is arguably the greatest art of all! You're using the materials of other artists, creating words of appreciation, and yours would be accurate, and they'd be eloquent, and they'd be directing people to what's good – what could be more creative than that? Or you could be on television, talking about music!'

Hugh smiles. 'People turn on TV to watch football, or a car chase, not some wordy bloke discussing music.'

'Maybe they will in the future,' I say.

'I'm sorry. I know you're all trying to help, but I don't want you to.'

'Why not?'

'Because it breaks my heart. I don't want you to see me like this. I don't want to drag you down, but I will because I'm lost. I just can't find my place.'

His voice is now calm, but a tear is running down his other cheek. I look at him, agonised.

Hugh, I want to tell him, no one really finds their place. I'm not sure I have. I've just found somewhere, and I'm trying to make the best of it. Hugh, I want to say, just kiss me, and take me to your bed. I think that might be my place.

'I can't go back there,' he says suddenly. 'I don't even want to fetch my coat.'

'OK,' I say.

'Would you say goodbye for me?'

'OK,' I say. I'm unhappy he's going, but I like the idea of being his representative.

'Just say I was feeling unwell, and you saw a Putney bus, so you put me on it.'

'OK.'

'Thank them both. Say I really appreciate them getting me out. But I have to go.'

'All right,' I say. I give his hand a squeeze. 'I'll bring your coat when I come.'

'Lucy Potts,' he says.

'Yes?'

'Thank you.'

I'm keen to talk sense into him. But perhaps I should trust him. I should let him speak.

'I love you,' he says.

'I love you,' I echo back.

My heart is beating hard. What will happen now?

'Simon will be worrying about us,' he says. 'Would you go back to him?'

I stand up.

'I'll come and see you soon,' I say.

'I'll be waiting,' he promises, and his smile is warm and paternal.

As I look back at him, I'm thinking: he's asked me to see him . . . he's said he loves me . . . what more do I want? And, turning away from him, I feel an unexpected sense of peace. As I walk across the bar, I'm struck by how beautiful it seems. The bottles behind the bar glitter like shells. The polished mahogany top has a glorious warm sheen. A pint glass stands waiting to be washed, and the Guinness foam has made lacy patterns round the rim. Heading for the door, I notice that the window has a beautiful curved expanse of glass. I turn to the table where I sat with Hugh.

He's gone.

With his exit from the scene, everything seems to fade. I step out into the street, and I can once again smell the musk of wet dust, but I can't hear the traffic. In fact the whole of Bayswater – the pubs, the shops – all fades to an outline. Somehow, I cross the street. I step into the entrance to the Tiroler Hut, but I can't see the white strips on the stairs. I feel like I'm stepping into a void. I know that Hugh is not going to recover, that I wasted my penultimate chance to change things, so why do I feel so light? I hear sad angelic singing. As I continue down the steps, I feel lighter and lighter. I feel I could step off these stairs, and I could just lift up, floating, into the sky.

And I open my eyes, and I see that's exactly what's about to happen.

I know where I am. I am on top of a Swiss mountain, and I'm with Simon, who's about to ask me to move in with him. While we're on a paraglider.

I remember this scene vividly.

A few weeks have passed since we saw Hugh in the

Tiroler Hut. I've started painting in Simon's basement. He hasn't just provided a studio. He's provided canvases. He's also – and this was the real surprise – supplied inspiration. Seen through the window at the front of the basement, the street is just above eye level. On the very first day I was there, I saw something through the window that was so wonderful I just had to paint it. A black cat was stepping out, right of frame. A man's feet were leaving, to the left. Then a bicycle swished through a puddle, and the water exploded joyfully upwards . . . I painted that in about three days, and I sent it off as an entry for the NatWest Painting Prize. After that I just painted everything. I painted the garden as seen out of the back window. I painted a daisy in a glass. I painted a study of Simon's back. (He has very strong muscles between his shoulders – all those wind sports.) Life has improved immeasurably, and much of that is due to Simon. When he comes home of an evening, he bounds down the stairs, and as he takes in the new work I've produced that day, his caterpillar eyebrows rise. He looks around, astonished and delighted by everything. In the evenings we go out and listen to music, visit galleries, eat in Chinatown. We treat London like it was our new-laid lover, and together we explore each corner, each crevice, each canal. We've not explored each other. I think Simon knows not to try. After each shared outing I go back to the Dog Basket. We are mates, we are allies. And here we are now, on a short holiday, on the crest of a Swiss mountain. Simon is on a business trip and has invited me along. He thinks it's the perfect moment to try something he's always wanted to do: a tandem paraglide.

He is standing before me now, a gigantic red paraglider laid out on the grass behind him. He's wearing a white helmet and a red jumpsuit, which is covered in straps and bits of metal. I'll give it to him, he looks good. The jumpsuit accentuates his lean physique. The helmet somehow highlights the little cleft in his chin. Seeing him now as a forty-three year old, I want to laugh. He looks so happy and so quintessentially Simon-like. Simon adores equipment. He's the king of gadgets. Only he would think that, before you pop an important question, you need carabiners.

'Turn your back to me,' he says, 'and press back against my front.'

I do just that. I am about half an inch taller than Simon, so with me standing below him on the slope, we are exactly the same height. We fit each other perfectly. I stand there as Simon busies himself with straps. There is one strap round my chest. There's another round my waist. And there are more straps – quite kinky ones, these! – which go round the top of each leg. Now I'm attached to him, I'm also attached to the paraglider. Behind me, Simon lifts up the straps, and the rig fills with air with a sudden whoosh, and at that moment I really take it on board: we're attached to a massive piece of canvas, *which can fly*.

Alarmed, I turn my head to look at him. I'm wearing a helmet too, and it bumps against his.

'You OK?' he asks.

'Yes,' I reply, but I don't mean it. I know that Simon – king of wind sports – has done this many times before, and that, almost every time, he was safe. But there was just the one famous occasion when his paraglider was dumped out of the sky by a freak gust of wind and he ended up in bed for three days. He *says* that won't happen today. He has given a long and confusing explanation, citing inferior equipment and weather conditions on the day of his accident. He says that everything, today, is perfect. But I'm feeling sick with fear.

'We need to fill the rig with air,' he says.

I look round. In wintertime this is a ski resort. A few hundred yards to our right there's a typical Swiss tourist hotel. It's a big white timber-framed building, squatting on top of a pizza restaurant. It's easy to imagine this spot covered with snow, skiers pausing here before starting their descent. In front of us is a patch of grass as wide as a tennis court. It is a dry day in late-November, and the grass is short and brown. This is our runway.

'Let's jog together,' says Simon.

I start running. I'm looking at my boots as I do. I'm trying to keep time with him.

'A bit more speed,' he says.

I'm still looking down as we run together. I say running. It's not easy to run well when you're strapped to someone else, and above your head there's a massive twenty-five-foot kite.

'A bit faster,' urges Simon.

Now the two of us are in time. Right foot, left foot, right foot, left foot. Our steps get longer as the paraglider fills with air. Then suddenly . . .

Oh my God!

The ground drops away, and we are gliding over ten feet of Swiss grass, and then, quickly, we're *thirty* feet up, and then we turn and – *ah! Oh, Lord!* – we're now over a *two-hundred-foot drop* above a Swiss valley. There are pine trees way below, which are spearing up towards us. The feeling of vertigo is intense. I sense I'm about to plunge, and I don't want to be over pine trees. If we're dumped to the ground, I want to be over grass. I'm tense with fear. Beyond the trees there is a grassy field. I want to be over that. We float towards it. We're flying fine. We're not crashing. Actually . . . I don't think we're going to crash.

I'm starting to feel calm.

I look further ahead. Beyond the field, in the distance, there's a majestic Swiss valley. The far side of it is dark green forest rising into a rocky blue mountain. I look down the valley, where there is a town. There is a road with cars moving on it; from here it looks like a glittering snail trail. I look beyond the town, down the valley, which becomes lilac blue as it stretches into the distance. And beyond that, hazy in the summer heat, there are taller mountains, and their blue is just slightly greyer than the deep blue sky, and hidden amongst their peaks there are secret patches of snow.

'Oh my God!' I say. In fact, I say it again and again and again. 'Oh my God!' We are doing the thing that every child dreams of doing. We are in the air! We are flying! *We are flying!*

'Lucy,' says Simon's voice. He's right behind me. 'Are you OK?'

'Yes!' I say. 'Yes! I am!'

'Are you sure?'

'We're flying! We're bloody . . . flying!'

'I know!' he says, loving my enthusiasm. He chuckles proudly.

'This is the most amazing thing I've ever done,' I exclaim. 'Are you OK?'

'Yeah!' he reassures me. 'I am flying, and I've always wanted you to do this, and – Lucy! Babe! – you're strapped to my front.'

Simon is really not an articulate man. For him, that counts as an elaborate speech.

'I'm happy too!' I say. And I am.

Simon is absurd, and he likes gadgets, but he is terribly sweet. He has given me a studio, and then he has given me this holiday. I do actually love him a bit. No. I love him a lot. I love everything. I am looking around, joyfully. In the sky, to our left, there's a buzzard. That's actually *below* us in the air. I've never felt as free and alive as I do right now. I feel that my life has recently lifted out of a trough of gloom and poverty, and Simon is behind that move. And he's behind me now. I can feel him pressed against me.

'Lucy,' he says, 'do you want to move in with me?'

'Gosh!' I say. 'That is such a kind offer!'

I am stalling as I rapidly consider it: would there be any

drawbacks to this highly tempting offer? *Yes, there would,* I want to say to my twenty-two-year-old self. *If you move in, Hugh will be jealous. He won't object because he's too polite. But soon after he will die.* I say nothing. I must not interfere.

'I would love to move in with you,' I say guardedly. 'But I'd be worried about letting down Gemma on the flat.'

'I thought you said she wants to go out to LA for Pilot Season?'

'Yes, she does.'

'So maybe you could just do it while she's away?'

'Yeah,' I say. And then I add something which I swear I didn't say at the time. 'But I'd be worried about Hugh.'

'Why?'

'Well, he left the restaurant the night you offered me the basement. Do you . . .' My voice trails off.

'Do I think he was jealous?'

'Yes,' I say.

'Yeah,' agrees Simon. 'And obviously we all want to help him, but we need to live our own lives as well.'

'I suppose,' I say. 'But he's not in a good way.'

'No.'

'He's got a lot worse than he was at college. I think he needs purpose and direction.'

'He does.'

'I wish,' I say, 'we could turn back time and keep him at college.'

'How are we supposed to do that?' says Simon immediately.

'Obviously you can't turn back time,' I say.

'Look,' says Simon, 'we are where we are.'

Of course what he's saying is right, but I feel irritated the way he's being so belligerently literal. I don't feel free as a bird any more. I feel trapped, like a woman strapped to the front of a man who's being belligerently literal. This angry feeling is painfully familiar to the forty-three-year-old me. It's the dull sense of resentment that poisons my marriage. Where does it come from? As I think about that, I feel I'm disengaging from the scene.

And it begins to fade. Sounds are growing muffled.

I'm conflicted. I know Hugh is going to die, and I've done nothing about it. Meanwhile the young me is anxiously scanning the ground below for the place where, Simon says, we're going to land. I look straight down. I shouldn't have done that. I see the space gaping beneath me. It makes me weak with sickness. And, worse, I see that the paraglider is flying high above a mountain waterfall. Far below, I can see water spuming into the air, and cascading on to sparkling rocks. And perhaps this has the effect of cooling the air above. Anyway, suddenly it starts to feel cold. It's unnaturally cold, I think. In fact, this whole scene feels somewhat unreal. I see something out of the corner of my eye. I flinch, and look again. Is it another buzzard? It looks like a witch on a broomstick. *But witches don't exist*, I think. *None of this exists.* And as I think that, the paraglider jolts suddenly. It starts to dive down.

We're falling! I didn't say anything, but we're falling!

'Simon!' I shout.

My stomach is leaping. I'm terrified about the loss of

height. But, worse, I have a feeling of mortal dread. *This did not* happen. *I know it didn't happen.* So if this isn't the past, what is it? And as I think that, my vision bleaches out, as if I'm watching a film that wasn't properly exposed. I can still see the waterfall beneath me, but the pine trees to the side of it – they've gone. The waterfall is exploding out into a white landscape, but I can't hear it. I can just hear a faint humming in my ears like tinnitus. I still feel I'm falling, but now I can't see where. I can't see what I'm going to hit.

I shut my eyes, and I pray that it will all go away.

For a moment I can hear choral singing. I'm just waiting to smack into the ground. I can feel how it will be. My knees are going to smash up into my face. Bones will splinter, teeth will crush. I brace myself. I'm going to hit the ground.

And I do.

Bang.

But I've not hit it with the force I expected. I land with a bump that's gentle but nonetheless disconcerting, as when you think there's another stair but there isn't. And I haven't landed on Swiss mountain rocks. Instead I am on my hands and knees on top of some paving stones. In front of me lies a sketchbook. It's open, and it's showing a photograph of some swimmers diving into a pool. The

Sellotape holding it has yellowed. Beside the sketchbook a black ant is crawling towards a pizza leaflet that has gone sodden in the rain. I am suffering from an acute sense of déjà vu, which makes me deeply uncomfortable. I can hear the breath catching in my chest. It sounds like a scared animal. I can feel a stone cutting into my knee.

'Hello,' says a voice.

It's a very familiar voice, it's deep and rich and soft as chocolate.

I turn and see Hugh. I am looking up at his double chin and shaved head. This is late Hugh – unwell Hugh. Still, I can't help it. It's Hugh, and his smile, though weakened, is full of warmth, and my heart leaps a *pas de chat* in my chest.

It's OK, I think. Hugh is still alive. I have one last chance to talk sense into him.

'You need to open the door yourself,' he says. 'The key is under the frog. Think of the book by Tibor Fischer. Or the Hungarian expression. "*I am so down,*"' intones Hugh, putting on a Hungarian accent, '"*I am at the bottom of a coalmine, down a deep well, under the arse of a frog.*"'

Looking down, I see the frog. I lift it up and find a key.

I unlock the door, and make my way in.

In the hallway I see a vast pile of mail. I step over it. At the bottom of the stairs, I catch a glimpse of myself in the mirror. I look good. I'm wearing the Hermès scarf which Gemma got me for Christmas, and the cashmere coat Simon bought me for my birthday. My hair is tied back with a couple of braided locks in pre-Raphaelite Princess style. This is good. I need to turn something on in Hugh, and I'm going to do it. I feel a brief rush of exhilaration. But as I go up the green-carpeted stairs, it drains away. I feel hurt he hasn't come out to greet me. Why hasn't he?

As I enter the living room, I think, for a moment, he's disappeared.

I look around, taking it all in. It's less of a room, and more of a lair. The windows are dirty, and half of them are smothered by brown curtains. In front of them a television teeters, balanced on some books. Across the floor there are magazines. Piled up all around the room there are books, and large wonky piles of homemade video cassettes. My eyes are still adjusting from the bright sun, and it's so dark in here I can barely see. I turn to my right, and I'm slightly shocked to see Hugh is sitting in a very low armchair that faces the TV.

'It's bad, isn't it?'

He looks ashamed. I bend and kiss him on his cheek.

'Hello,' I say.

'I heard you won the NatWest Painting Prize,' he says. 'That's spectacular. That makes you the best young painter in the country! You make me very proud!'

'Thank you.'

'Sit down,' he says, waving airily at a wooden upright chair. I don't sit. How do I begin?

'So,' I say. 'I've found something I'd like to paint next.'

'Oh, yes?' he says politely.

'I'd *like* to paint this,' I say.

I take the sketchbook out of my bag and place it on his

lap. I open it to the picture of the swimmers. As I do that I'm leaning over him, and a lock of my hair falls against his head. I quickly brush it back. The picture seems to provoke regret in him.

'Oh,' he moans. 'That's where it all went wrong.'

'Really? Why?'

I thought it'd be flattering and amusing: this picture of him leaping into a pool. But, no.

'Well,' he says, 'because I should have won it for a start.'

'Why should you have won it?'

'It was two hundred metres butterfly – four lengths – I was Greek Junior champion at that event. The Greeks are not necessarily a country of athletes. We don't like to train, for instance. Instead we like to lie on the beach thinking about the Good Old Days. But Greeks do know how to swim, and I was a national champion. Of course it's all about fitness, and I wasn't in great shape, but I should still have had enough to win a race against first-year students.'

Leaving the book, I sit down on the chair.

'So why didn't you win?' I ask.

'Didn't you see?'

'No. I was cold. I left after the first length.'

'Oh,' he says. 'I was winning after the first length. There were just two swimmers with me, to both sides of me. At the end of the second length, they were still with me. They were closer, in fact. Five feet behind. It unsettled me. I decided I was going to outsprint them on the third length. I put in the fastest strokes I could do. Reaching the end of the length, I looked right. The guy was two yards behind. I looked left. The guy was *still with me*. I couldn't believe it. I looked to the front . . . and that's when I crashed into the end of the pool. *Smack*.'

'Did you?'

'*God, it hurt!* I took the entire impact on my face. I was dazed. I was spitting out a bit of tooth. I was trying to clear my head. There was some guy shouting at me, some PE teacher type. "*Come on*," he was shouting. "*You can still do it!*" But I just couldn't.'

'Why?'

'My accident was an opportunity for everyone else. I just stood there looking at them take it. I could see an expanse of churning water, and all the other swimmers surging off into the distance. Even Simon went past and Cocky is many things, but he's no swimmer.'

Hugh pauses. I don't say anything.

'Life is like that race,' he says quietly.

'Why?'

'Everyone cares only about the winners. Nobody else gets a look in. Nobody else even gets a job.'

'But *you* could be one of the winners!'

'That's what everyone says!' says Hugh. 'That's what keeps them going. But I couldn't be a winner.'

'Why?'

''Cos I made a good start. But then I smacked a wall. And that little trauma seems to have started the ME.'

At this, Hugh goes quiet. I can see he's in a depression, but there seems something obstinate about the way he clings to it. It annoys me. What am I supposed to do or say?

'Where did you go,' I ask suddenly, 'when you left college?'

'I came here. Though I also had a lengthy stay in the Psychiatric Wing of Ealing General Hospital.'

That chills me. 'Why were you there?'

'I enjoyed the food. Plus I was made to stay there after I tried to kill myself.'

I feel sick. 'Did you?' I say lightly.

'Yup. So then I was sectioned. It's a sign of madness, apparently, trying to kill yourself. Don't know why. It's a sign of sense, if you ask me.'

Inside I'm panicking, but Hugh is horribly casual. He picks up a biography of Descartes and starts to roll a joint on it, using a tiny rabbit pellet of hash. He looks far worse than he did in the Tiroler Hut. He looks squashed under a huge weight.

'There are too many of us,' he says. 'Good manners alone dictate we kill ourselves. And why not? To be or not to be? Sartre says it's the only real question.'

'That's because Sartre never met Simon,' I suggest, 'or he'd have posed other questions. Like, what is his obsession with Jackie Chan? And when will he realise that it's not cool to wear golfing visors?'

Hugh smirks at this. He loves talking about Simon.

'And, of course, Monsieur Sartre could have asked many other questions,' I continue, 'such as: does this top go with those trousers? Which do I prefer – the smell of jasmine or the scent of wisteria? Is there a cure for the Human League? There is so much to live for!'

Hugh flashes me a grateful smile.

'See, when you're with me,' he says, 'it lights a little fire in my heart. But then you go. And I feel an icy loneliness which fills my head with emptiness and my heart with sadness.'

'Is that a quotation?'

'That's what Satie said when his love left him,' says Hugh, then looks at me ruefully. 'Do you ever feel education is a burden? Your head fills up with the words of other people, and you lose room for your own.'

He gives me a blank look then, which takes the wind out of my sails. I'm starting to feel like him – like I can't move, like there's nothing to do but sit here waiting to die. I watch Hugh as he slowly sprinkles hash into his joint. His depression is raw and visible as an open sore. His gloom is a big brown ocean, and I'm just a tiny fish, pressed down by its weight. What can I do? What can I say? Looking round the room for inspiration, I notice an *Evening Standard* opened at the Movie Listings. I notice that tonight is the first night of the Jackie Chan film Simon wants to see. It occurs to me . . . I could buy seats. Simon only works in Hammersmith. I could walk there in twenty-five minutes. I see myself striding across Putney Bridge and turning up at his office waving tickets.

Hugh's finished rolling his joint now. He points at it, as if to say: Do you want some? I shake my head. I want to say: Are you sure you want to smoke that?

'Can I open the window?' I ask, getting up suddenly.

'Be my guest,' he says.

I yank open the brown curtains. I pull up the window on the right. I try to lift the big one in the middle, but it's stuck.

'My mum always tries to open the windows when she comes in,' says Hugh. 'I tell her . . . I have ME. It's not going to be cured by a spot of fresh air.'

He is fumbling for a lighter. He has a grain of sleep on his face. Could he not at least have wiped that off? I feel really angry suddenly.

'Do you know who's the only person who accepts me as I am?' he says.

'Who?'

'Simon,' answers Hugh. 'That man comes here, and he just keeps me company. It's the kindest, sweetest thing that anyone does. That man is a saint. You know how hard he's been working? He's still found the time to watch an entire series of *Ballykissangel* with me. And I suspect he hates *Ballykissangel*. Fair enough. If I weren't clinically depressed, I wouldn't watch it myself. He's a bloody saint, Lucy Potts. I think you should marry him.'

Hugh flicks the lighter, but it doesn't spark. Throughout this conversation, the forty-three-year-old me has been lurking in the back of my mind like a tumour. I feel prodded into action. I feel it's now or never.

Speak to him, I whisper. *Say what you feel.*

My young self feels thrown. I was feeling faint anyway – what with the smell of hash and the burning

Rizlas sizzling away in the ashtray – but now it's worse.

'Well,' I begin, 'Simon has asked me to move in with him.'

Hugh's face freezes in a polite smile.

'And will you?' he asks. He's artfully disguising how much this means to him.

'I don't know,' I reply. 'I wanted to find out if you'd mind.'

'Why should I mind?'

'Because I think you love me. Just as I love you.'

About to flick the lighter again, he pauses and studies me for a beat.

'I'm no use to you,' he says. 'You should marry Simon.'

'Stop telling me what to do!' I say, goaded. 'I don't *want* to marry Simon. I want to marry you.'

He flicks the lighter again. This time it sparks. Hugh drags in smoke.

'OK,' he says, smiling, 'but I don't think I can make it to a church. We'll have to do it here.'

'Would you not leave this house,' I ask, 'even to marry me?'

'I left it last month to see you guys,' he says, 'and it damn near finished me off.'

He gives me a slightly pathetic smile. I know we're joking, but I still feel really angry that, even within the confines of a joke, he wouldn't contemplate leaving the house – to marry me. The older me is also slightly irritated he just lit that joint. The smell is now suffusing the room, adding to the air of unreality. The corners seem to fade away. I am staring at Hugh, sitting in his collapsed chair, but I can only see his outline – the contours of his face, his drooping mouth and depressed eyes.

Say what you feel, I repeat.

'I love you,' I begin.

'I love you,' he replies, a bit mechanically.

'Then do one thing for me.'

'What?'

'Get out of here. Walk to the river, lean on the rail, and have a look.'

His eyes crinkle in a sad smile.

'I can't,' he says.

'It's a minute's walk away,' I say. 'Can you not make a bit of an effort?'

'I've got ME,' he says. 'It attacks your effort.'

It's attacking my effort now. I stop talking. I wonder: am I being intolerant and unreasonable?

'Please don't move in with Simon,' he says quietly.

I am astonished by this.

'I'm sorry I've got ME,' he continues.

There's a tear in his right eye. Is it from emotion or the drugs? I don't feel sympathetic. I feel irritated.

'Your problem isn't ME,' I tell him.

For the first time he looks angry. His face hardens. 'You don't believe I have it? When I tell you my bones feel like lead, and all I want to do is sleep?'

'I believe you have ME,' I assure him, but already I'm getting worked up. 'I just believe it's grown like ivy on the cracks in your make up.'

'What exactly do you mean by that?' Hugh's tight-lipped. He doesn't want me saying this. I don't care. I feel angry now.

'I don't believe your ME was started by some stupid race that happened in our first term,' I say. My heart is pumping. I feel I'm venturing where I shouldn't. 'You have to go back *way* further than that. Our view of ourselves is formed by our mums and our dads, especially our dads. If they love you, you're like Simon: you have a cheery voice inside that says you can cope with anything. But if they didn't it becomes an evil goblin, hissing: *you're shit, you need to be dead!*'

I spit out those last words with a savage fury. I don't feel this is the young me talking. This is the old me taking control. I know I'm interfering, and indeed reality is truly dissolving. I can hardly see Hugh. The outline of his eyes is all I can make out in a bleached blur of nothingness. I don't care. I feel I've ripped through a veil. I have one chance to shout back into the past, and I'm going to do it.

'Your dad wanted you out of the way,' I say, 'and what's happening? *You're obliging him!* You're not even angry! You keep up this air of cheery levity, but when you're alone the bile oozes out. That's what depression is, Hugh. It's the state where you don't feel any anger, except with yourself. *Be angry with your motherfucking dad!* You need to *fight* him with your youth and your spirit! And how do you do that? You *change* the past. You *fight* the gloom. Each day you find *one* thing you like, and you take *pleasure* from it. And if you can't find something to take pleasure from, at the very least, you *look*. If you don't want me to move in with Simon, you need to come to the river, and do that now.'

'OK,' says Hugh, smiling slightly. 'Just give me a moment to finish this joint! It'd be a shame if I were arrested for walking through Putney smoking drugs!'

He's still making jokes! He hasn't listened to a fucking word I've said.

'**No!**' I shout. 'The offer is for *now*! It's for fucking *now*! Now, Hugh! *It's for NOW!!! NOW!!!*'

I'm shouting so loud it's hurting my throat. But he's still not listening.

'I'm not asking you to run a four-minute mile, Hugh. *I'm just asking you to come outside and look!* **Look**, *just* **look!**'

CHAPTER 11

As I've been talking, I've been staring vehemently into the faint outline of Hugh's eyes.

They've disappeared.

I've whited out like never before. Now that I've stopped shouting, I breathe in slowly. Cool air enters my lungs, and it makes my vision clear once more.

I realise I'm no longer looking at Hugh.

I'm looking at an old man in a white robe. And I'm not sitting in a gloomy room in Putney. I'm sitting upright in a field, looking at the man who's sitting in front of me, before a tree-covered slope.

He smiles.

'So,' he says quietly, 'you believe we learn our view of ourselves from our fathers.'

'What?' I say. I feel very disoriented. Did he hear

everything I just said? 'I was talking to Hugh,' I say, 'not to you! Why has he gone?'

'Probably because you started to think about the memory, so it dissolved,' he explains. 'But what you say is valid. In the counsel we give each other, we learn what we wish to teach ourselves. What view of yourself did you learn from your father?'

'I don't remember my father!' I say, trying to swipe his question aside.

'Do you wish to?' he prompts.

'No, I don't! I cannot think about my father. I need to think about Hugh!'

The old man is scrutinising me with his blank look.

'Why is this man so important to you?'

'Because he died, and I loved him, and I could have helped.'

'May I ask: when he came back into your life, did you immediately go and see him?'

'What?'

'Did you go to him immediately?'

'No!'

'Why not?'

'Well, he was depressed. He didn't want visitors.'

'Or perhaps you didn't want to see him.'

'I'd waited so long, I could wait a little longer.'

'Just as you can wait to see your father.'

Why does he keep talking about my father?

'I don't remember him!' I plead.

'Do you feel you need to?'

I'm not sure. That chest is closed for a reason.

'I don't remember him!' I protest. 'What's the point of thinking about him?'

'Well,' says the man, with a mysterious smile, 'I think I'd give you the advice that you gave Hugh.'

'What was that?'

'Look. Just look.'

'Look at what?'

'Say it: I need to look.'

'I need to look,' I repeat.

The old man smiles as if he's made some important point. Why? What's happening? He purses his lips, and blows out his somniferous breath with its smell of mud and earth. Instantly drifting off, I see the truth of what he's been saying: he isn't in control at all. I am! I'll go into a memory if I need to. 'Need' is the magic word, and I've just said it. My eyes are shutting. I can hear the sheep in a nearby field. I can hear a blackbird in a tree behind me.

Then it all muffles away.

I drift.

I can hear piano music. It is 'Au Clair de la Lune' by Debussy. It's a delicious and calming tune designed to engender a pang of nostalgia in all who hear it. But for me it's even worse. My dad used to play it every night, after we'd turned out my light. I'd forgotten that. How have I just remembered? I'm suddenly filled with a burning thought: *Perhaps it's Dad who's playing it now! Perhaps I could see him!* But can I? Where am I?

Eyes open.

I see a Fisher-Price family camping on the carpet nearby. I am on a mattress on the floor, in my childhood bedroom. I, however, am not sleeping. There are several reasons for that . . .

A party is going on downstairs. I can hear people laughing and talking and I can smell cigarette smoke drifting up. Also, the curtains are not closed, and the moon is shining in, so in fact the whole bedroom is currently *au clair de la lune*. Also . . .

Gemma is here.

I can see her silhouette. She is standing at the other end of the room, and she's looking out of the window. As my young self surveys my best friend, I become aware of my thoughts, and thus I become abreast of the whole situation . . . Gemma and I have been holding a bit of a party of our own up here. I sneaked up two packets of crisps. Gemma produced a bottle of Coca-Cola, and we drank it and it made us tingly and far too excited to get to sleep. Gemma told me all her latest secrets. Her dad recently went to live elsewhere. Gemma doesn't mind. She's going to stay with him, next weekend. He's got a new house. And he has also – and this is the really good bit – got one of those paddling pools that is so deep you can actually swim in it.

Gemma is climbing up on to the little red sofa, and she looks out. From here, I can see the perfect half-circle of the moon. Its blue light is touching the top of Gemma's cheek. I think if she is allowed up, I am probably allowed up. Anyway, I want to look. So I quickly get out of bed, but I am scared. I don't want Mum to catch us. I climb up on the sofa and I look at Gemma. She is staring out of the window and her eyes look round and mad.

'Oh my gosh!' she says in an awed whisper. 'I just saw a witch!'

'Really?' I say.

'Yup,' states Gemma. 'Definite witch. She took off from the top of a tree over there and she was flying.'

Now she's got me interested. 'Where was it?' I say.

I look out and I see the wonderful view. I can see our garden sloping down. I can see the bird bath sparkling in the moonlight. I can see the lines of blue trees stretching into the distance, and beyond them the hills looming like great grey whales in the darkness.

But I can't see any witches.

I feel disappointed. Gemma has raised a terrifying idea – I thought witches were just in books, but I wasn't quite sure – and now I find there ARE witches I am definitely afraid. Definitely. But I also think: if there ARE witches, and they can fly around in the sky, I would like to see one.

'Where is the witch?' I enquire.

'She just flew off,' says Gemma (a bit cross now), 'from the top of that spiky tree.'

I see the one she means. It's just the sort of tree a witch would land in. It's in our neighbour's garden, and half of it is dead. I can actually see a crow sitting on a top branch.

But I cannot see a witch.

I look at Gemma. I don't want to be too mean about this, but I do feel I need to say something.

'Gemma,' I declare, 'I can only see a crow. I cannot see a witch.'

At this Gemma gives me a really nasty look. She shakes her head at me and says: 'Well, SOME crows can turn into witches, but you *just didn't see*!'

She says the last bit very loud. She's really cross that I doubted her testimony, and that makes me uneasy. Now I want to get away from her. I start to climb off the sofa. As my foot touches the carpet someone must have opened a window downstairs because the noise grows much louder. It's definitely my dad playing the piano. I can hear him singing and everyone is laughing. What is he doing to make them laugh? Inside my head, the thoughts are flapping round like crows in the night. I'm terrified Mum will find me out of bed. And my older self is worried too. If I see Dad, what will he be doing? And what will I do? I don't think it will go well. But then I think: look, just look.

I head for the door. Gemma flashes me a jealous look. If anyone should be allowed out, she feels it should be her.

'Where are you going?' she asks.

I don't want her to come with me.

'I need to have a wee,' I say.

'Oh,' she says.

That was actually a really good thing to say. Gemma wears a nappy at night. Any talk of toilets shames her into silence. She resumes her inspection of the garden.

I open the door, and I'm out.

Peering at the long expanse of the forbidden corridor outside, my young self listens out for Mum, the way a vole does venturing into owl territory. I, however, am drinking in a sight I've not glimpsed in forty years: the upstairs corridor of The Old Vicarage. It is a thin one, with a wonky floor and exposed beams. I step on to the wonky floor, and I creep stealthily past my brother's room to the stairs. They are very steep windy ones covered with a brown hair carpet, which is all rough like doormat. I tiptoe down the first four steps. Then I stop because there is a little hole you can peep through.

I crouch down and look.

I can see into the corridor outside the living room, and I can see the backs of two ladies, one of whom is smoking. The singing has stopped, which makes me sad because I really longed to see my dad in action. Someone comes out.

Oh my God! It's Dad!

I can see his face properly. He's got a thick black moustache! Now I see it, I remember it tickling when he kissed me. He has got on a very natty checked suit with flared trousers, and he's wearing a green waistcoat and a very bright shirt with ruffles on the front. My dad looks good. He's got sideburns, and mad curly dark hair, and very twinkly eyes. I can't help it. I feel a great surge of love for him. I feel awestruck as he strides down the corridor until he's almost under me. He's reaching in the pocket of one of the coats hanging on the wall by the front door. A lady appears. It's Miss Lindhurst from Sunday School.

She doesn't notice me. She comes down the corridor and smiles at my dad.

'What are you doing?' she asks lightly.

'Just getting my fags,' says Dad.

Now she doesn't know what to say. She looks at him expectantly.

'Where's the bathroom?' she asks.

'Just in there,' says Dad. 'I'll turn the light on for you.'

She walks past him, and he looks at her back. They disappear, but before they do I think I can see my dad reaching out his hand to touch her. Then I can't see him any more, but I really want to, so I start edging further down the stairs on my bottom. I'm just shuffling round the bendy bit when someone appears.

It is Dad.

I freeze. I am terrified he'll be cross because I'm out of bed. What will he think of me? It seems vitally important. He's looking at me. His face is big as a Space Hopper and it's taking me in.

He smiles.

I feel warm.

'Are you all right?' he says gently. His voice is a little husky. It's a very attractive voice.

'I couldn't sleep,' I admit.

'Why?'

'Because it was all noisy and Gemma said there are witches.'

Dad smiles even more. He seems to be in a very good mood.

'Ah,' he says. 'And do you think there are witches?'

'Nope.'

'I think you're right,' says Dad. 'Although I have my suspicions about that lady in the sweet shop.'

I can tell he's joking so I laugh.

'Will you ask Mummy to come and give me a hug?' I ask.

'I'm afraid not,' says Dad, 'because she is with her friends and you are supposed to be asleep.'

I think he's telling me off, and I feel like crying.

'But also you don't need a hug,' says Dad. 'Because if you saw a witch in the sky, you would do your magic trick on it.'

'What would I do?'

'You would squeeze her down like this,' says Dad, demonstrating the witch-squeezing system, using his thumb and forefinger. 'So you'd squash her 'til she was as small as a ladybird. And you'd say the magic words: "Ladybird, ladybird, fly away home/ Your house is on fire/ Your children are gone . . . "'

When he says this, Dad raises his eyebrows, as if to say: And that's what you do to witches!

I need to be quite clear about this.

'Can you do magic on witches?' I ask.

'Of course,' answers Dad. 'Witches are magic themselves, so you can magic them back.'

As he talks, his face is very close to mine. He has brown eyes like dark honey and they have lots of speckles in them. I feel that Dad is a bit magic himself. As he speaks, I definitely feel OK.

'Right,' he says, 'I'm going to carry you back to bed, and we'll check there are no witches.'

He reaches down and lifts me up. Soon I am next to his shoulder and he is carrying me up the stairs. I feel as if I'm on a horse but it's safer and more comfy. When we get to the corridor, Dad does a funny, sneaky walk, and whispers: '*Don't wake the bear!*' I remember this. It was a joke we had about my little brother. I smile. As he carries me down the corridor, I twirl my finger in his thick black hair. I am so happy to be with my dad, especially when there are just the two of us, and he is being so smiley and lovely. I want it always to be like this.

'Dad,' I whisper.

'What?'

He stops walking.

'When it's my birthday party, will you play the piano in Musical Bumps and Musical Statues?'

'Of course,' he promises.

'Because you can do funny music and make everyone laugh.'

'I'll definitely do that,' says Dad. Then he gives me a kiss on my forehead. It makes me feel instantly calm and safe. 'I love you,' he says.

Then he opens the door.

Gemma is still on the sofa. She looks up at us, terrified as a mouse caught in torchlight.

'Gemma,' says Dad quietly, 'you need to get into bed. It's time for sleep.'

She scurries off. Dad puts me down on the floor a moment.

'Wait,' he says, looking out. 'I'll just check for witches. Yup . . . I can see one. I'm going to shrink her.'

Against the window I can see him going for the witch-shrinking pinch.

'Yup,' announces Dad. 'I've shrunk her down. She's now the size of a ladybird. If you shut your eyes a second, you might hear her. She sounds like a cross ladybird.'

I shut my eyes, and try to hear the sound he's described: the sound of a tiny and furious witch, who sounds like a cross ladybird. I strain, but I can't hear it.

I keep my eyes squeezed shut.

For a moment I have a strange feeling, as if I'm not standing on the floor of my bedroom but on a boat, which is moving. Then I hear something else . . .

'Lucy,' says Mum, 'do hurry up.'

I open my eyes.

I'm looking at her. She's about thirty years old, and she's standing beside the car and looking back at me. She's got permed hair, and orange eye shadow, and a brownish shade of lipstick, but all that is failing to conceal the crossness in her face.

'We don't have much time,' she says.

I feel very confused.

I see I am standing by a gleaming car, in sunshine

which is hot as the Sahara Desert. I'm standing next to a little pile of melted pink bubble gum, which has got stuck to my nasty shoes. Oh, God. I realise I'm back in the same memory – we're in Maidstone High Street again, about to go shopping for Kickers. What's going on? I think. We've already done this one, and it wasn't a high point last time.

'Get a move on,' says Mum.

I stand still a moment longer. I'm panting like a black Labrador stranded in sunshine. Mum walks off up the pavement pushing my brother in his buggy. I look for a moment at her bum, encased in the shiny skirt, and her rope-soled shoes. She's walking towards a row of small terraced houses. Beyond them I can see the shops. Words blow into my mind: 'Just look.' But what am I supposed to be looking at? The stretched bubble gum? At the same time, my five-year-old self is thinking it too: what am I doing? Then I remember . . .

I'm buying boots!

That's it! I'm buying Kicker boots, like the ones Gemma has! I am filled with purpose and energy. Better buy them quick before Mum changes her mind. I love those Kicker boots, and they are my escape from the ketchup-poo sandals. I feel like a cow pushed with the cattle prod.

I set off after Mum at speed.

Quickly I catch her up. Indeed I overtake her. 'Wait a moment, Lucy,' she warns, but I don't. I carry on sprinting up the pavement. I'm oblivious to clumping sandals, to

Mum, to the terrible heat. I run right to the end of the row of houses.

'*LUCY!*' yells Mum, shouting my name like a slap. '*Wait* for me to cross the road.'

So I stop running.

Panting, I wait for Mum. And meanwhile I turn, and I look through into the front room of the last terraced house.

Look. Just look.

The front room looks like any front room in Maidstone. It's small. It has a mantelpiece made from ugly grey tiles, and on it huddles a collection of little porcelain figures that frankly need smashing. To the left of that stands a television, and on its screen I can see Bjorn Borg. Sitting beside a display of Robinson's Barley Water, he is staring out like he's trying to become Wimbledon Champion at being boring.

The couple on the sofa are moving.

The man is kissing the woman. Not only that, he's actually touching her breast with his left hand. That's easily done. The woman is wearing a low white top. The man has long sideburns growing down his cheeks. Perhaps inspired by Bjorn Borg, he's wearing very short shorts which are covering very little of his legs. It's still not enough for the woman however. She seems intent on removing them. She sets about the task now, and meanwhile the couple carry on kissing and squirming about like maggots. Everything about the scene is so shocking and nasty it makes me feel sick. But it's not just the sweaty horrid things the woman is doing. It's the man.

It's Dad.

I am so flabbergasted I stare for far too long.

Obviously I should have run off. I should have sprinted at Mum. I should have begged her to forget the Kickers. But I don't. Something about the scene has robbed me of all my energy.

I'm still staring when I'm joined by Mum.

She looks through the window. And then she gasps. And she grabs hold of my hand, and yanks me away. She picks me up and she carries me back to the car with my head pushing against the handle of the buggy and she shouts at me and she hurls me on to that scalding back seat as if she's a witch thrusting me into a big steaming pot. I protest that we're supposed to be buying boots. I stick to my rights like a little lawyer. I insist that she *promised*. Whereupon she gets into the car, and crushes all protest by slapping my bare right thigh so hard she leaves the imprint of four fingers. She also shouts that I am 'a very spoiled and greedy girl' and assures me that, when I get home, I'm going 'straight to my room'.

So really the incident ends up much as before.

Except this time, even as Mum is shouting at me so loudly that spittle rains into my face, I feel removed from the whole scene, like a guard watching it through a monitor. I am not Lucy, the five-year-old girl. I'm a forty-three-year-old adult, watching all this again and longing to find a way of telling Lucy that she has misunderstood, it's not her fault, she'll be fine. But I'm not yet ready for that. I squeeze my eyes shut. The world lurches away.

I open my eyes.

The world settles. I see I am sitting in my childhood bedroom. I am alone, except for a Fisher-Price farmer, and a Fisher Price wife, and a Fisher-Price dog. (Why is that dog wearing a bow tie?)

I'm sitting on the floor, leaning against my wooden cupboard, wearing my hated red-brown shoes. I'm moving my toes up and down, which makes the butterfly patterns on top of the shoes move. Then I look up, and I see myself in the mirror. My cheeks are very round, and the tears have left wet tracks down them. My bottom lip is thrust out. I crawl forward until my face is so close to the mirror the breath is leaving little ovals of moisture on the glass. The left nostril is making more than the right. I study that for a moment. Then I look into the sad wet eyes of the five-year-old Lucy Potts. And I know this child is me, and I know I've been travelling, in her head, seeing things again, as she sees them.

But at the same time, I feel quite separate from her.

I note she's as calm as she is likely to be. I observe she's alone, and sitting on the floor. I consider that conditions are as perfect as they're ever going to be. If I'm going to do this, I figure, I should do it now. So I whisper.

Lucy, it's OK. It's OK.

My watchful young eyes widen with surprise. I am shocked to hear the voice. I freeze, staring into my own wet eyes. I feel a little faint and sick. I breathe out on to the mirror, through my mouth this time. The nausea passes. I'm OK.

So I continue.

I know Mummy shouted, I whisper, *but she is not angry with you. Don't worry. In a few weeks you'll get the Kickers, and you'll wear them a lot. We always get what we want in the end, just not when we expect it.*

Then something strange happens . . .

The young me talks back.

'Who are you?' she whispers, staring at her own reflection in the mirror.

I'm you, I tell her. *But I'm from the future.*

At this point my childish mouth falls open with surprise. 'From the future?'

Yes.

I stare, amazed, into the mirror. Then my quick young mind asks the obvious thing.

I say: 'Tell me some more things that will happen.'

I pause at that. It feels like an awesome responsibility to tell the future to a five year old. I look into her wet eyes. I flick through the events of her future, but I don't know where to start. I realise that, when I think of my past, I usually concentrate on the tragedies – my parents' divorce, my struggles with food, the day in 1982 when we get the phone call from Canada saying that Dad has died . . . But no five-year-old girl should hear all that. So I do something I've never done before.

I start to tell the story of my life, like it's a happy one.

Well, I whisper, *in a few months' time you are going to move house, but you'll have a nice room, and you'll get a brilliant dog called Judy. You will have a different school, but you will still see Gemma and she will still be your best friend. In fact, you and Gemma have something that happens to very few girls: you will stay friends all through school, and then you'll even go to college together . . .*

At this, I trail off.

I want to tell her about Hugh. Amongst all the figures of my life, he seems to loom so large. But really . . . who is Hugh? He's just a very handsome, very charming man that I meet at college. Whereas . . .

And at college, I say, and for some reason, this is the bit that makes me start to cry, so I have to start again. *At college, you meet a man.*

Shall I tell her who the man is? Best not.

He's very handsome, and he's kind, and he really loves you. All he wants is for you to be happy, and the only thing that makes him sad is when you don't love him. And you have two children. Tom is a very funny boy, and he is MAD about animals. He makes you get a dog, and a newt.

My young self smiles. I am listening intently. 'I like dogs,' I whisper. 'I want a beagle.'

That's the sort you get, I say. And then something about the subject of dogs troubles me, so I move on. *And you have another child,* I say. *A boy called Hal.*

'Oh,' says my young self. 'I prefer girls to boys.'

Why?

'Because boys show off, and they always want to play football, and they make a mess and they shout.'

Well, I say, *Hal is not like that at all. He also likes books and cooking and he's the sort of boy who always knows if you're worried and he tries to help.*

My young self likes the sound of Hal. Who wouldn't? The boy's irresistible.

'What else does he like doing?'

He has his own recipe books and his own chef's hat, and he can be very funny. Like . . . if you put on the television, he says 'Televizzzioneee!' and waves his arms like a chicken. I wish you could meet him. I think you'd really like him, I say. And then my voice trails off. *Oh,* I add, *but of course you will . . .* And for some reason, that makes me cry so much that my voice goes squeaky, and then, for a moment, I can't carry on.

My young self is staring, riveted, into the mirror. I really want to hear more.

But then I think about Hal a moment. I think of the wisest thing about him: he knows that, when someone is upset, you shouldn't talk to them too much. You need to let them talk themself.

But are you OK? I ask.

'I am cross because Mum shouts at me and she says I'm a bad, spoiled girl.'

And do you think you are?

'No.'

What do you think she should say?

'She should be more kind,' I say. 'I was only trying to buy some boots for my birthday, and I only didn't move because I saw Dad, and it wasn't my fault she saw him.'

I know, I say. *It wasn't your fault.* I'd love to say more, but now I'm crying too much, and something else is happening. I feel I'm fading from this scene like the vapour that is fading from the mirror. I'm drifting away.

Mum will come in a minute, I say. *Now remember . . . she's not cross with you. And you're not greedy at all. In fact, you don't have to lick the bowl. Cake mixture is tasty but it makes you fat.*

'What do you mean?'

You'll see, I say. Then: *She'll be along any moment. Blow your nose and wipe your eyes. I love you.*

That seems a strange thing to say, but I feel so sorry for this sad lonely girl, sitting sobbing in front of her mirror. I do love her. I love her watchful eyes, her wide clumsy shoulders, the little butterfly hairclip in her hair. She takes a tissue from the roll of Andrex by her bed. It looks familiar. She wipes her eyes. And she blows her nose. And, so doing, she shuts her eyes. At the same time, *I* shut my eyes, because I am Lucy. She is me.

Drifting a moment, after the encounter, I feel sad and deeply uneasy.

I just did the thing that's forbidden – I interfered – and I didn't say a few words only. I had a whole conversation. I'm fearing that, somehow, the man in white knows, and will exact furious revenge. I fear I'm being taken somewhere so the punishment can occur.

I can hear sad piano music.

It actually is Erik Satie – the steady downward chords of *Gymnopédie No. 1*.

I open my eyes.

I'm in the car, and music is playing. Mum is driving. My brother is lying on the back seat in his carry cot even though he's so big his feet touch the end. There isn't much space so I'm squashed against the right-hand door. I'm looking out of the window as we go down Linton Hill – past the pub, past the little thatched cottage – till we arrive at The Old Vicarage.

Dad's light blue Morris Minor is waiting in the driveway.

Mum sees it, and says: 'Oh.' At the same time, I think *Oh*, because, straight away, I know what is happening: this is the last time I saw Dad. We're now hovering in the middle of Linton Hill, waiting for a break in the traffic so we can turn right into our narrow driveway. The sky above the wonky roof is a light watercolour blue. I briefly consider it as a painting. I see words appear in the sky, painted in red – a title. It says: *The Last Time I Saw Dad*. I mentally remove the words. I don't want to interfere. I don't want even to think. I need this to happen.

A space in the traffic appears. Mum crosses the road. She parks outside the house. She turns.

'I'm going to talk to Dad,' she says. 'Could you stay outside a minute?'

I nod. Mum opens the back door and gets out my brother.

'Don't go in the road,' she says.

I nod again, but my young mind is thinking: why would I go in the road?

Mum enters the house, but she leaves the front door a little bit open. I can clearly hear her talking to Dad in a very serious whisper. She is saying: 'So are you *going* to talk to her?' and my dad is saying: 'Yes, of course I'm going to talk to her!' Just hearing them makes me so worried my stomach is clenched with tension.

The door shuts with a loud bang.

I'm scared that Mum and Dad are going to come out and they'll see that I was listening to their conversation, so I decide I should start doing something quick. I look around and I see the flowerpot Mum gave me. It's looking dry. Luckily my watering can is nearby. When I pick up the can, I find a woodlouse under it. It looks like a very small dinosaur. The woodlouse starts hurrying into the lawn, as if he's forgotten something. I'm wondering what Dad is going to say. Is he going to be like Gemma's dad, and I'll only see him at the weekend? I think that would be all right especially if he gets a really big paddling pool. I would like that, but I would also need armbands because I can't swim.

I'm just filling up my watering can at the tap when my dad comes out holding a big leather bag.

I try to be normal, because I know I shouldn't have heard Mum and Dad talking, but straight away it's hard because I'm trying not to cry. Dad puts his bag down on the lawn. I look at his shoes – they are old brown leather ones – while he sits down on the low brick wall next to the tap.

'Lucy,' he says.

I look up at his face very quickly. I can see he's trying to be all smiley but it's clear he's got something terrible to say.

'I need to chat to you,' he says.

I nod. I'm still looking at the shoes.

'I'm just going away for a bit.'

I nod again. Then I dare to look up at him.

'Am I going to come and see you at the weekend like Gemma does with her daddy?' I ask.

'I'm afraid not,' says Dad. 'Because I've had to find another job quickly, and I've found one but it's in Canada.'

I wish I hadn't looked at him. Now I'm in danger of crying. I say: 'Oh.'

'It's going to be a lovely job,' says Dad brightly. 'I'm going to be working in a place where they do summer camps and I'm going to be in charge of all the music and the singing, and in the holidays you're going to come and stay.'

I don't like the sound of that one bit. I don't understand how to get to Canada. You would have to go on a plane and how could we go on the plane if Daddy isn't there? He is the only one who knows about all the tickets and things.

'Dad,' I say, 'I don't want you to go to Canada.'

'I know,' says Dad. 'But I must. At least for a few months.'

Now he gives me a quick hug. It doesn't really work, because his knees are in the way, and I don't put my arms around him. I don't know what to do.

'I love you, Lucy,' he says. 'And I will see you soon.'

When he says that, I feel a bit calmer, because of what he's said, but now he's confirmed that he really is going and that makes me feel as if I'm standing over a massive hole, like a person in a cartoon, and it's only a matter of time before I start falling. I don't say anything. I am trying to be very brave. I know that Dad has to go. But then I think of a plan. It's brilliant! It will mean that he *can't* go to Canada!

'But, Dad!' I say. 'You *will* still be doing the piano and the singing at my party!'

'No,' he says. 'I won't be able to do that.'

When he says that, I feel crushed – not just because he's going, but because my plan didn't work.

'But you *promised*,' I say.

'I know,' he replies.

Now I feel angry. I understand that maybe he has to go, but why did he have to ruin my party?

'But you can put on a record!' says Dad.

'But . . .' I begin. I know we can play a record. Is that really the point? 'But, Dad,' I say, and just then I get a giant frog in my throat, so I stop and quickly wipe my mouth with the back of my hand. I try again. 'But,' I say as reasonably as I can, 'who will be in charge of the games?'

'Well,' says Dad, 'Mum can be in charge of them!'

'But she can't!' I argue. 'Mum doesn't know the games!'

Dad is being quite serious, but he smiles at that. 'Oh,' he says, 'Mum knows the games! And Gemma knows the games. And also,' he says, and when he says this, he lifts his finger in a funny way and continues, '*you* know the games.'

I smile at that for a moment, and Dad is pleased. He pulls me towards him and gives me a kiss on the top of my head. He holds the back of my neck in his hand, which feels all nice and warm. For a moment, I think: I am OK. Dad is here.

But then he stands up and walks to his car.

'Anyway,' he says, 'I'll see you soon!'

I don't say anything. I'm very confused, but I know this . . . If Dad is going to Canada, he *won't* be seeing me soon. So he is a liar. I'm really cross with him. And also I'm really angry with myself. If I hadn't made us get the Kickers we would never have seen him and Miss Lindhurst on the sofa. It's all my fault. I'm a very greedy girl. That's the trouble.

Dad puts the bag in the back of the car, and then he walks to the driver's door.

He looks round at me. 'Lucy,' he calls, 'are you OK?'

While he's speaking he squats down to my level. He's showing me he's ready to talk if I want to.

I look back at him. I nod. For a moment, I'm about to say something. But then I don't know what to say. So instead I just gulp a few times. Then I have an overwhelming urge to escape. I run for the front door. It's got one of those strange old-fashioned latches, and it's stiff, and my young hands can't get it open. I'm too stunned. Watching this whole scene again, as a forty-three year old, I realise I'm stunned too. But I feel I have to intervene.

Lucy, I whisper. *This is your only chance. Go back and say what you feel.* Then instantly I'm tense. Have I just said the wrong thing? What will happen now? It's too late to take it back. My young self turns. I feel very angry. Dad can see that. He looks worried.

'Lucy,' he says nervously. 'Are you OK?'

'*No, I am not!*' I shout.

'Lucy!' says Dad. Now he's the surprised one.

I walk towards him furiously. 'Dad!' I say, very loud. 'I know you want me to be nice because you are going away. But I do not want to. I am *very angry* with you! You are leaving me alone with Mum, just because you wanted to kiss Miss Lindhurst.'

Dad is staring at me with his mouth open. I go right up to him, and I stab my finger angrily into his chest.

'And I am also very angry because you are going to *ruin my party*,' I shout. 'Mum is good at making lunch. She is good at shouting at people. She is *not* good at games! She is *not* good at games at all!'

With this, I push him so hard in his chest that he rocks backwards, and has to stop himself falling over with his hands. Now I'm scared I'm going to get in trouble for what I've said. So I quickly run for the door and luckily this time I manage to open it. I'm not surprised by that. It felt good, turning on my dad like that. As I walk down the dark hall, I feel powerful. I feel as if I've just won three fights. I walk quickly into the kitchen, where I stop.

My brother is sleeping on the floor in his carry cot.

I am really cross with my brother too. He wakes up every night shouting, and I think that is one big reason why Dad doesn't want to live with us. My brother's face is all pink like a balloon. I think I could easily just stamp on it and he would die. But I don't. I look at my mum. She is boiling the kettle but she's not looking at it. She's looking out of the window at the orchard.

'Did you talk to Dad?' she whispers.

I nod.

'I'm making some jelly,' she says. 'Will you help me to pull the pieces off?'

I don't know why we are making jelly. It annoys me.

'Mum,' I say, 'I know you think I am a spoiled and greedy girl. But I am not.'

'Of course not!' she says, looking very surprised.

'I am good and I am nice and I'm *trying my best*,' I say. 'And I am *fed up* of you saying I'm bad. It is not kind and it is not fair.'

I have been trying to whisper all this, but by the end I raise my voice in a furious snarl.

'Lucy . . .' says Mum. I can tell she's about to tell me off for waking up my brother.

'And I am fed up of you only caring *about my stupid brother*!' I say, and I really let rip with this. I want to wake him up. It's the least I could do. '*I matter as well!*' I scream. '*I matter as well!*'

And, shaking with fury, I walk past Mum, and past my brother, and I go out into the garden. When I'm outside, I'm scared that Mum is going to follow me, and I do not want that. So I slam the door very hard.

Bang.

As I march off down the garden, I've never felt so strong. I just shouted at my mum, and I know that everything I said was completely right. I would shout it again. Feeling angry but fantastic, I stride past the bird bath. I go over to the side of the garden, so I can stamp down the jaggedy steps past the vegetable patch and the raspberries. At the fence I reach the place where you can peer down the side of the house, and I do. I can see Dad. He throws a cigarette on the ground, looks back at the house. *I could go after him*, I think. I could get into that car, and I could go all the way to Canada, where I could have a long happy life, hunting moose and playing ice hockey. I could tell him not to leave me with Mum.

But I don't.

I turn my back and tramp down to the lowest part of the garden, past the weeping willow tree. I am still cross with Dad. Even if he came running out, begging me to go with him, I would just pinch him down like a witch, and say: 'Ladybird, ladybird, fly away home,' and then I'd squidge him like a grape.

I have reached the hole in the hedge at the bottom. I've actually never gone through it. I figure: That's going to change. *Right now.* I'm going to see those giant chicken-legged dinosaurs for myself. I crawl through. I have to shut my eyes at one point because there are prickly plants in my face, but I am afraid of nothing. I sweep them aside. For a moment I get the floating feeling.

CHAPTER 12

Then I open my eyes, and look around.

It is not the sight I was expecting. I do not see a huge dinosaur with feet like a chicken. I do not see an orchard, with line upon line of apple trees, stretching off into the distance.

I see a car that is lying upside down.

Beside it there's a very tall man standing with his back to me. He looks as if he's playing Granny's Footsteps, very slowly. As I look up into his pale, red-rimmed eyes, I smirk. I feel cheeky and excited.

'You look different,' he observes.

'I just saw my dad. I said a few things that I always wished I had. I did some things that I wished I'd done too. He still left.'

The man looks anxious. 'Why is that good?'

'I did what I could, but he still went. There was nothing I could have done to stop him going. I feel released!'

I feel angry with the old man now.

'You said,' I accuse him, 'that if I interfered with reality, I may die. But I didn't.'

'I didn't say you may die if you interfered with reality,' he answers. 'You may die because you've had an accident, and when you're in a memory then time is not passing.'

'So what would have happened if I'd stayed in that memory?' I ask. 'I could have stayed for ever! I could have gone with Dad to Canada, and had a whole life there.'

'You could, if you could have believed it. But you must not try to do that.'

'Why? I wouldn't be harming anyone in my life, I would just be making a whole new one.'

Then I stop talking. I've just had an idea. It occurs to me that everything I said to Hugh was actually right: his ME didn't start with a stupid race; he needed to go back further than that. It occurs to me this whole journey went wrong, right at the start, when I left my bedroom, and went through a door, and found myself in a shed. Why did I do that? I could have stayed with Hugh – when he was beautiful. I *should* have stayed! I could have kissed him, and we could have slept together, and then the next day he would not have left college, he could have stayed, and done his exams, and got better, and he could have left with a degree, and got some wonderful job, and he could have had a great life that brought pleasure to him and to everyone who met him. And I could go back now, and that could happen, and no one would be harmed. I wouldn't be cheating on Simon. At that point, my relationship with him hadn't yet happened. I could help Hugh, I could love Hugh, and then I could love Simon later, and what harm would be done? None! None at all! And at least I'll know what would have happened!

I start crawling backwards.

'Where are you going?' says the man, alarmed.

'To Hugh,' I answer. 'I'm going to save him.'

'You cannot change other people,' he says.

'Not by shouting at them,' I say, 'but maybe with love.'

'And you cannot change the past.'

'But you can,' I say. I feel drunk with possibility. 'You can make a new one. You've just got to see each sight, and smell each smell.'

I duck my head as I go back through the brambles.

'You cannot do this,' the old man says. For the first time, he's angry. 'This is very dangerous! I will *not* let you do this.'

'Like you said: you're not in charge!' I call. 'I am!'

He's out of sight now. I'm back in the garden. He's still in the field. I feel childishly happy. I feel naughty, but in a good way. Maybe I've been too careful all my life. I stand up and I look for a moment at The Old Vicarage. I'm scared I'll be stopped – that Mum will come out, or the Old Man will hook a long arm through the hedge. So I don't waste time. I hurry back towards the shed. For a moment I sniff the shed scent of spider web and wood varnish.

Then I shut my eyes.

I open the shed door and step inside. Meanwhile

I whisper under my breath: *I need to go back to when everything was good. I need to see what could have happened.* For a moment I get the light feeling, as if I were floating in an underground tunnel.

Then I pull the door shut with a bang.

And, opening my eyes, I see I'm looking at a self-portrait of Filippino Lippi, which is stuck on a door.

It's worked.

With my left hand, I am clutching two cups of tea. Everything is perfect! I turn, and, to my delight and relief and wonder, I see my Isis House bedroom. It has a double mattress on the floor, and on it, Hugh Ashby is waiting for me in the soft morning light. Sitting up in bed, wearing a white t-shirt and black dress trousers belted with a tie, he's looking healthy and handsome and more delicious than any man has ever looked before.

'I'm back,' I announce.

'Lucy Potts,' he says, giving me a lazy happy smile. 'You're looking more gorgeous than ever. You seem different.'

'I am.' I smile. 'And I brought tea.'

I sway my hips slightly as I go over. Already I'm enjoying this. I sit in front of him on the mattress, and I pass it over.

'Thank you,' he says.

He holds his tea up to his lips, and blows across the top. I do the same. We smile. Now we are both sucking the tops of our tea. His lips are pursed, but his eyes are still sparkling. So are mine. Without even trying, our actions are synchronised. We both take a long, slow mouthful of tea, and then we both place our mugs on the floor by the bed.

'Hugh,' I begin.

'Lucy,' he counters, smiling.

Looking into his pale blue eyes, I have a sense that something momentous is about to happen. I am about to enter into a fabulous future.

'Ooh,' he says. 'I brought something.'

'What?' I ask.

He reaches in the pocket of his jacket. He holds up a cassette.

'Tape.'

'What's on it?' I ask.

'Candidate Number Two,' he says, 'in the contest to find The Most Beautiful Piece of Piano Music Of All Time.'

'What is it?'

'Chopin.' He beams. 'Piano Concerto Number One, the Larghetto. Do you have a tape player?'

I indicate the machine behind him. I've got the same Sony ghetto blaster I had all through school. It's still got the Duran Duran stickers that Gemma stuck on it.

'May I?' he asks.

'Be my guest.'

He reaches over and puts the tape on. He presses play. Music starts.

'A bit like Beethoven,' he says, 'it starts with deliberately bad strings. Which I love.'

'Why?'

'I like to feel you must journey into the music,' he says. 'You have to peel off its outer layers, to find the bit which is tender and exquisitely beautiful.'

God, he looks well! Right now I'd like him to peel off my outer layers, to find the bit which is tender and exquisitely beautiful! Chopin's introduction has finished. The piano comes in, with a tune that is heavy with longing. It's ripe and fertile, like a pear filled with juice. I can't put it off any more.

I put my mug on the floor.

Then I take Hugh's mug away from him. He knows what that means. The moment is a pear filled with juice.

I lean towards him.

Hugh leaves his head pressed against the wall, and his irises widen as I approach. I place my right palm on his broad cheekbone, and then I go closer 'til my nose is softly touching his, and then, at last, I place my lips against his. I kiss him once. I move my nose to the other side of his. Then I smile and I kiss again. As if I've now decided that was really the best position, I move my nose back again to the first position, and I press my lips against his until I can feel the stubble around the mouth. Then, as if on a signal, we both open our lips and tentatively, tenderly, I reach my tongue out to touch his. My tongue brushes gently against it, lazy as a fish in a stream, and now I can't stop it. I press myself to him, till my breasts are squashing his chest, and my lips are clamped over his, and my tongue is reaching deep into his mouth and it feels huge and hot and it tastes just slightly of tea.

His hands stay by his side. He is passive. He seems slightly nervous.

I stop kissing.

'Are you scared of love?' I ask him.

'Well,' he says. 'There are a few bad associations.'

'Perhaps they can be changed,' I suggest.

I smile. He smiles. I kiss him again. I kiss his big stubbly cheek. I kiss his neck. I gently kiss the brittle tent of his Adam's apple. I can't believe it. I have Hugh Ashby in my bed and am free to experience, as fully as possible, the wonder of his muscular body, at its peak of perfection. I lift up the white t-shirt, and I kiss between his large swimmer's pectoral muscles. I lift the t-shirt over his head. I kiss his navel. I look down at his trousers with the tie. I could take them off, I think. You're a very spoiled and greedy girl, I think. I kiss him on his hip.

Finally I've goaded him into life.

This is good. He rolls over me, so that I'm now on my back, and his glorious body is right over me like a tent. I'm looking up at his beautiful arms, with their triceps bulging like satsumas. I look down the little sequence of his abdominals, each one round and separate like dumplings. I look at his dress trousers, and I think I could take them off, and I could find another part of him which would be like a ripe pear filled with juice. Well, I'm not afraid of that. I feel absolutely open, and relaxed, and fearless.

He smiles.

'I think I could change my associations,' he says.

Good, I think. I've got him. I've woken the fire inside him. I need to get it hotter. *Don't do this now*, I whisper to myself. *Make him want you even more.*

Nothing happens.

But of course, I realise. There is nobody to talk to, in this memory. Because none of this happened. For the first time, a shard of worry starts to poke through. It's never good to look up at someone's face hovering over you. The flesh hangs down. The eyes look piggy. I feel a dizziness. It's only slight, but it's like the ominous onset of sickness.

'I'm so glad you could change your associations,' I say. 'But you won't be changing them tonight.'

I roll out from under him.

Hugh lies down on his side. He props his head on his hand.

'Fine,' he says. 'But, out of interest, why not?'

'We must stop here,' I say, flighting a gentle kiss on to his lips. '"Lest too light winning make light the prize".'

'What does that mean?'

'You're not filling my "parfait hole".'

'What does that mean?'

'I don't fuck on first dates,' I say. 'And we should sleep.'

He says: 'All right', and we smile at each other, and then we kiss again. I feel loving and safe and sleepy. And this, possibly, is the most delicious moment of the whole encounter. I rest my head on his thick swimmer's arm, enjoying how perfectly I fit him. I place my hand on his chest. I turn my face into a space between his neck and his naked shoulder. He smells of wood and sea and man. And

I listen to Chopin who's reaching the end of his Larghetto, and I fall asleep.

And it's confusing, because I have a most disturbing dream.

Is this a dream?

I'm on the sea front outside Kiters' Paradise. Leaning on a pillow made from rolled-up coats, I am in a deckchair and I am looking out to sea. I can see men on surfboards, to which they've attached kites. They speed towards the waves and leap high into the sky, as if hoping to achieve flight. The air is brisk with sea and spray. My bare toes are scrunching into sand. On my lap I have a sketchbook. With a few quick lines in ink, I've captured the waterline. I have also sketched in the elegant sweep of the bay in the background. The lines are thick, definite. I have put a heavy black frame round the picture. It looks like something Heath Robinson would do, if he were illustrating a book of fairy tales. I am surprised by this. I like this style, very much, but I've never drawn in it.

I am hit by a gobbet of wet sand.

To my left is Kipper's bottom. He's wagging his ginger tail as he applies himself to digging. No dog digs more industriously than Kipper. He sticks his bottom up still further as he tries to grab a stick. He runs round the hole to the other side. He looks at me excitedly then he leaps on the prize. And now he has it! It's a brown, gnarly piece of wood. He carries it over to me – I lift my sketchbook – and reverently deposits his slimy prize on my lap. 'There you are!' he seems to say. 'Now you can THROW IT!' I don't want drool on my fingers. But then I think: this lovely dog won't always be around. All he wants is for me to throw his stick. Is it so much to ask? And I stand, and I give his stick a magnificent fling, and he surges after it, and I feel a great wave of happiness. It crashes in my chest and then turns instantly into foam and aching sadness.

Wiping a hand on my trousers, I sit.

I return my attention to the sketch. It is missing what would appear to be its main subjects. To my right are two boys, who are digging too. Indeed they have dug so deep they are down past their waists. With their backs to me, they are scooping out sand with their spades, and they are putting it carefully on the edge of their pit.

The smaller one turns.

'Hi, Mum!' he says.

Oh my God! It's Tom! But he's about seven! He's lost his snotty nose and his baby fat. My little boy looks good-looking.

'Hi, Mum!' says the taller one, turning too.

It's Hal! He's older as well. He's ten! He's grown into himself. He looks even more sensitive and gorgeous, but his hair still sticks out at the back.

'You're not going to believe how far we've dug,' says Tom.

'You must be very strong!' I say.

'We are!' he agrees. He raises his fist and shows me his muscles. I laugh. His brother does the same.

'Mum!' he says. 'You should draw us!'

I look at them both. At their naked chests, their proud biceps, their grinning faces. They're right. I should draw them. They look so beautiful, so happy, so why do I feel so damn melancholic? I feel I'm about to burst.

'Hey, darling!' shouts a man.

I turn.

It's Simon. He's walking towards us up the beach. He has a surfboard under one arm, and a bundled kite under the other. His hair is wet with saltwater. He looks very healthy and gorgeous, and I love him.

'Man!' he announces. 'That was awesome!'

'Dad!' shouts Tom. 'How high did you jump?'

'Probably about thirty feet!'

'Did you?' says Tom, much impressed.

'Didn't you see me?' boasts Simon. 'I flew like Superman, and mid-air I let go. I flew like this: "Wehayyyyy!"' Simon throws down his kit so he can demonstrate his Superman-flight. 'My mouth was wide open! Then I smacked down and drank about three million gallons of sea.'

'Did you?' asks Hal.

'It'll probably be on the news later,' says Simon, now putting on his newsreader voice. '"Sea levels round Britain went down one foot today, after three million gallons were *drunk* by Simon Cockburn, the self-styled Superman of Hythe."'

The boys are gazing at their dad with naked admiration.

I've rarely seen him so infectiously happy. He's now looking above their heads towards the building. I turn and look that way too, and I'm surprised.

I don't see a café made out of reclaimed timber. I see a five-storey hotel.

And it's glorious. Incorporating all the best features of seaside buildings in Brighton and the South Coast, it's got a white stucco frontage, and every one of the big Georgian-style windows has a metal balcony. Strangely, the bottom floor looks like the old Kiters' Paradise, though way bigger. It's a hall, fitted out with reclaimed timber, and in front of it there's a terrace strewn with cactus and anchors and strange maritime objects. There seems to be a line-dancing class going on in there, which has a nautical theme. I can see four rows of four dancers and they're all springing round as if they were the spokes of a wheel. I know what dance they're doing. It's called Raise the Anchor, a hilarious, camp recreation of an anchor-raising dance. That must be why the dancers are wearing white sailor's hats. They all seem very good-looking and very happy.

I recognise one of them! It's The Amazing Gemma Weakes! And I recognise the musician! It's Edmundo, who's playing the accordion! Actually I recognise several of the dancers. They are Simon's regulars. I know all about them. He discusses them all the time. He gives them nicknames, based on what they eat. I can see Peter the Pieman (who eats pies), I see Trevor the Cider Drinker (who drinks cider), I see El Greggo (who dines in Gregg's). All of them are dancing!

I'm distracted by Simon. He's stashing his board in a big timber shed.

He gazes with proud affection at his sons.

'Yup,' he says to me, 'it was a good idea making a giant sand pit. That's the only trouble with Hythe: no sand.'

'It's true!' I agree.

I look at the boys, who are happily digging, and I realise it . . . There is no sand on Hythe beach. This is a beach that Simon *might* make in the future. But it's certainly not one he's made now. This hasn't happened. Perhaps this will never happen.

The wind gusts.

It ruffles the pages of my sketchbook. It pushes the book off my lap. I lunge forward to catch it. At the same time I close my eyes against the sand stinging my face. My emotions are changing as violently as the weather. I feel terrified. As my eyes shut, I have the feeling that I'm shooting somewhere, like debris gushing down a pipe. I need things still, I think. I need things still and quiet and safe.

The movement stops with a jolt. My hands are touching glass.

I open my eyes.

I'm pushing the door of a shop. And it's not sand that's stinging me. It's dust being blown by a freak gust of wind, up St Aldate's in Oxford. I must get inside. The door opens with a ping.

I find myself in an old-fashioned chemist's.

It has those square tiles of rough carpet in blue and cream. It has dark wooden shelves behind the counter, which are filled with wonderful glass bottles. The place couldn't be more vivid. It's got that chemist's smell – a heady mixture of TCP and plasters. It's also got a clock behind the counter, stamped with the name of a drugs company. It's 2.09 p.m.

I blink. I breathe in the scent of Germolene. I catch up with my thoughts . . .

Nine hours ago I was waking, in my bed, to find Hugh lying beside me, like the best present I've ever received in my life. It is eight and a half hours since we fell asleep in each other's arms and I dreamed I was on a beach drawing pictures. It is six hours since he suddenly woke, and bolted from bed, saying he had a tutorial at twelve and needed to write an essay. I've not seen him, now, in six hours. I love him, I think. I love Hugh Ashby. It's like a heavy weight in my stomach. Does he love me? When will I see him again? Will I see him tonight? I've never felt such lovesickness. I must see him again soon or I'll die.

I hear a muffled cough – the sound of a very quiet man announcing his presence.

I turn, and I realise that an elderly Indian gent is watching me from underneath the bottles, and I flush with embarrassment.

'Can I help you?' he enquires.

Why am I here?

Ooh . . . I remember. Hugh and I have just got together.

I want condoms. I want to be ready, in case the moment comes. And here they are. How many do I need? Sixteen? That seems optimistic. I'll go for three. No, nine. Oh, God, the idea of making love to Hugh Ashby nine times makes me feel a bit unsteady. I quickly take the packet of nine, and then, mindful of the Indian gentleman, I grab a couple of other items to cover my embarrassment. I've got extra-large Odour Eaters and a knee support. I place the items and a note on the counter before worrying I've made things worse. I'm now implying, to the very reserved-looking Indian pharmacist, that I shall be having sex, nine times, with a man with huge, stinky feet, after which I shall have a sprain. I cover the pile with a packet of Fisherman's Friend. Does that make it better? I am scared the Indian gentleman will ask: 'What actually is wrong?' But of course he's the soul of discretion. He slips the condoms into a paper bag, and hands over change.

The clock on the wall now says it's ten minutes past two.

Hugh's tutorial will have finished an hour and a half ago. Where is he? I only left home ten minutes ago. He could have come to see me. He should have, in fact. My happiness bursts. I feel fraught. Why didn't he come? We just spent the night together. We kissed, but nothing more happened because I pushed him off. Was I too prudish? Oh, God, I was prudish and repressed and I pushed him off like I was an uptight matron! He's seen the error of his ways! Oh, God. Will I see him tonight? Will I see him again? Does he like me? Does he love me like I love him?

He couldn't! No one could feel like this! Oh, God, if he doesn't love me, I'll die. I couldn't live without him. I couldn't. I don't like being in love. I feel scared.

My composure is utterly gone.

I'm thinking: Hugh Ashby doesn't love you, like you love him. This kind of love drives people away. It's like Simon. Dear Simon, who loves too much. I feel woozy and wilting and I could lie down. No! I must concentrate. I must focus.

Before me looms a bottle of eucalyptus oil.

Perfect. I take it off, unscrew the lid, and gingerly sniff it. The scent attacks my sinuses like paint stripper. Good. This vivid smell is grounding me in the here and now, though I'm anxious in case the Indian man is still watching. I screw the lid carefully back on the bottle. I read the words on the front. Eucalyptus Oil. Underneath there is some smaller writing: 'This isn't happening, and you know it. This is a chance to review, not to invent.'

I immediately feel sick.

Hurriedly I put the bottle back on the shelf and look around in desperation. I glance over to the wall – the wall that I was looking at only moments ago. It had a shelf full of verruca pads and a mirror. Now it's gone. In front of me there's a shelf full of nail clippers and pumice stones. Beyond that there's just white space.

The shop is disappearing! This isn't happening! None of this is happening! I feel faint!

'Are you all right?' says a kind voice beside me.

It's the Indian pharmacist. But I can hardly see him.

He's just a misty image near the counter. I can only see the outline of his beard.

'I need air,' I tell him.

I bolt from the shop.

The door closes behind me with a clunk, and I'm out in the hot day. It's blinding out here. I can feel the strength of the light, but *I can't see anything*! Perhaps that's just because my eyes haven't adjusted. I'm hearing the traffic. I'm smelling the asphalt. Detail is returning a little.

I sink to the pavement.

I place my hands on it, and smell the dusty pavement smell. I can see an old piece of bubble gum stuck to a stone. There is some graffiti next to it written in thick purple felt tip. It says: 'You are in danger.'

Terrified, I stand up. I turn to the right.

There's a pub. A pubby smell is wafting out – fags and carpet soaked in beer. Fags? How come they're smoking in there? Surely that's against the law . . . Of course it isn't! What am I thinking? Oh, God. Stop thinking!

I hear a familiar voice. 'Lucy!'

And – thank the Lord – here he is! It's Hugh! Immediately the world steadies and becomes focused and real. He's striding out of the pub. He's wearing black jeans and a black mac, and his hair is just slightly disordered, but he is huge and he is Hugh and I love him and I am holding his waist!

'Hello,' I say. My voice sounds faint and faraway. 'Have you been in the pub?'

'I just popped in.' He smiles. 'Nothing like a glass of ale to pep you up after a tutorial.'

'Were you on your own?' I ask, failing to hide the slight note of disapproval.

'Yes,' he says, lifting a cigarette to his mouth.

I can see the filter. It's a Benson & Hedges. It seems so long ago that people were smoking Benson & Hedges! *I mustn't think that! I must stay here!*

'How did the tutorial go?' I ask.

'Good!' says Hugh.

'Great!' I say. 'You're not worried about your dad, are you? You've just got to forget him, and you've got to forget you once did the best A-level in the country, and forget you haven't worked enough. You've got to forget everything, just sit down at those exams, and do your best!'

I realise I'm burbling.

'Are you all right?' says Hugh.

'Yes!' I say, with terrible brightness.

'What's the matter?' he asks.

Oh, Lord, can I tell him? I want to say to him: the trouble is that loving you is scary. I feel I'm standing on the edge of an icy pit and starting to slide. I'm here, and I'm with you, but at the same time I know that something terrible has happened, and none of this is real, and if I stop believing it, if I stop feeling it, it'll all melt. But I don't. That would be weird.

I just reach forward and kiss him on the mouth.

His stubble has got longer since last night. It feels sharper too. I can smell the cigarette smoke on him, and the beer. I don't care. It is real, it is Hugh. My tongue thrusts into his mouth and is touching his and it's all rough and beery like a pub cellar and it is utterly vivid and I love it. I love him. I love Hugh Ashby. I feel steadied.

'Ooh!' says Hugh. 'I guess you're pleased to see me!'

I pull my face a few inches from his, but I continue holding him.

'Yes!' I say. 'I am!'

'Good,' says Hugh. 'Shall we do something?'

'Yes!' I say. 'Let's go somewhere together!'

'Where?'

'It must be somewhere vivid, where we're both intensely aware of each stone, and each gust of wind.'

'Why?'

'Just because . . .' I begin. Can I tell him? 'Otherwise I'm scared all this will fade away and I'll be lost.'

Hugh smiles at me. 'You're unreal,' he says.

'You don't know the half of it,' I say.

'What shall we do?'

'We could climb to the top of the University Church tower. Have you ever done that before?'

'Let's go,' he says.

'Let's run!' I suggest.

'Run?' he says, horrified. 'I don't think I can run!'

'Hugh! You're an athlete!'

'I used to be an athlete,' he corrects. 'I'm now a smoker.'

'Let's focus on what you can do, right now,' I say, taking his hand and dragging him up the pavement. 'You can run to the tower. And if you do that, I will let you have sex with me at the top.'

Hugh guffaws.

'That puts it in a different light,' he says. 'Let's run like the wind!'

We set off jogging up the street.

Minutes later, we arrive, panting, at the church.

I look up at it. The steeple is looming over our heads. Clouds are surging past, and it seems to be toppling forward. I've never been up there before. How do you get in? I see a door to the church, through a small paved courtyard which has a bench where tramps often sit. There are no tramps there today.

I see a sign. There's an arrow and underneath it says: 'Entrance to the church this way'.

'Look,' I say.

'I think it's a sign,' says Hugh.

We smile at each other. Then we run, more slowly now, round the back of the church, where we find the way up to the tower. You have to pay four pounds per person to the lady in the little booth. Hugh presses a ten-pound note on her. 'Keep the change!' he says. She is about to object but we move on. Holding hands, we run some more. For the first flight, there are wide wooden stairs. Then we come to the church roof and have to duck under flying buttresses till we reach another flight of steps, stone this time. These are steep and claustrophobic but very vivid. We have to let go of each other's hand as we climb up and round. There's an earthy smell of wet flagstones. In the walls are gashes which look hundreds of years old. Very soon we are both gasping heavily. I'm getting hot flushes but I'm not faint.

'I feel like a cork,' pants Hugh. 'Being yanked out of a bottle . . . *Wait!'*

Looking up, he's spied a couple of tourists about to descend. They have fanny packs wrapped round their waists, and they're both about six stone overweight. It's a terrifying thought: having those two blocking our way out. 'Would you be so kind as to wait one moment?' Hugh calls.

The couple pause.

We both sprint the last flight, as well as we're able. And then, dodging past the tourists, we come through a low stone door, and then—

Oh my God! We're out!

We are hundreds of feet up and there is Oxford spread out below us. We are seeing it, as the bird does, or the helmeted airman. We can see over Oriel and Merton Lane and, beyond them, there's Christ Church Meadow. We can see people, small as ants, lounging on the grass outside the Bodleian. It's wonderful. And, better still, we are alone. I've never felt so elated in my life!

I look at Hugh, and I beam.

'Look!' I say. 'It doesn't get much better than this!'

'I know!' he says, and suddenly I feel desperately happy and terribly sad all at once, and I really don't want to talk. I come towards him and my mouth flows up to his.

Quickly, we are both panting into each other's mouths.

My hand is inside his coat. It snakes inside his shirt, I place my palm against the mighty muscles of his back, and I squeeze my fingers into them as we kiss more. I feel him getting turned on. This is good. I want him roused. I want him to change his associations. And besides, I just really really want him. I place my hand over him, then, on a mad whim, I fumble with the zip at the front of his trousers.

'What are you doing?' says Hugh, but he doesn't object as I reach down and push my hand through his zip and down the front of his pants and take him out. He is large and hard and surprisingly hot. 'People will see,' he says quietly.

'There's no one here!' I protest.

'But there might be.'

'And if they appear, they won't see!' I say. 'Keep your trousers up. Keep your mac in place. No one will know what's going on! It will be our little secret.'

He pauses. I look into his beautiful pale eyes and I can see the thoughts passing behind them. He likes the outrageousness of the scheme.

'Here!' I lean against the stone parapet. 'Just lean against me, no one will see!'

I pull him towards me. I make sure his mac is closed round me, then I hitch up the back of my skirt. He leans over me. I can feel him against my buttocks. He kisses my ear. I can smell the cigarette smoke on him. I reach my head right round and he presses his mouth to mine and we're kissing again. God, I love him! Meanwhile his hand goes round my front. It lifts up my skirt. Oh Lord. I hope no one can see down below. He pushes his hand into my pants. It is cold and the sense of discovery is fantastic as he touches the top of my thighs. I go still. I'm waiting. And now his cool fingers move slowly inwards, and it's like the Beethoven piece. The introduction is over, we're reaching the essence, and it's tender and exquisitely beautiful.

I stop kissing him for a moment. I turn to look out over the parapet.

The wind is rushing up the High Street into my face. Nearby, a seagull is hovering in the air. That is how I feel. I feel like I'm soaring in the air. I love him so much. I want him so much. If we do this, then we're changing the past for ever. He pulls my pants a bit more; they are halfway down my thighs. I grip his mac with both hands. I want to make sure it's enclosing me. I can feel him all hard and hot against my buttocks. He squats down slightly, and now I can feel him beneath me. I'm sitting on him like a horse.

'I have condoms in my bag,' I breathe. 'Put one on, and we can do it right now.'

'You're not going to get pregnant, Lucy Potts,' he whispers into my ear.

'How do you know?'

'I know like I know,' he says.

I want to challenge him on that. What he's saying seems to go to the heart of what's troubling about this situation. At the same time, his finger is tracing a circle round and round me and I feel soft and terribly alive.

'Hugh,' I breathe. His name is meant for breathing. 'Just do it then.'

'What?'

'Come inside me,' I pant.

He doesn't need asking twice. He bends his knees. They buffer gently against the backs of mine. And then I can feel him against me. He's far too big. I can't see he'll ever fit. I tilt my buttocks towards him. It's the most pornographic movement I've ever done, but I don't mind. There are sea-gulls on the wind and I am high up on a church tower and Hugh is with me. Nothing must stop this! *Nothing!*

'Hugh,' I pant. 'Just do it!'

And he thrusts, and—

'Ohhhhhh! Oh, God!'

It actually really hurts. But then it is a bit like diving into water, because after the shock I relax and think . . .

Oh my God, Hugh Ashby is inside me!

I calm. I turn my head. I reach for him again and he fills my mouth with his tongue. I place my hand on the right side of his face.

'Hugh!' I sigh. 'You're inside me!'

'I know!' he says.

'I love you so much!' I say.

'I love you so much!' he says.

I relax a little more. He steadies himself and I can feel him entering higher inside me. For the first time he sways slightly, and he moves as gentle as a boat by a buoy.

'I love you, Lucy Potts,' he breathes into my ear. Then he kisses it. 'I love you now. I loved you the first moment I saw you. And have ye no doubt,' he says, and kisses my ear again, 'I will love you every moment of your life.'

He is steadying himself as he moves slowly in and out of me. He moves his head to the other side and kisses my left ear. I reach to the left, and kiss him again. I am calming now. I am slowing and moving my hips, letting him ease gently in and out of me. It feels so astonishingly intimate. I love him. I love him. Nothing could ever be better than this. He is moving a bit faster now. He's going to do it! Hugh Ashby is going to come inside me and that *has* to change everything! We can have children! *Maybe Hal is his!*

But . . .

'Oh, hello,' says Hugh genially.

I open my eyes. I look to the left.

A couple of tourists have arrived on the balcony. Instantly Hugh and I stop moving. He carries on leaning against my back of course, but we are both smiling a polite smile at the couple. The man looks like an academic. He is thin, and wearing metal-rimmed glasses. Everything about him is small and neat, apart from his eyebrow hairs which are badger-grey and unruly. The woman with him is in a dress which has flowers in an unwisely chosen purple and green colour scheme. Her hair is short and grey and she has ratty front teeth. So does he. I think they are brother and sister. They look like a pair of human rats.

They are also standing right next to us.

'Which college is that?' asks the man, pointing.

'I think that's Oriel,' answers Hugh, always polite.

'Oh, yes!' declares the man. 'And so that must be the back of Christ Church!'

'Yes!' confirms Hugh, with an enthusiasm that I can't match.

'Thank you,' says Rat Lady. 'Very nice to meet you!'

'Lovely to meet you too!' says Hugh.

The couple disappear behind the tower. I turn and look at Hugh for a moment. He has softened in the interlude, but his love is there . . .

'Have they gone yet?' he asks.

'Almost,' I say. 'They're just disappearing behind the tower.'

'What a shame!' he says.

'Any second now we can resume,' I say.

But at that moment some new arrivals burst on to the balcony. They are cubs – one, two, three, four – followed by a hilariously overweight Akela. 'Oh, dear!' I say.

'Indeed,' whispers Hugh, his mouth twitching with amusement. 'You know, no one likes cubs more than I do, but they should never become mixed up in coitus.'

He pulls himself away from me. By silent agreement, we both begin putting ourselves away. The cubs are all holding papers. I think they're looking for something. By the time they reach us, my pants are up and Hugh's trousers are zipped. We don't move though. Hugh kisses me, almost chastely, on the lips.

'I told you the condom wouldn't be needed,' he says.

The cubs are disappearing again. They're young. They don't want to linger. But the ratty people are still on the other side of the tower, gazing out at the view. It doesn't matter. I feel calmer now that we've done that. Something happened, just then, and Hugh is with me, and he's mine. I still have my hand on the warm small of his back. I slide it up higher between his shoulder blades. His lips part slightly, and I feel his breath on my cheek as he exhales. We both smile.

'Amazing, isn't it?' he says. 'We don't ask to breathe, and yet the breath goes calmly in and out, giving life.'

'Yup,' I agree.

'Do you ever feel there's a divine force?' he asks. 'It flows through everything, easing breath into our chest, pushing leaves from the tree.'

I am slightly taken aback by this. Is Hugh religious? If he is, it's the first I've heard of it.

'Well, it would be wonderful,' I say, 'if it were all true.'

'Yup.'

'Imagine you could be bathed in water, and every sin would go. Imagine you could see angels, flying above you in the sky.'

'Perhaps you can,' he says. 'Just not at the same time. But perhaps every moment is always with us, and if you want to feel it, you've just got to let go of fear, and the flesh.' He smiles. 'Though,' he adds, 'flesh does have its pleasures.'

I feel myself smirking. It actually just happened: Hugh and I made love and it was glorious.

'Yes,' I say. 'I'm not ready to give it up.'

The humour fades slightly in his eyes.

'No?' he says.

'No,' I say.

I feel a momentary twinge of alarm. I thought, we are doing what we always do: we're just talking, and nothing matters. Why is he looking so serious all of a sudden?

'And is that Magdalen?' says a voice.

I look round. The ratty lady is addressing us.

'Excuse me?' I say.

I want to be polite and helpful like Hugh.

'Is that building Magdalen?' the woman is saying.

'I'll show you,' I say.

I go over to join her. She and the man are both pointing out a college with golden limestone walls. Their gestures are exactly the same. I'm sure they're brother and sister.

'Yes,' I say. 'That's Magdalen.'

'Thank you so much,' says the woman. 'I just can't find it on the map.'

She has a paper map open. Her finger has traced up the High Street. She's pointing to where Magdalen should be.

'Have you got any children?' she whispers.

'What?' I ask her.

The question terrifies me.

'Why?' I ask, alarmed.

But she's not looking at me. She's looking over my shoulder.

'Is that your boyfriend?' asks the man.

He looks very worried. He's turned away to glance back at Hugh.

It's funny how you have an instinct.

Instantly my stomach leaps and a feeling of cold terror washes over me.

I turn round and am just in time to see Hugh. He's climbed up on the parapet of the stone balcony. He's standing right on top of it. He looks strong and invincible silhouetted against the sky. The Great Ashby. He also looks in terrible danger.

'Hugh!' I yell. 'What are you doing?'

'It's like you said,' he says evenly, 'it can't get better than this!'

'No!' I shout, and lunge for him.

But I'm too slow.

His face looks blank and sad and very ashamed as he turns away and leaps like a diver into the sky.

I run forward.

It's surprising how long it takes for him to fall.

By the time I reach the wall, he hasn't yet hit the ground. For a moment I think he won't. He'll land on the roof of the church. But he doesn't. I hear a terrible crack as his arm smacks against the church roof. It doesn't stop him. It makes him spin, so that, as he falls down past the church, his body turns; so that, for a heart-stopping moment, he's looking up.

Time goes so terribly slowly.

I have enough time to see his face. He's looking up as if contemplating the sky above him. I have enough time to notice that – thank God! – there is no one in the little courtyard. And then I hear a muffled thump as his body smacks on to the ground. His head smashes like an egg in an explosion of blood. His limbs seem to burst outwards. And then he goes very still.

I know he is instantly dead.

I've not breathed since I saw him fall. I still haven't. I just look down at him. I watch a star of blood starting to seep out of his broken head, and only now do I start to feel something.

Then I think . . .

None of this should have happened! This is all some long insanity, and I need to get out of it as quickly as I can. Then I think: maybe I could do it too! Maybe sometimes you need to let go! And on a mad impulse I clamber up on to the wall, and, before I can stop myself, I *leap* off into the void.

Plummeting downwards, I shut my eyes . . .

CHAPTER 13

The sheer length of the fall is terrifying.

How hard am I going to smash? I am ready for it. My eyes are shut and my shoulders are hunched and my whole body is squeezed tight like I'm a walnut, falling from a tree. Why am I not landing?

I feel a hand touch my shoulder.

Startled, I fall down and backwards. I am somersaulting on to long grass. I am sitting in an untidy sprawl, looking up at the man in white. He surveys me with a gaze which is cool and blank, like a buzzard looking for prey.

'Who are you?' I ask, still panting.

'It doesn't matter,' he answers. 'I don't want to influence you. I am just here to help you be clear.'

This again.

'What exactly do I need to be clear about?'

He studies me a moment. Is his gaze growing softer?

He no longer looks so like a buzzard. He looks peaceful.

'Whether you want to die,' he says.

'Of course I don't want to die!' I answer.

Immediately he stands up.

'Then come,' he says. 'It's time.'

He begins striding towards the trees. He is stepping over the ones I hit with the car. They are young hazels, their silver-grey stems flat on the grass. I am very irritated by the way he's stalking off ahead.

'I know who you are,' I say, following after him. I feel furious loathing towards him.

'What did you see just now?' he asks, looking back over his shoulder.

'Hugh,' I say. 'I saw what could have happened.'

'How was it?'

'Wonderful,' I say. 'Right up to the part where he killed himself.'

'You can't change the past,' says the man, 'only your attitude to it.'

'*You've already said that!*' I shout. I have a powerful desire to hit him.

He's climbed up through the bank of trees. We've reached the road.

'Who are you?' I ask again.

He turns and looks at me calmly.

'Who do you want me to be?' he responds.

'I don't know!' I say. I just want him to be infinitely wise, so I can get out of this.

'Who is it that you think that I am?' he asks.

That gives me a chill. I stop walking. Isn't that what Jesus said? *Is he Jesus?* Is he Jesus tall as a basketball player and aged two thousand years? Is that what's happening?

'Who do you want?' he asks again.

Simon, I think. That's who I need. But this guy isn't Simon.

'I want Hugh,' I say. 'That's who I've always wanted.'

The man smiles.

And as he does, sounds seem to muffle away, as if I'm underwater, and everything seems to slow as the hair spreads inexorably over his bald pate then turns brown. The blotches fade from his skin. The lips acquire more flesh and become plump and red and smiling. The eyes remain pale blue, but a light comes into them, as – how the hell did I not see this before? – the man reveals himself as Hugh. Not just Hugh, but Hugh, young and at his best – Hugh at the garden party in New College. Why didn't I recognise the white robes? They are his Lawrence of Arabia outfit.

'Hugh,' I say.

'Lucy Potts,' he replies, with the faintest ghost of a smile.

For a moment, looking into his face has the old effect. It's like seeing the Mediterranean from a dusty cliff top. I feel briefly uplifted. Calm. Then a murderous hatred fills my heart.

'Why are you here?' I ask.

'Because you wanted to see me again. And I thought I could help.'

I don't say anything to that.

'Also,' he says, 'there is one question I'd like to ask.'

'What?'

'On that last time you saw me,' he asks, 'why did you go?'

He's touching on the source of so much guilt.

I pause. 'I'd seen something in the paper,' I answer.

'What?'

'A listing for a Jackie Chan film,' I say bitterly. 'So I went to get tickets to give to Simon.'

I feel disgusted saying this. It seems a terrible reason to leave someone, before they die.

'So you left me because you wanted to see Simon?'

'Yes.'

'Why?'

'Well, you were depressed. You were also clinging to your depression. I couldn't help. Whereas Simon – I could! I could give him Jackie Chan tickets. Anyway, why shouldn't I have wanted to see him? He's fun and loving. You have a massive brain, and more potential than any man alive. What Simon has is guts! Gusto! Energy! I can't believe it, Hugh! I tried to give you love and you just died! What sort of thing is that to do to someone who loves you? You poisoned my life for years. I can't believe I loved you. You're a selfish, pathetic coward!'

I've been advancing on him while I speak. He doesn't retreat. I punch him on the side of the arm, as hard as I can.

'I despise you!' I shout. 'I despise every way that I'm like you!'

I hit him again, harder now. He looks at me blankly. I hit him again and again as the fury boils hotter and hotter, but the hitting doesn't seem to affect him, and it does nothing to dull my rage. Eventually I stop. Now I'm panting, staring into his face, and he's looking at me with sadness and calm.

'So,' he says. 'You chose Simon?'

And I suddenly see it. 'Yes,' I say, and for some reason I want to cry. 'I chose Simon.'

'As long as you're clear,' he remarks.

He turns.

'Follow me,' he says. 'I need to show you something.'

'What?'

Jesus Christ, I am not ready for any more of his stuff.

I briefly delay following him.

We have climbed up the wooded slope, about twenty yards from the fateful turning. Looking down it, I can see a trail of crushed branches and, at the bottom, my upside-down car with its rusty bottom, and the body of a dog lying nearby like a macabre sacrifice.

I turn away and look down the road.

The other vehicle is a hundred feet down the slope. It must have hit me, then blundered down a surprisingly long way before it veered off the road into the trees. It didn't go right into the field. It went off the road and nose-dived into the first tree it hit. From here I can see its underside.

Seeing what I've done, I feel numb with shame and dread.

'Who is it?' I call to Hugh.

He doesn't answer. He strides down the muddy road on his long legs. I follow behind, hardly daring to breathe. As I approach, I can see that the van is black, and so already I'm starting to fear. I am fairly sure who it is now, I'm just hoping the accident hasn't been so bad. But as I go down the side of the van, I see it was a brutal crash. The van must have slipped off the road, and then dived down into the base of a strong sycamore which smashed through the middle of the roof. The windscreen shattered. The driver shot forward. He's now lying over his own steering wheel, amidst a lot of blood, which is already congealing. He doesn't look like a person, he looks like a corpse, but there's no avoiding who it is.

It's Simon.

The discovery is made worse by the awful knowledge: I did this. And because I know this means that my children will have no parents. And because it's Simon. All sound fades. All colours bleach away. But this time – though I wish it would – the scene doesn't disappear.

'Simon,' I whisper. I hope that somehow I can wake him. 'Simon!'

But there's no movement. Is he dead?

'Lucy,' says a voice.

I had forgotten about him. I turn and see Hugh watching me, standing there in his long white robes.

'What do you want?' I ask.

'I am trying to help,' he says.

'Did you somehow cause all this to happen?'

'What?' says Hugh. 'Of course not! I just saw that the crash had happened, and so I came. I saw this as a chance for you to review, to understand, to become clear. And you've done that. Whatever happens, you must take some comfort from that.'

'What?' I exclaim. *Comfort?* I have rammed a car into my husband, depriving our kids of parents. I take no comfort from anything!

'Lucy!'

'Leave me alone!' I scream. 'I wish I'd never seen you!'

'You don't mean that!'

'I do!' I yell. '*I wish I'd never been born!*'

And I turn away from him.

Not knowing where I am going, or what I'm doing, I drift slowly away. I glide past the Newsomes' farm, and Mrs Eden's cottage. Somehow – like a dead spider washing towards a plughole – I'm still moving. On instinct, I'm heading back to the sanctuary of our home. If I have any thought it's a numb desire that I could join Simon. But as I reach the gate to our house my thoughts move on, and I'm thinking clearly, with that terrible clarity that you get in moments of extreme danger.

The boys, I'm thinking. *I just need to help the boys.*

I'm moving more quickly now, more definitely.

Going round the side of the house, I check the window into the living room. They're not there.

I look out into the muddy expanse of the back garden. I can't see them. I look at the great beech tree. They're not sprawling in the treehouse. They're not bouncing on the trampoline. The bikes, unridden, are lying on their sides. No one is on the swing, which is limply dangling from the oak. Under the apple trees there are plastic water pistols lying on the grass, but no child is squirting them. The place is chillingly empty.

I go through the open door into the kitchen.

There are knives by the toaster, but there's no sound of boys. My boys. My longing for them is so strong now, I hurry up to their bedroom.

I can't see them.

A thought occurs to me . . . Perhaps this is what happens when you die. You drift around unnoticed, and all alone, and you can't see anyone. A wave of cold panic spreads over me. This is what Hugh meant when he said what I was doing could be dangerous. By wishing for him, was I somehow willing my children out of existence? Is that why I can't see them? Have I killed them too?

I scan their bedroom for signs of them.

Tom's duvet has been thrown back. On the wrinkled sheet there's a jumper, a drawing of a dog, and his favourite teddy – Mr Paddywack the Snow Bear. I look at the picture. It depicts a brown dog. It is huge – about as big as an elephant – and a boy is riding him. It's a superb piece of kiddie art. It's anatomically weird, of course. The dog is far too big. Also his legs are stuck on the bottom of his trunk like stilts under a house. But the boy is clearly smiling. And there's a sun bravely peeping over a hill, and in the sky there are clouds, and all of them have smiley faces. Tom has plainly loved doing this, and looking at it, my heart feels gashed open like an octopus cut on jagged glass.

Down at the other end, Hal's side of the bedroom is strikingly clean.

His trainers are standing neatly together under the bed. On his little desk he has an exercise book in which he has been working on a homework project entitled: *When I Grow Up*. A note from Ms Pemble, Hal's teacher, suggests that he should use what they have learned about Wow Words. I don't know what Wow Words are. But I can record that Hal's writing reads as follows . . .

'When I gro up, I would like to be like my dad. He is very good at sports, and he really loves kite serfing, and also he is very funny, for egsample my dad has made a funny song with the A-Team theem. It goes Der DUM DUM, and its got all the words . . .'

At this point, Hal's writing changes.

It's easy to see what happened: he must have stopped. He must have realised he wanted the exact *A-Team* intro, and gone to the computer in my bedroom, Googled the text, and copied it out very carefully. In his reverence for the *A-Team* text my son does not make a single spelling mistake as he faithfully transcribes the introduction right up to the famous last words: 'If you have a problem . . .'

I want to read what else Hal has written in his exercise book.

But I realise I can't turn over the page.

And it hits me: I shall never again turn over another page of his work. At the Open Day at school, I'll not be there to admire his sums. I also won't be there to watch with tearful pride when he performs in School Assembly. When he enters running races, it won't matter how hard he bravely tries, I'll never be there to cheer him on. And now the shame and guilt hit with numbing force. How could I ever have been so stupid? All this questioning about lovers – why am I cross with my husband? Could I have saved Hugh? – seems so irrelevant. Yes, I am a wife, a lover. But I am also a mother. I am a *mother*. That is the most important thing I am on this earth, and I am horrified I've even contemplated not being there to give love to my children. That's all I want to do in this world. I don't care if they don't want me for years and years and years, I am a mother, and if those boys need me, I'll be there to give them my love. But where are they?

Maybe they're upstairs in our room.

That's it. They've sought out the comfort of our bed. As I speed upstairs, I know the boys won't be there. But I think that, somehow, Simon will. Possibly he, like me, has become detached from his body, and, if he has, it stands to reason he would make for our bedroom, like a salmon makes for its spawning ground. As I reach the door, I *know* it . . . he *will* be there and it will be like all the other crises we've faced – the times boys got sick, and cars got pranged

– we'll talk it over in the sanctuary of our bedroom. He'll be there. He'll know what to do.

I come into the room.

On his bedside table there's a bottle of massage oil with the top open. On a spa holiday Simon did a massage course where he learned a technique he called Lymphatic Drainage. I still don't know what that means, but it began with him blowing on the backs of my knees. He did that two nights ago when he massaged me. Dear Simon. His presence is all over the room. His favourite naval-style jacket is on the back of the chair.

But he is not here.

In his absence, I lie on his side of the bed. There's a faint smell on the pillow (a trace of the coconut gel he uses on his hair). On his bedside table there are photos: the two of us, up on a Swiss mountain – the day he asked me to move in; another of me, in subfusc, the day we graduated from college; another of me, smiling proudly outside the gallery in Whitechapel where I had my first exhibition. All Simon's pictures contain me, and I notice something obvious that I somehow forgot . . . He loves me, and I rammed a car into him. How did I do that? What have I done?

Scared that even this comfort will be snatched away at any moment, I breathe in the smell of Simon, and I shut my eyes. I squeeze them tight shut against the shame and pain. I immediately feel that I'm falling.

I stop.

'Mummy,' calls a little voice. 'Muuuuuuuummmmyyyy, are you awake?'

I open my eyes with a start, and I'm instantly reassured.

I'm still here in my bedroom. Thank God. I love this room. Simon and I have a king-sized bed, with huge plump pillows. The walls are white, as walls should be. Not for me the fashionable nonsense of wallpaper: why have wallpaper when you can have a view? And a view I have. I sit up and see it. Through the window to my right is a grassy hillside, which slopes steeply up to a forest. The grass is long and green and it is dotted with sheep that are backlit by the morning sunshine. I love a backlit sheep. I love my home. Is it wrong to love your home as much as I love mine?

I look round.

On Simon's side table there's a book, *Ubik* by Philip K. Dick. I remember that. He read it a year ago. Beside it, there's the Prime Blade Catalogue 2013. That doesn't make sense. Simon would never have an old catalogue. I look at my side. There's *Beautiful Ruins* by Jess Walter, piled on *The Great Gatsby*, *The Bell Jar*, *Brideshead Revisited* and *Where'd You Go, Bernadette*. I loved all those books. I read them a year ago and then gave them to Oxfam.

This isn't happening now. This is the past.

'Mummy!' trills the child's voice again. 'Are you awake?'

'Yes,' answers my voice.

To my right, a little face peers around the edge of the

door. It's Tom. He looks to be about four. His face is younger, chubbier. He is beaming, though.

'What's happening?' I ask.

'It is . . .' he begins. He's obviously trying to say a speech. 'It is Daddy's birthday today,' he says.

'It's not Daddy's birthday,' snarls a hidden voice (Hal), 'it's Father's Day.'

'It is Father's Day,' says Tom. 'And . . .'

Now Hal appears. He looks younger too. He's wearing a white tea towel tied chef-style round his head. 'And to celebrate Father's Day,' he says, 'Daddy is making you breakfast in bed.'

'Great!' I say.

The mini-chefs disappear. There's more whispered conversation. Then Tom appears, proudly holding up a glass of orange juice, like a priest holding a ceremonial cup. He's followed by Hal, who's carrying a tray on which there's a Full English Breakfast. Hal is followed by Simon. He is dressed in jeans and white t-shirt, and his big eyes are smiling, and his square face is full of manly vigour and affection.

'Simon!' I say. 'It's supposed to be Father's Day!'

He grins and shrugs.

'This is very kind and loving of you.'

He grins more. He doesn't know what to say.

'Am I kind and loving to you sometimes?' I ask.

He grins and nods, tossing his head from side to side. This isn't something he wants to discuss. He just wants to serve the breakfast. But I am deeply bothered by the question. Do I love him enough? Do I show it?

Simon is followed into the room by Kipper, who's eyeing that tray like a doggy magician intent on performing a spell. And it seems to work. As the tray is lifted up on to the bed, a sausage rolls off the plate and on to the floor. Instantly Kipper grabs it. He gets the sausage by one end, and he tips back his head. For a moment he looks like a beagle smoking a fat cigar. I can't help but laugh. Kipper does look funny. And this scene is so pleasurable, I could stay in it for ever. But, alas, I lean my head back against the wall and I shut my eyes with contentment.

Then I see it: none of this is happening.

These events are just thoughts, flashing through the mind of a dying woman. I haven't showed Simon enough love, and that's one reason he is not in the bedroom serving me breakfast. He is in his van with his head bleeding. I feel sick. I feel I'm falling fast.

Chapter 14

I open my eyes to stop it.

I'm still here. But the boys are gone. Instead Hugh is standing against the window.

'There's an ambulance out there,' he observes.

I hurry over. The ambulance is driving towards the field where my body is lying.

'The ambulance is going to me,' I remark. 'Why not Simon?'

'You matter.'

'Why not to Simon?' I stress. 'Does this mean he's dead?'

'You're important too,' he insists. 'You're a mother, and a wife – and a painter.'

'Ugh,' I say. I feel disgusted even talking about that.

'You're a great painter!' he continues. 'In the year 2042, one picture sells for twenty-eight million pounds. Another is copied on to five million posters.'

'Which one?' I ask.

'I'm not making it that easy,' he says, smiling a little.

'Look,' I say, 'I don't need to know.'

I can just see, in the distance, the ambulance reaching my car. Perhaps they haven't seen Simon. Perhaps they'll see him now!

'There's only one thing I need,' I say. 'And that's for Simon to live.'

Hugh says nothing. He continues to stare out towards his friend.

'Is there anything we can do?' I ask.

'Yes,' he says. 'Be clear.'

I tut.

'We've all heard of miracle recoveries,' he says. 'Is Simon dead, or just injured and concussed? How bad are his injuries? It's in the balance. Thought matters.'

'Look,' I plead. 'I realise that thoughts may have got us into this situation. But they cannot change the fact that Simon has had a terrible accident, and is potentially on the verge of death.'

'But if he is,' says Hugh, 'there's only going to be one thing on his mind.'

'What?'

'Whether you love him.'

'Of course I love him!'

'How does he know? Last time you saw him you rowed. And then you rammed a car into him.'

I see he has a point. I feel sickened.

'So it's not quite clear,' he continues, 'that you are radiating love like a lighthouse.'

'But how, practically, is my thinking supposed to save him?'

'Truthfully,' says Hugh, 'I don't know. I don't know how badly injured either of you is. Your crash seems worse, but actually momentum was broken gradually. How bad are your injuries? I don't know.'

I feel desperate. 'But what could actually happen to change this?' I repeat.

'I don't know. But I'm thinking you might go back once more, and this time you'll be clear and trusting, and the events that caused this will happen again. Except this time you'll leave, up that hill, and you'll turn that corner, but you won't crash. And then you'll wake up, and you'll have survived . . . Or that's what I'm hoping anyway. That's why I've come.'

I'm touched by this devotion. It also makes me ashamed.

'Hugh,' I say. 'I'm so sorry about what I said earlier.'

'I know.'

'I was angry.'

'I know.'

He studies me calmly for a moment. Then he asks another question.

'Why do you think I died?'

'You had ME,' I answer, 'and you didn't think you'd recover. You also had a deep-rooted sense of worthlessness instilled by your father. And a profound cynicism about the world. So you wanted to leave it.'

He offers no comment on my analysis.

'Why did I do it that day?' he asks.

'I think you saw I'd go off with Simon,' I suggest. 'And that made you feel disgusted with yourself.'

'So do you feel angry with him about that?'

'No.'

'Do you feel angry with me?'

'No.'

'So why can't you get over it?'

'I'm still angry with myself.'

'Are you?'

'Yes. Sometimes I want to scream: "*Lucy . . . He'd fucking told you he was suicidal, and you left him to go and see a fucking Jackie Chan film – you fucking idiot!*"'

The anger of my words seems to be spitting and spluttering round the room. Hugh pauses a moment to let my rage subside.

'And if you wanted to be fairer,' he says, 'what would you say then?'

'I'd be more kind,' I answer. 'I'd say: "His death was because of an illness, not because of you. And I know it makes you feel very bitter, but it needn't. In our lives we have so many relationships which are empty, you can be happy that in this one you both truly loved each other, and you must thank him for that, and let him go.'

'Indeed,' says Hugh.

We both look again out of the window. Another ambulance appears, and this one turns up the hill towards Simon. I'm so relieved. I look back at Hugh.

But there's no one there.

There's just an absence, and a terrible silence, like an orchestra who've stopped playing. Oh my God, I realise, he really has gone. And, closing my eyes, I sink down onto the bed.

And when I open them, I find that, appropriately enough, I'm at Hugh's funeral.

It took place two weeks after I'd found him dead, on the island where he was brought up. I flew out with Gemma and Simon, and we went to a service in a white stucco church, that stood on a hill with a view over fifty miles of glittering sea. Simon made a speech which was unwittingly hilarious. He said: 'Hugh was my friend . . .' Then his voice went squeaky, so he stopped, and started again. 'Hugh was my friend,' he said. But then he started squeaking again. He started a third time – 'Hugh was my friend' – but then he started crying, and the priest escorted him back to his seat. Whereupon Gemma leaned over and said: 'Simon . . . *Awesome speech!*' and I got the giggles. Gemma got the giggles, too, and Simon got all hurt. At the end he walked quickly out, and we followed him and everyone else down to the home of Hugh's mum – Caroline Ashby – which turned out to be a heartbreakingly picturesque two-bedroomed house, perched twelve feet above a little rocky cove.

I'm there now.

It's a small living room with a tiled floor. There are

about twelve mourners – mainly friends of Hugh's mum, older Greek ladies who are sitting around in black clothes. The shutters are closed, in the Mediterranean manner, which emphasises the cloying sense of grief which hangs over us. Simon has just gone out of the back door, and a light is spilling in and gleaming on the tiles. He is still being prickly, and, actually, he's been weird with me for a while now. A few weeks ago, arriving in the basement, he tried to kiss me. I was taken by surprise. I was completing a painting. I evaded him, and he blurted out: '*OK . . . Yes . . . I'm sorry, Hugh is the only one you're allowed to love, I forgot!*' and then disappeared. Ever since, he's been stiff and horribly formal.

This is very much on the mind of my younger self. I'm figuring: Today is Hugh's funeral. If this can't bring us together, what will? I get up. Hugh's mum, deep in conversation, gives me an anxious smile. I smile back. Then I take two glasses of wine from the table. The wine is a rosy pink, and there's vapour on the glass. Desperate to escape, I dodge out the back door into the blinding light.

Wearing a tight Gucci suit, Simon is standing on the edge of the rock, staring out to sea.

I stand beside him and give him the wine.

'Thanks, babe,' he says.

'Pleasure.'

'You OK?'

'Yip,' I say.

He looks sideways at me with his round brown eyes.

'Simon,' I begin. 'I'm sorry we got the giggles.'

'Doesn't matter,' he says. 'I just felt I let him down.'

'You were a good friend to him,' I say, 'and he loved you.'

'Thanks,' he says. He raises his glass in the air. 'To Hugh. God, he was a nice man!'

'He was,' I agree. 'He was clever and handsome and kind and funny – at least he was before he got sick.'

'Yup,' says Simon, and he gulps. Then he quickly drains his wine. I do the same. It's delicious. It's cold and it's got a taste of raspberry. Simon puts his glass down on a pot that contains a beautiful red geranium which has remarkably long stems.

'Hugh told me about this terrace,' he says, looking out to sea.

'Oh, yeah?'

'He said you could go out of his mum's house, and jump straight down into the water.'

'Well,' I say, 'there's only one thing to do then.'

'Yeah?' he says, and this is one of the moments that makes me fall in love with him. Because he doesn't say 'What do you mean?' or 'Sorry, this is a Gucci'. He just says, 'OK then,' and reaches for my hand.

I reach for his.

Then I shuffle to the edge of the rock and look down. It's actually a really long drop, I'm not confident about the depth of that water, and I'm wearing a full-length black dress. But Simon is smiling confidently. And you can slag off Simon, but he's superbly competent. If he reckons it's safe to jump, you know it is. And somehow we're both putting down our glasses, kicking off our shoes and mouthing, 'One, two, three.'

On three, we *leap*.

As we go my heart leaps to my mouth and I feel acute panic. Plummeting towards the water, I see a large piece of timber that's beating against the rocks. I'm scared we'll hit it. It seems to take too long as we flail through the air. I'm also aware that my dress is flapping up above my pants. And then we *smack* the water. Yes, we're in the Mediterranean. It's still March, and I'm wearing a full-length dress. It feels cold and wrong and my body tenses up a moment, and I gasp.

But then the relief floods my system. Still holding Simon's hand, I look out. The late-afternoon sun is sparkling on the sea. On the horizon there's an island, pale blue in the haze. I turn to Simon, and see he is beaming. He looks quite absurdly handsome, standing, all wet, in his Gucci suit. I think of how Hugh was so endlessly entertained by him, and how fond Hugh would feel, seeing his friend standing fully clothed in the sea, and something softens inside and I burst into tears.

Meanwhile, out at sea, some big ferry must be passing, because out of nowhere the water rises in a deep swell. As the first wave passes, there's a loud bang. Startled, I turn to see the timber clonking against the rock. I've turned to Simon and I'm holding his waist with my right hand. Another wave passes. The water rises up our necks. Looking into each other's eyes, we make a decision.

We both crouch down.

It's quiet under the water. I can hear vague sounds of rushing water, and muffled now, the timber hitting against the rock. The sound doesn't matter down here. Nothing matters. I feel calm. I feel I'm being baptised and every wound is being washed away. I wait till I can feel the waves have grown weak and I can't hold my breath, and then, suddenly desperate for air, I leap up as high as I can.

Surging up like a salmon, I realise Simon is grinning and leaping up with me. I also realise a strap of my black funeral dress has been pushed off my shoulder, and my left breast is making a bold bid for freedom. I don't mind. I feel raw and earthy and very alive. I also realise I'm still holding Simon, who's looking perky and handsome and very much alive himself. We land. The sea splashes round us and there are drops of water in Simon's long sexy eyelashes and he's beaming his delighted grin.

I can take it no longer. I pull him softly towards me. I kiss his eyelid. I kiss his other one. I kiss his cheekbone. I kiss his ear. I lick his forehead and I taste the salt. I rub my nose against his and his mouth opens and now I press my lips against his so hard our teeth touch. I grip his back. Something changed while we were underwater. Now I feel triumphant. I feel like we're two rutting mermaids who've just discovered their love. I feel filled with a passion that's big and timeless as the rocky hills around us, and loving how manly and muscular he feels, I pull him towards me and I thrust my tongue into his mouth.

Another big wave is passing. ***Bang.***

The front door just slammed shut.

Startled, I leap from bed. I'm back home in Kent. Just now I was having a dream where I was in the sea. Now I'm in my bedroom, and I see it's cold and windy outside.

I don't mind. This is where I need to be. I run down the stairs, and, panting slightly, I enter the kitchen to find Simon cooking a giant Man Breakfast. He's crunching a spitting pan of bacon down on to some eggshells.

'Morning, babe!' he calls.

I beam at him.

'Morning, Simon,' I say. 'I'm sorry about last night.'

'Nah nah nah,' he says. 'I'm sorry I didn't consult you before buying Kiters' Paradise.'

'I'm still glad you got it though,' I concede. 'It's got loads of potential, that place!'

'I know!'

'You should do food. You should make it into a hotel.'

'I'm gonna!'

'And might I make one more suggestion?'

'What?'

'Pies,' I say. 'Blokes like pies. We should invent our own special recipe.'

'I could do that!' calls a voice from the dining room.

I lean round the corner, and there they are – my two lovely boys, eating breakfast.

'Hal,' I suggest, 'I think you should start trying out different recipes, straight away.'

'I will!' he promises.

'Mum,' asks Tom. 'Can we get a new dog?'

'That is an excellent question,' I assure my young mad-eyed son. 'And if you get into the car straight away, you and Dad can chat about what animals we might need. He's thinking the café might need a dog, but maybe also a rabbit, or a parrot, or some fish, or maybe even a giant tortoise. Dad just can't decide! Do you think you could go and tell him your opinion?'

Tom can. He's already running for the car.

As he runs out, I smile.

Moments later, I'm sitting in the front seat of the A-Team van. The clock says 6.08 a.m. I can now clearly hear the angelic chanting that's been calling me all this time. It's Jeff Buckley singing about Lilac Wine. Simon is next to me, wearing his special sunglasses. He turns to me, and lifts them up.

'You sure you want to go to the beach?' he asks.

I smile. 'Sure!' I say.

'I had put High Tide on the calendar,' he says. 'But you hadn't looked, had you?'

'I'm an artist,' I inform him. 'I don't work to schedule.'

'You're very sexy,' he comments. 'But what are you going to do there?'

'Just come and be with you all,' I answer. 'I might draw.'

'Good,' says Simon.

I smile at him.

'I love you,' I tell him.

'I love you,' he tells me.

'I love everything about you,' I repeat.

He holds up a CD. 'Even this?' he asks.

'Except for the Monster Mix,' I correct. 'I consider that a sort of aural torture. But it's not a view shared by our offspring. So, please, pretty please, put it on, and turn it up loud.'

Simon needs no further encouragement.

'My darling,' he promises, 'I will.'

He slips in the disc. He reverses. The van fills with the sound of choppers and drum beats.

In the back, some amateur percussionists are beating along to the rhythm. I turn to admire them. They look very happy – Hal, the tall kind one, and Tom, the little mad one, who's patting out the drum beat on the top of Kipper's head. Kipper doesn't mind, but he's blinking a lot. The text comes, and they both lip-synch along. '*If you have a problem, if no one else can help, and if you can find them, maybe you can hire . . . the A-Team.*' My lovely darlings, I think. You are my A-Team! No one else can help! The chorus kicks in – DUM Dum DUMMMM – and in time with it, Tom lifts up Kipper's ears so he looks like Superdog, flying to the rescue.

And then suddenly I realise it . . .

Kipper is dead: none of this is really happening.

It *could* have happened, but I got out of the van because I was petulant and cross. This is just a fantasy flashing through the head of a dying woman. But then I reason that, if I can believe it enough, it could somehow become true. And I know the secret to that. I must just hear every sound, I must smell every smell.

The chorus kicks in again, and Simon skids off up the road at speed.

In moments we pass Mrs Eden. We pass the Newsomes'. We start heading up the hill, towards the sharp right turn. We go into the copse. I look ahead. It's very early. There are no cars around. There *should* be no cars, heading in the opposite direction, around that corner. The A-Team van *should* be safe, and if it does hit anyone, it can't possibly be me it'll hit, because I'm sitting here, with my family.

We should be fine.

We should be fine.

I have a sudden desire to call up Gemma to say I love her and could I see her soon? Then I think: Focus on the here and now. I open my window. I can't hear any cars. As Simon picks up speed, the dawn air blasts my face. I can smell the forest wet with dew. I can smell bark and mushrooms and moss. I glance at Simon. He has his sunglasses down, and he's concentrating. I want to tell him to drive more slowly. But equally I don't want to interfere. I'm aware the A-Team van is a left-hand drive, which will give it an advantage at the corner. And, besides, it's Simon. I trust him. I love everything about him, and I'm hoping, just hoping, that's enough.

We're into the copse of trees now, we're approaching the bend.

Simon toots his horn, but he's still driving fast. If another car comes now, it could be quite a smash. I find I'm leaning towards him, craning to look around the corner. I can't hear any cars. I'm thinking: I love this family so much. Please keep us safe. As we round the corner, I shut my eyes. I'm praying to God, I'm praying to Hugh, I'm praying to the A-Team. I'm thinking: please, let us be safe. I'm thinking: please, sweet God in heaven, let us be safe.

We speed round the corner.

I open my eyes.

A Volvo is hurtling towards us. It's driven too fast by an older lady with a short Judi Dench haircut. I shut my eyes. I brace myself. I feel that my whole body is tensed up, and my legs are crushed, and my head is so full of pressure it could burst.

Chapter 15

I open my eyes.

I'm awake. Really awake.

Blinking – once, twice – I see I'm not in a car. I'm also not under a car. I'm in a room.

It's a hospital room. The flooring is white rubber.

At the foot of the bed stands a locker. It is covered with flowers and cards. There's one from Kriss, a Manga-obsessed boy in my A-level set. He's drawn me, very flatteringly, as a Manga heroine and written: 'Ms Cockburn, you're the best teacher I ever had. Please get better, lots of love, Kriss xx'. I am stunned that a teenage boy used the word 'love'.

Beside that there is more artwork, rendered by more familiar artists.

There's a picture of a monster – really a hairy scribble, with feet and arms and a face. The text reads: 'Luv Monste

Say GET WEL MUM!' The spelling is erratic; the sentiment is painfully clear. The artist clearly likes this approach. Beside the monster there is another monster, then another monster, then a dog, then a dog, then a dog, then a monster who looks like a dog. Behind the card there's a gigantic bunch of flowers. The card with it reads: 'Lucy, you're my best friend. I love you. Please get better. Gemma x'. My eyes travel intently around the whole display. I scan every object and every card, three times, and am forced to this conclusion: none of them has been sent by Simon. I go cold.

A nurse walks in.

She looks to be in her forties, with sallow skin and her hair in a ponytail. She's clearly not expecting to see me awake. She goes to the foot of my bed and checks my chart. She's walking out when she looks at my face and visibly starts. She stares for a couple of seconds, stupefied.

'Hello,' I say.

'Hello,' she tries. 'Are you . . . How are you feeling?'

'Alive,' I reply. 'How long have I been here for?' I enquire.

'Erm,' she hesitates. 'A few weeks.'

'A few weeks?!'

'Yes,' she says guiltily. It's as if she feels personally responsible. 'I'll get Doctor.'

She disappears.

After that there's silence for a moment. I look around, and I see there are objects on my bedside table – a picture of us all at Kiters' Paradise, and a sprig of lilac in a glass, and my phone. Did someone reckon it was one of my familiar objects? Did they try to lure me back with ringtones? The phone's presence is a bit sad. But it's also very convenient. I turn it on, and am surprised to find there's power.

Then there's a noise at the door.

It opens very cautiously.

Who is this going to be?

A face slides round it. First some hair appears. It's short and grey, in a hairdo modelled on Judi Dench's. Then some very surprised eyes appear.

'Hello,' says Mum.

'Hello,' I say.

She doesn't say anything more. She stays like that – her head poking through the door at a diagonal.

'Are you all right?' she enquires.

'Yes,' I say.

She doesn't know what to say after that.

Silence.

'Mum?'

'Yes?'

'Have you been looking after the boys?'

Silence. Then . . . 'Yes.'

'How have they been?'

Her eyebrows go up still higher. 'All right,' she says.

'Thank you for looking after them.'

'That's all right!' she says. 'They've eaten jolly well. They've had steaks and spaghetti and a lot of fruit juice.'

'Thank you.'

More silence.

'Mum?'

'Yes?'

'And thank you for looking after me too.'

'Pardon?'

'When I was a child.'

'Oh,' says Mum. 'That's quite all right.'

I've never seen her less loquacious. She really doesn't know what to do. Then she adds something very surprising.

'I'm sure I could have done a better job,' she says. 'Of looking after you.'

'But you did your best,' I tell her. 'Thank you.'

'That's quite all right,' she repeats. Why is she being so formal?

'Mum?'

'What?'

I'm not sure how to put this. 'Did he make it?'

'Pardon?' says Mum.

'Did Simon . . . you know . . . pull through?'

There's a long silence like a chasm. Mum is looking agonised at me. But then she's distracted by a voice outside the door. It sounds like Tom.

'Have you got the boys?' I ask.

'Yes!' she says. 'Would you like to see them?'

'Of course!'

'But,' says Mum, 'don't you think we'd better wait 'til the doctor comes?'

'Mum,' I say, 'sod the doctor!'

'*Lucy!*' warns Mum.

'*Send them in!*'

At that point, the matter is rather taken out of Mum's hands.

The door is flung open so hard it smacks against the wall.

And there they are – both of them, standing frozen in the doorway with identical looks of astonishment on their faces. They're not nine and seven. They're as they should be: Hal is seven and he's got big eyes like a deer and his hair is standing up in the air. Tom looks like a mad snotty frog. His face is crazed with excitement.

But then that melts like ice cream in the sun.

His bottom lip comes out, and his eyes fill with tears. 'Mum!' he says. 'We thought you was dead!'

'Well,' I say, 'I'm not.'

Mum's got them very well trained. They're terrified of that doctor. They don't think they're allowed to move from that doorway. Finally I help them out. I spread my arms wide.

Still they don't move.

'I am de Love Monster!' I say, in a slightly Polish accent. '*Come to me! I am yours!*'

Now they both run for me. It's lucky the doctor isn't here to see this. I'm hit by a full broadside of child. Both their heads are squeezed against me and I'm smelling the delicious smell of Pears shampoo and hot Weetabix and boy. We stay like that for quite a while. Who was it who said 'You don't have much time'? That's so untrue. I have all the time in the world, and I don't want to move. But after a bit both boys pull back. They seem to be in a state of shock. They don't know how to behave.

Mum is still hovering in the background like an owl.

'I'm going to nip to the café,' she says. 'Can I get you anything?'

I realise she's offering to leave us alone together for a moment.

'I'd love a Ribena,' I say. 'Thanks, Mum.'

She edges out of the door, and I'm alone with the boys.

Tom puts a hand tentatively on the bed.

'Mum,' he asks, 'are we going to go home soon?'

'Yes.'

'Will it be like it was before?'

'Yes,' I say. 'Except . . .' I begin. Is Simon alive? Do they know?

'Except what?' says Tom.

'Except,' I continue, 'I think we should get a new dog.'

Tom looks surprised by that. But he's not against the suggestion.

'And I think,' I propose, 'it should be a brown dog, and it should be a hairy dog, and it should be so big you could ride on it.'

Now his mouth opens.

'Though actually,' I tell him, 'dogs don't really like being ridden on. So maybe we should get another animal for that.'

'Like what?' says Tom.

'Like a horse?' I suggest.

Tom develops the big sleepy grin he gets when he's just eaten a huge sweet. I look at Hal, who's eyeing me anxiously. It occurs to me: I bet Hal knows about Simon, but Tom doesn't. I'm dying to talk to Hal.

'But what sort of dog do you think it should be?' asks Tom. He's warming to this subject now.

'Tell you what,' I say, handing him my phone. 'Why don't you Google the words "Big Dog" and then click on "images"? That's spelled "B, I, G, D, O, G".'

I click on the internet on my phone, and pass it to him. Tom handles the phone carefully, as if he's holding a holy icon. As he prepares to take it off to the corner, I notice the phone opening up on to the Horsebridge's website, which causes me a moment's worry. I wince.

'What's the matter?' asks Hal.

'Oh,' I say. 'Before I had the accident, I was supposed to e-mail the Horsebridge Gallery because they are having an exhibition of my work and they wanted to know what the title would be.'

'Really?' says Hal. 'The whole gallery will just be filled with your pictures?'

'Yes! And I was really worried,' I explain. 'Because it was impossible to know what the title was going to be when

I hadn't even done any pictures! It had to be something along the lines of Things We Love, but I was so tense I couldn't even think of anything I loved.'

Just explaining this now, I'm remembering how anxious I'd felt. And I'm worried Hal might sweep my worries aside and say: 'I suppose that all seems silly now.' Or maybe even, 'Could you not think of *anything* you loved?' But actually his big deer's eyes fill with concern.

'That must have been a *real* worry!' he says, with wonderful feeling.

'It was!' I agree.

'But did you have any ideas for pictures?' he asks.

'Well,' I say, 'I think there should be one of you and Tom, and you could be digging on the beach, showing your muscles. It should be called *Musclemen*.'

Hal smiles a bit uncertainly.

'And there should be a big one which shows four young men, diving into a pool. That's called *Where It All Went Wrong*.'

'I am glad you're giving them names,' he says. 'I hate it when they're just called *Untitled*.'

'I agree,' I say, and then I take a slow breath because I'm in danger of crying. 'The next picture,' I explain, 'would be a scene viewed from the air. In the background there are mountains. In the foreground there's a buzzard. It's called *The Proposal*.'

'Wow!' says Hal.

'The next one shows a gap in a hedge, and it's filled

with sunlight so you long to go through it. It's called *There Might Be Monsters*.'

'Mum,' says Hal, 'it sounds like you've seen these pictures. How come?'

'Well,' I explain, 'while I've been lying here, I've been having sort of . . . dreams. I've been seeing all the people in my life, and I've been thinking about the things I'd miss.'

Hal stays silent for a moment.

'That,' he says at last, 'would be a brilliant title.'

'What?'

'*The Things I'd Miss*,' says Hal.

'It would be good,' I agree. My voice goes a bit squeaky because I'm really crying now. But if Hal notices, he's too kind to say.

'But do you think it would be a good exhibition?' he asks.

'Well,' I answer, 'I can't tell if it'd be good, or bad, or interesting, but I think any exhibition tells a story, and this would be the most truthful tale I could tell.'

'But what about Dad?' asks Hal, a bit anxiously. I look at him. Is Simon alive? Does Hal know? I'm desperate to ask him. But he's a very mature child; I still don't think he should be charged with telling his mother that her husband is dead. 'Is Dad in any of the pictures?' asks Hal politely.

'Well, he's sort of in all of them. He's one of the divers. And he was the one who made *The Proposal*. And you and Tom, you wouldn't be here if it weren't for him.'

'Yeah,' says Hal, 'but if there was one of Dad, on his own, what would he be doing?'

I think of Simon for a moment. I think of him dressed for paragliding. I think of him behind his DJ decks, punching the air, looking happy and carefree.

'I'd like to do a picture of Dad,' I explain, 'which would be set in a place called Christ Church Meadow in Oxford, which was where *Alice in Wonderland* was written. It's got a wide avenue of giant trees, and Dad is running off, and he's sort of bobbing from foot to foot in that funny Dad way. He looks a bit like a dog, running to catch a stick.'

'I do know what you mean!' admits Hal. He seems in danger of crying too. What does that mean?

'And I think there should be another one of Dad,' I continue. 'Where he's just come off his kite-surfer and his arms are wide and he's got a huge grin on his face, even though he's about to smack the water. That's called *The Superman of Hythe*.'

Hal smiles, but now he's definitely holding back a sob.

'Do people go to art galleries,' he asks politely, 'to see pictures of kite-surfing?'

'Well, kite-surfers do,' I say. 'Also I would like it. And after the exhibition, we could put the picture up at Kiters' Paradise.'

Hal looks up sharply, and now I have no doubt: he knows his dad is dead.

'But,' he starts, very uncertainly, 'will we still be keeping Kiters' Paradise?'

'Of course!' I say. 'We're going to have a lot of fun there!

And we're going to have to do a lot of work, to make it as good as possible. I think we should do food there, and I think you, Hal, need to think up some recipes. Could you do that?'

'Definitely!' he says, nodding.

The door opens and my mum reappears.

'The doctor is here to see you,' she says. 'Boys, shall we leave Mummy alone for a moment?'

Tom looks annoyed. He feels he's just got his mum back. He doesn't want to leave.

'And if you come now,' says Mum, 'we'll go to the café and buy some Chocolate Buttons.'

That changes Tom's view on the matter entirely. He bolts through the doorway like a rabbit going down a hole. Hal stops at the door.

'In the café,' I suggest, 'see if there are any ideas we can use.'

He gives me a brief professional nod – the sort that a chef gives before going off to investigate ideas. Then he's gone.

Now there's just Mum, stopped in the doorway.

'Mum,' I whisper.

'Yes?'

'What happened to Simon?'

Mum gives me a long look. 'Has no one told you anything?' she asks.

My heart tightens.

'No.'

She doesn't know what to say.

'Darling,' she begins.

'What?'

'I'm afraid he won't be kite-surfing for quite a long time,' says Mum. 'He's broken both legs, and several ribs.'

I start to smile. 'Who cares?' I say.

'I heard that!' says a voice outside the door.

It's pushed open. And there's Simon in a wheelchair.

I can't believe I'm seeing him again.

'Hello, gorgeous,' he says. He's clearly already adept with that chair. He comes forward smoothly.

'Hello, my darling,' I say.

Mums slips out. Simon pushes himself in, and then he just stops, beaming at me with a smile that's as big and wide as a windswept beach. I don't think I've ever felt such emotion as I do now – staring into his brown eyes with their furry caterpillar eyebrows. I feel like I'm holding my breath. I want to get down and I want to hug him.

But there's something I must say.

'Simon,' I begin. 'I'm so sorry.'

The caterpillars climb higher. 'Why?' he says.

''Cos I loved Hugh.' Simon says nothing to that. For a moment, I'm scared that somehow he knows everything – that in some other realm I just kissed Hugh, that I made love to him in a tower. But actually Simon is totally comfortable with that statement. Who understands Man Love more than Simon?

'We all loved him!' he says.

'It's easier to love someone like Hugh, who's not there,' I explain. 'Because I've got a soft loving heart, but life is hard, and my heart's been covered with a shell. And if I let myself love you, Simon, that's like taking the shell off, and then it's like cutting a slit in my soft loving heart, and letting it bleed.'

Simon still says nothing. He's just staring at me with his round brown eyes.

'And that doesn't feel safe,' I say.

'But I'm doing the same thing,' he says, 'so we're both safe, as long as we stay together. Though personally I don't find it hard to love you. I'd find it hard not to.'

I don't know why I think of myself as the sensitive, artistic one. I realise that, in its blokey way, his words were a hundred times more articulate and more loving.

'And Simon,' I continue. 'I'm really sorry, because I smashed a car into you.'

'I know!' he says. 'I couldn't believe it! You totally trashed the A-Team van!'

'Get another,' I suggest. 'You need it to carry your kite-surfing equipment.'

As I say this, Simon continues staring at me with his eyebrows up. But then, quite suddenly, he gulps and a tear springs from his eye. That's so Simon! Come out of a coma, and tell him you love him – he barely moves. But tell him to buy a new A-Team van, he weeps like a big girl!

'I'm not going to get a new van,' he declares. The tear is now rolling down his broad cheek. 'We don't have any money, and I'm not going to be kite-surfing in a long time, if at all.'

Oh God. Why are we still talking about the A-Team van? Why won't he just wheel forward and kiss me? I've never needed anything so much in my life.

'Simon,' I tell him, 'you must get another van, because you will have money, and you will kite-surf again, and because, Simon, I love you. End of.'

ACKNOWLEDGEMENTS

I started this book in happy circumstances. We'd just moved to the countryside and we had no TV or internet or friends or ballet classes (I spend 70 per cent of my leisure time driving girls to ballet). I'd also been reading *The Artist's Way* which encourages you to write like Cézanne who took a line for a walk, and it was August and *everyone* was away, so I sat down one day and wrote the scene where Lucy leaves her children to buy rice but she has a crash, and the one where she wakes up beside the man she truly loved, and the one where she finds herself back in her childhood garden . . . That night, I felt exhilarated. *Finally*, I thought, *I've learned to invent!* But now, eighteen months on, I've finished writing, and it's been like the end of *The Usual Suspects:* I've seen everything in a different light. I've realised the whole book has been about Derk Van Raaij . . . Derk and I were friends at college, though we met at school over a Bunsen burner. We once went on a blind date with Richard Scott and a girl who had clumpy sandals and white woolly socks. We both got wild teenage crushes on a witty, artistic girl called Lucy. I really loved Derk – how could I not? – he was tall and kind and athletic and clever and he had twinkly eyes, and the gift of being able to tease without a trace of malice. We had a lot of fun together. One summer, we windsurfed round the Isle of Wight with our friend Callum.

Then one day, twelve years on, I bumped into Callum. 'How's Derk?' I asked. 'Oh,' said Callum, 'he took his own life.' I was stunned. I'm still stunned. I knew Derk had got ME – I'm sure it wasn't the happiest chapter of his life – but I just wish I'd seen him, and shared some of it with him. I wish I'd seen how wonderful were the times we had spent together – how precious they were, and how terribly limited . . . But perhaps it makes me feel extra appreciative of the people who've helped during the writing of this book.

Thank you to the dancing girls – Grace, Cassady, Livy and Iris. Thank you to the team – Philippa, my agent Lizzy Kremer (she chose the story) and my editor Gillian Holmes (she edits so gently and so wisely!). Thank you to the writers whose work has particularly inspired this one: the classics – Sylvia Plath, Scott Fitzgerald, Evelyn Waugh, P.G. Wodehouse, Charles Dickens, Philip K. Dick and Will Shakespeare – and the contemporary ones – Jess Walters, Maria Semple, Julia Egan, Jonathan Dee, Lisa Jewell, Polly Williams, Christina Hopkinson, John Green, and Stephen King (this novel started with an 8,ooo-word short story, which I wrote, the day after reading *The Man in the Black Suit*). Thank you to Silvia Polivoy who gave me Ayahuasca, and an experience like the one in this book. If you want one, Google www.spiritvine.net. Thank you to the gorgeous friends who've helped me – Becky Promitzer, Tony Grounds, Josephine Ross, Paul McKenzie, Rod Liddle, Liz Tatton-Brown and Dominic Collier (we love you, King Dominic! Dominic Collier, step in time!).

And thank you for reading my book. Could I ask you to do something? Might you get in touch with a friend – right now – someone you really like? It doesn't matter what you do – give them a hug, give them a book, drink some wine – but might you also light a Bunsen burner in memory of my friend Derk?

www.andrewclover.co.uk

ALSO AVAILABLE IN ARROW

Learn Love in a Week

Andrew Clover

'The funniest book I've read about relationships in years' Lisa Jewell

After ten years of marriage, Polly and Arthur are at crisis point.

Polly
'Arthur is the IKEA wardrobe of husbands. He looks good in the pictures, but if you ask him to hold anything, his back pops out.'

Arthur
'I have the libido of the Giant Panda. I know what sex leads to. It leads to a small person who likes to post toast in the DVD player.'

Can they learn to love again? And if they can, will they still choose each other?

'The kind of book that draws looks from strangers as it will have you laughing so much. Also a saucy modern fable about thwarted dreams and working out what is really important' *Daily Express*

arrow books

THE POWER OF READING

Visit the Random House website and get connected with information on all our books and authors

EXTRACTS from our recently published books and selected backlist titles

COMPETITIONS AND PRIZE DRAWS Win signed books, audiobooks and more

AUTHOR EVENTS Find out which of our authors are on tour and where you can meet them

LATEST NEWS on bestsellers, awards and new publications

MINISITES with exclusive special features dedicated to our authors and their titles

READING GROUPS Reading guides, special features and all the information you need for your reading group

LISTEN to extracts from the latest audiobook publications

WATCH video clips of interviews and readings with our authors

RANDOM HOUSE INFORMATION including advice for writers, job vacancies and all your general queries answered

Come home to Random House

www.randomhouse.co.uk